Trey Roberts
and the
Ancestor's Wish

~

Book 2

By
Lee Magnus

Cover by Levierre

Tanarkin House

Tanarkin House
An imprint of Michael Matthew Publishing
First Tanarkin House paperback edition November 2019
The Library of Congress Catalog 2019952258
ISBN 978-1-7340748-3-3 (Ebook)
ISBN 978-1-7340748-2-6 (Paperback)

This would not have been possible without my boys.

Table of Contents

Nick's Secret

Trey Roberts settled in his room after showering off the day. He sat in a chair and stared at the sword he acquired from a flying cat-man.

This has to be a dream, he thought. There's no way I did all these things: fought a bunch of scary undead goblins with a mysterious woman named Lyza, befriended an electric furball, was captured and escaped from Centaurs, defeated a multi-sized bug in a riddle contest, teleported to Egypt, China and the Highlands.

Trey shivered as he thought about the Etherios where he had an ominous conversation with his Grandpa's spirit then finished soff befriending a dragon.

This is completely unreal, as he continued with his thoughts, *I mean look, the house looks as if nothing happened there are no rogglets or enormous snakes. Teleportation doesn't exist. I'll wake soon and be freaked out at how real this dream was.*

He gathered the disk artifact he pulled from the snake demon, the Discolursor Annular that revealed Seth's true form, the bag holding the key to the Etherios spirit realm, an odd shaped gold coin and a small case containing a fireproof, an energy and a cloaking potion. He then placed them all into the chair next to the sword. He removed the picture of him and his father from a drawer and displayed it on his nightstand. After a few minutes he fell asleep from exhaustion.

Trey stood yards away from the edge of a desolate cliff which rose above an ancient bustling city a distance below. It was surrounded by desert. Sitting together, a woman and infant sang a pleasant song amid sand colored structures. A thin lonely cloud drifted in the distance. A small grey bird stared keenly.

Trey asked, "What is it bird? What do you say?"

A whispered thought of foreboding. An image of a man, no something much worse, a red demon with flaming sword in hand.

"Shriek! Shriek! Shriek!" screamed the bird hopping up and down.

Instant fire and destruction ravaged the city. Screams of women and crying babies filled Trey's heart. The long dark face of the demon turned. Blood red creases painted stony cheeks. Black hole eyes, as if no light could escape, transitioned to yellow with crimson pupils. Proud of his deed, the scarlet demon raised the sword toward the cliff of which Trey helplessly stood. A blinding bolt of plasma blasted Trey into consciousness.

"Treeeeey! Treeeeeey, it's tiiiime to wake uuuuuup!" he heard his mom sing from down the hall on a peaceful Friday morning. He opened his eyes slowly and shivered off the surreal dream. Rubbing them clear he focused on the sword leaning against the chair where he left it the night before. He tossed his head back and said, "It can't be real! There's no way! Arggg!"

"Trey? Did you say something?"

"No Mom!"

"Hurry up, breakfast is getting cold!"

The small house overflowed with aromas of sage and biscuits. Trey's stomach roared.

"Ok! Be there in a minute!"

He looked back at the pile of items in the chair and became startled when he noticed something was missing. "Olerand's Disk! Where is it!"

He looked on and around the chair. Nothing. "Where'd it go?"

Trey ran down the hall, "Mom! Have you seen -" He brushed the pocket of his red and black checkered flannel lounge pants. "What's this?"

He pulled out the disk.

"Did I put that there?" he said confused. "I thought I left it on the chair."

"What was that, Trey? Do you need something?" him mom asked from the kitchen.

"Uh, no mom. Sorry."

He put the disk back in his pocket, then joined his mom for a breakfast of scrambled eggs, biscuits and smoked sausage.

"Thanks, mom. Breakfast is great," he said stuffing a piece of sausage into his mouth like he hadn't eaten in three days - which was mostly accurate.

She stepped from the sink, set her hands on her hips and said with contempt, "Did you leave your manners back at Marcus'? Use a fork, please."

He mumbled with a mouth full of food, "Sorry, Mom. I just forgot how hungry I was. Why the big breakfast anyway?"

"No reason. I've barely seen you these past few days. I missed you and just wanted to do something nice."

"It's nice. Thanks," he said smiling then forked in another piece of sausage.

Trey set his fork down while he struggled with a strong thought. He then asked, "Mom?"

She sat next to him and said, "What's bothering you, Sweet T?"

He temporarily felt abashed with the nickname. It usually didn't bother him (he normally welcomed it) but somehow, today, he felt a little too grown up for the childish name. He brushed his feelings aside and asked, "Did you know Mr. Smith? Don Smith?"

She studied her son, "No. I never met him. I've only met Clara once. She was very nice at the time and never mentioned her husband."

Trey thought she seemed to be holding back details.

"You know? The rumors aren't true." He continued with his breakfast.

She seemed ashamed but may have been more surprised that Trey knew what she was thinking.

"Rumors? What do you mean?" she said as if she didn't already know.

"Mom," Trey said frustrated. "I know everyone thinks he left her for another woman. It's not true."

"And how do you know that?" she asked like she didn't expect an answer.

"He came home yesterday."

"Oh-my-god," she said slowly. Her eyes were buggy. "After all this time?" She looked off in the distance. She returned her attention to her thirteen-year-old son. "How do you know that?"

"I, uh, found him – I mean, I found out, uh..." He struggled for the words. He hadn't expected to be questioned today about how he rescued Don from a dragon in another world with the help of his dead Grandpa. "I, uh, Nick! I mean, Mr. H told me on the way home last night." He breathed a sigh of relief.

"Mr. Hampton? Really?"

"Yeah. He, uh, said he found him while travelling in Egypt."

"Egypt? What was Don doing there? What was Mr. Hampton doing there?"

"He, didn't say," Trey replied with evasive eyes.

"Huh." She said. "Imagine that. You never know what to expect from day to day do you?"

Trey couldn't hold in an uncomfortable chuckle, "You sure are right about that, Mom."

"So, why all this talk about Mr. Smith? What does he have to do with you?"

Trey shifted in the seat. He chopped his eggs slowly. His next words were difficult to say – as were all the times before since his dad left them. "Did you know that Dad and Don knew each other?"

She looked at him like only a mother could when her child was hurting. She placed her hand on his and said, "No, baby. I didn't know. Your father never mentioned him."

Trey, a little more anxious replied, "Did you notice he and Mr. Smith left about the same time?" He shuffled again and continued, "You say you hardly talk to Dad anymore and he hasn't come to see me in over three years. Do you think that maybe he's in trouble too? Like Mr. Smith was?" He couldn't help, just like any other thirteen-year-old, hide a hopeful expression.

"Honey," she said in a soft voice. She touched his face. He looked down. "I don't know what your father's doing. All I know is that whatever he's into is more important that you or I." She then grasped his hand firmly, "I know it's great that Mr. Smith is home."

Her closed-eyed grimace held back all but one tear. She wiped that one away then continued firmly, "Your father is different. You can't remain hopeful that he will dramatically return home one day."

It was just like she slapped him. The truth, as painful as it was, is what Trey expected.

Trey thought to himself, *I know it's improbable that Dad will ever come back to us. Even if he were in trouble like Mr. Smith, what are the chances I could actually help?*

"I know." Trey replied. He thought he was stupid for believing just because Mr. Smith knew his father that maybe he could bring his own father home too.

He held his head for a second then a thought crossed his mind, *that's right! Mr. Smith knows my dad!* He brightened up and said, "Thanks for the talk, Mom! I love you!" He then tossed his plate in the sink and rushed back to his room where he wrapped the disk in a sock and placed it along with the Etherios key and potions into a drawer. He picked up the sword, jabbed and sliced at the air a few times then hid it between his mattress and box spring. He gathered his backpack, then left for school.

His mind stirred endlessly on the way to school. Where was his father? Does Mr. Smith know? Does Lyza know? Would he be able to save him if he needed saving? He walked the sidewalk anxious and full of hope.

~ ~

"Kid! Where've you been?" Marcus said. He had too much gel in his hair. It was slick and shiny – distracting Trey from the conversation. "What's the deal?

You don't answer texts anymore? Are you breaking up with me?" said Marcus jokingly to Trey in a school hallway.

"No, dork. I'm not breaking up with you. I was, uh, sick the past couple days. Sorry I didn't call."

Trey easily recalled nearly dying several times at the hands of ghoulish creatures in his house, Egypt and China; battling a zombie dog in a magical realm in the Libyan desert; literally dying when he defeated a demon in a fairy kingdom; and outrunning unwavering henchmen in a tiny oasis town. He believed his "sick" excuse was unsatisfactory at describing the past couple days to his best friend. He wanted to tell him. He wanted to share these experiences with him. He felt he needed to warn him of what might happen – no – what will happen (according to Grandpa and the Keeper).

But this information is too much for Marcus now. He thought. *Marcus won't understand. Plus, Lyza said we'd be safe for some time so there's no urgency in bringing him in...just yet.*

Trey had a terrible feeling Marcus would be involved. In every movie he had seen, the bad guy always goes after the protagonist's family and best friend. It's already been necessary to protect mom. It's only a matter of time that they discover Marcus.

I have to keep him safe.

Marcus looked at Trey. Disbelieving eyes revealed he knew there was more to the story, but decided to wait it out and said excitedly, "You've missed a lot. Jenny Jacobson broke up with Tom. Do you think she'd go out with me?"

Trey pulled his attention away from the past days and Marcus' hair gel, "Jenny Jacobson is one of the smartest girls in school."

"Don't forget she was also homecoming queen last year."

"Exactly. Unless you pick up your grades or

become a handsome jock, I think your chances are slim. But what do I know. I've never had a girlfriend."

"I think she'll dig my quirky comedian personality."

"No doubt. I think, however, you'll find more interesting news this week besides who dumped who."

"Like what? You have good dirt on someone? Wait. I'm talking to the strait-laced Trey Roberts. If it's not dirt, then what could be more important than Jenny Jacobson? Oh, crap. Don't look, it's Donald."

Marcus turned toward the lockers, trying to become smaller so he wouldn't be seen. Trey stepped out to greet his new friend.

"What's up, Trey?" Donald said happily.

They high fived after which, Donald gave Trey a quick manly one-armed hug.

"Nothing much," Trey responded with a playful smile.

"You have time to hang out before your game Saturday?" Donald asked.

"Yeah! Absolutely!" Trey wanted to talk to Don personally about his dad. Maybe he could make that happen Saturday with Donald. "Want to meet around 11 at the park then grab some lunch?"

"That'd be great. See you then!" He hugged Trey again just a little longer than before – he closed his eyes to feel it more. He then said with a whisper so only Trey could hear, "Thanks again. Dad told me what you did to rescue him. You don't have any idea how much you mean to me and my mom."

"It was my pleasure. I'm happy it all worked out."

Donald pulled away. His eyes were watery and a little red but no tears. "See you at eleven. What's up Marcus!" he said before walking off. Marcus stood bug-eyed as if he witnessed the most unbelievable occurrence of his life. His gaping mouth could hardly form the words, "What ... the heck ... just happened?"

"I told you something more interesting than Jenny Jacobson happened."

"No. Seriously. What just happened."

Trey smiled.

"Did Donald Smith; the guy that chased us through the playground earlier this week, the guy that I've been avoiding all week, the same guy that tormented you for years, just hug you?"

"Yeah."

"What the heck. What happened? What'd you do to make him not pound you?"

"We made up."

"Really? That's all you have?" he said with low cut eyes.

"I helped him out with something."

"Like algebra? Don't tell me you're doing his homework."

"No. Nothing like that. I can't really tell you right now. Maybe later."

"You have to tell me. I can't wait for later," Marcus pleaded.

Trey smiled and turned. Marcus chased him down the hall.

"You mean like later next period later or after school later?"

"Just later."

"Dude! You're killing me! I have to know. Please?"

Trey stopped. "Look. There's Jenny Jacobson."

"Yeah." Marcus said. He looked at the girl and said to Trey, "You suck you know."

"I know. You gonna to talk to her?"

"No. I'm gonna go make her laugh," he said with a level of confidence only Marcus Bouer could possess.

Marcus straightened his tucked in shirt then crossed the hall targeting a tall girl wearing a tight-fitting knee length skirt, blue top and long brown hair braided to one side. She smiled when Marcus casually approached with a quirky strut. Trey made out "Hey Marcus" from her lightly painted lips. She was easily half a foot taller than Trey's enthusiastic friend. He said something to her at which she giggled, then returned a comment Trey couldn't make out. Marcus waved bye, then returned to Trey.

"So, how'd it go?"

"She thought I was funny, just like I said."

"Good for you Marcus. That's the power of intention at work. Now all you have to do is ask her to the Homecoming Dance."

"Holy crows I forgot about the dance! You think she'd go with me?"

"I don't know buddy. You're on your own with that one."

"What about you? Who are you taking?"

"I'm not going. I've got too much on my mind lately."

"Yeah? Anything I can help with? But none of that boring sciency stuff you're into."

"No. Just some personal things that I have to work out on my own."

"Well to add to that, I'm still mad you didn't text me."

"I know. I didn't mean to hurt you."

"I'll get over it when you buy me ice cream after the movie this Sunday."

"Sure thing," Trey said.

"Uh Oh. You have one other thing to add to your personal list," Marcus said looking up the hall.

"What do you mean? What is it?" Trey asked curiously – convinced Marcus couldn't know of anything

that would stand up against his issues with Commerand –
but he was wrong.

"There's someone else that would've liked a heads
up," Marcus said urging Trey to look ahead at Sarah
waltzing down the hall toward them.

She wore a flower print sundress that waved as she
swayed gracefully. The alluring article rose into two broad
straps that barely draped each shoulder. Her rolling
blonde hair fell to one side exposing a luscious neck on
the other. She flaunted a smile that would suck the wind
from the largest sail.

"Oh no! I told her I'd walk her to school
Wednesday. Ahhggg!" he said putting his face in his
hands.

"Yeah, she asked where you were. I told her I
didn't know. She didn't seem mad or anything. More
concerned. I'll let you take it from here," he said as Sarah
took his place in the conversation. She settled on one hip,
closer to Trey than Marcus but not so close they could
accidently touch.

"Hey Marcus."

"Hey Girl!" he replied giving her a high five. "I
have to get. I'll see you two later."

He shot Trey a knowing glance as he walked off.
Trey eyed him several seconds silently screaming for help.

Trey turned a forced smile to Sarah then said
slumped in a disappointed posture. "Hey Sarah,"

"Hey Trey. Are you ok?" she asked with a
scrunched brow. She held a couple books in one hand.
Her voice was friendly and compassionate. "I figured you
weren't feeling well. It's not like you to miss school two
days in a row."

She notices when I'm not here?

"Yeah. I was pretty messed up. I'm sorry I couldn't
meet you Wednesday morning. I would've enjoyed the

walk."

She shifted hips. "It's ok. I waited a while for you. I thought you stood me up."

"No!" Trey said with too much emphasis. "I mean," he tried to correct his tone, "No, I didn't do it on purpose."

"I know. It's ok. Kenny Parker picked me up and took me to school."

Trey replied startled, "Kenny Parker? I didn't know he could drive."

"He got his driver's license a few weeks ago. His parents bought him a new car last week. A convertible. It's really nice, especially this time of year. Wednesday afternoon was a great day for a cruise."

Anxiousness and fear crept into his voice. "So, he took you home too?"

"Yeah. We also stopped at Danucci's for ice cream."

"That's cool," Trey said dismayed. He felt his heart sinking. His stomach churned.

"He's friends with Rhonda's brother. I've known him for years. He's a nice guy."

Trey replied in the friendliest manner he could muster, "He plays on the varsity soccer team, but I don't really know him." He hoped she wouldn't recognize his anguish.

"Yeah, he does. I went to his practice yesterday. They're pretty good."

"So, I hear. You went to his practice too?" He looked away then back to her and said, "That's cool. So, you two are a," he shuffled, "a couple?"

Trey felt embarrassed after the comment. He wished he could take it back. He didn't want to know the answer – unless it was definitely no.

"No," she said quickly. "Well, I don't – I, uh – he's

just – we like talking to each other and it's kinda neat hanging out with the high schoolers," she finally finished.

She didn't say 'yes' but Trey knew 'yes' was her answer. He looked at his aged shoes then said, "It's really none of my business. I shouldn't have asked."

"No. Really, Trey. It's ok."

Trey thought she seemed genuinely concerned and awkwardly ashamed for answering like she did.

"I, uh, have to get to class now. I'll see you later Trey. I'm glad you're feeling better," she said uncomfortably before strolling away.

Dang! I really messed up. That stupid disk! Why me? Why did all this happen to me! Kenny Parker of all people. Arggg! How do I compete with a high schooler with a car?

He hung his head, then pressed it against his locker. When he pushed away something clanged against the metal door. He reached in his pocket to find the disk.

"Wha – How'd this get here? The spell Aunt Kathy told me about when she gave me the disk. The spell must force the disk to always stay with me. Kathy didn't intentionally keep it in her purse. That's just where it stayed. I guess I'm stuck toting this thing around with me forever. The weirdness just doesn't end," he said to himself as he turned toward science class.

He greeted his science teacher as he strolled into class, "Hey Mr. H. Nice to see you again."

"Yeah Trey. Long time no see." He moved closer lowering his voice, then said, "That was a crazy few days huh? Are you ok?"

"Yeah, I guess. I messed up with Sarah and woke up this morning realizing the past two days weren't a dream. I'm having a really hard day."

"Sarah huh? Is there already trouble in wonderland?"

Trey gave a discontented expression.

"Sorry," Nick offered. "That was inappropriate. Seriously though, I think we've gotten ourselves into a big mess. Come by the lab after school today. I need to show you something."

"Sure."

Trey took his seat while Nick began discussing simple machines.

After science class Coach Rafiq caught up with Trey in the hall.

"Trey!" Coach Rafiq said urgently with a slow intentional Spanish accent.

"Hey Coach."

"Where have you been? Tomorrow's game day and you haven't been at practice."

"I know. I wasn't feeling well."

"You could have said something you know. You gonna be well enough to play tomorrow?"

"Yeah! I'll be there for sure."

"We are doing well with the 4231 with Davis at striker."

"Davis? Argg! This day!"

"I know you are disappointed. I'm starting him in the position tomorrow. You'll take his place at right midfield," he smiled then continued with a soft chuckle, "assuming you remember how to play the position."

He looked away from Rafiq and replied in a disappointed voice, "Yes sir. I understand. I'll be fine at midfield."

"You'll be at practice today right?"

"Yes sir," he said continuing his disappointed low

voice.

"Great. See you then. Remember Trey, communication is the key to fútbol as well as life. Don't leave your friends and family out of the loop again. Ok?"

"Ok Coach. Thanks."

He turned to find a girl resting against the adjacent locker.

"That's tough about your position," she said wearing only a concerned smile for makeup. She held a book with both hands over her belly. Long auburn hair dangled in a ponytail as she leaned her head to the side. She looked up to make eye contact.

"Oh. Hey, Leslie. You heard my conversation with Coach?"

"Most of it. I'm sorry."

He felt embarrassed she knew considering he hasn't yet had time to process the news.

"It's ok. I'd probably do the same thing if I were him. I'm lucky to be in the game this weekend."

"If it matters, you played a great game last weekend."

"Thanks," he said smiling. "You came to my match – again?"

"I haven't missed one yet this year. You're fun to watch," she said in a pinchy voice then straightened her posture. She briefly looked toward her athletic shoes before regaining eye contact, "You move the ball so well, like the other guys are standing still. That last goal for a hat trick was unbelievable."

Trey looked over her head down the hall at two boys shoving each other. When the brief scuffle was over, he brought his attention back to the sparkling emerald eyes of the girl who pleasantly invaded his space – he failed to realize he didn't mind her closeness. He lost his concentration in her gaze – like peering upon a lush green meadow after a spring rain. He could almost smell budding flowers and hear bees gathering their spoils. He forced himself back to the conversation, "Thanks. But many of them are standing still," he said dismissively. "It's just middle school soccer," he said shrugging a shoulder. "Some of the other schools don't have the pool of talent we have."

She shifted her eyes toward the lockers then back to his. Her face brightened. "I joined the girl's team last week!" she said gently bouncing on her toes and with a slight squeal as she completed the remark. "I don't start," she said lowering her voice. "But I'm fast," she continued in her previously chipper tone. "Coach says I could be a great winger," she said with a faultless smile.

"That's fantastic," he said casually – aware of his heart beating a touch stronger. "Let me know when coach plays you and I'll come to a game."

"Really? You promise?" she said with wide hopeful eyes. A light splash of freckles danced high upon her cheeks and nose when she smiled.

"Yeah, uh, sure. I'll be there."

"I hope so! See you later Trey!" she said then skipped off down the hall.

Trey watched her ponytail bop side to side as she flittered away like a butterfly bouncing against invisible objects along an undetermined flight path.

On his way to meet Nick in the science lab, a short stocky kid strutted toward Trey. He wore a smug grin.

"Davis," Trey said in a condescending tone.

"Trey! Nice to have you back," he said significantly overdoing the sarcasm. "See you at practice today," he said staring coldly at Trey then roughly bumped his shoulder as he passed.

Trey shook his head then moved on to the lab

Nick met Trey at the door of the science lab. "Come see this."

Nick took him to an object inconspicuously located in the corner by the far window.

"That's the rock you were testing for conductivity, right?"

"Yeah. It is. But I'm not testing it for connectivity. I wasn't really sure what it was I built until Lyza brought us back home."

He uncovered the object revealing a dark igneous stone encased in a copper housing. A flat four-inch by four-inch panel remained accessible. The copper housing attached to thick shielded copper cables connected to long grounding rods buried just outside the window.

"I forgot about this after that morning. The stone looks just like..."

"A portal stone" Nick finished.

"Lyza was right."

"Right about what?"

"That Khaitu or someone related to him wanted you to build this and get the Eye of Kartho. We did just what they wanted us to do. But it's useless without a key to power the portals and Lyza has that and the Eye is missing."

Nick held up the opened ceramic box displaying a copper colored key he recovered from the bird spider cave in Asia over the summer.

"You have a key too! We're in it deep. Who else knows?"

"No one. Just you, me and I guess Lyza. But she doesn't know I have a key."

"And the creeper that led you to do it."

"Yeah. I suppose that's true. But why go through

all that effort? Why not just send others loyal to Khaitu, or Commerand himself?"

"I don't know. It looks almost the same as Don's." Trey ran a finger across the cold surface of the portal. "Maybe when his didn't work out, they tried you. But if Commerand knew you had a key, he'd be here. Without the Eye, there's no other way for him to get to the other dimensions."

"At least none that Lyza has mentioned," Nick countered. "Remember, Don said he thought Commerand could open the portal. Maybe he has a key."

"Oh yeah. I forgot about that part. How many keys do you think are out there?"

"I have no idea. I didn't even know I had one until yesterday. You know," he said to Trey sincerely, "we talk about her a lot like she's this great guardian doing us favors. What do we really know about her? I mean, I'm not positive, but I feel quite certain she was responsible for Seth and I getting jumped at the Cairo airport."

"Really? That's what happened? Her and a guy named the Phoenix were talking about that. Said you gave 'em hell! That's awesome!" Trey responded excitedly.

"We nearly died."

"Oh yeah. That would've been bad," Trey said tempering his excitement.

"All I'm saying is that I'm not sure we can trust her. Think of the mess she's gotten you into."

"I've been having the same thoughts. She did conveniently show up at my house right before the rogglets attacked us and she did haul me off to nearly get killed in the desert. And I just followed the plan and won the Eye for her. I'm so stupid!"

"No, Trey. You just did what you thought was right at the time. But just in case you see her again, don't tell her about this portal or that I have a key. By the way, do you know how it works?"

"Yeah, she said you have to know the shape engraved on the stone to where you want to go and then think about where you want to go. Then as you saw, touch it to the stone. I wouldn't try it though. If you get it wrong, bad stuff happens."

"What do you mean bad stuff?"

"She tried to describe it to me but all I could imagine is falling forever until you die of old age which shouldn't be too much longer for you, huh?" Trey said jabbing Nick in the arm.

"Very funny, funny guy! It's about time for soccer practice, right?"

"Yeah, I need to get going."

"Did I hear right that Rafiq moved you to midfielder?"

"Yeah. Said I missed too many practices this week. It makes sense since I don't know how the team utilizes the new formation. It'll be ok. Davis will be a good striker."

"And you're wicked fast. You'll do fine," Nick said proudly.

Teamwork

"Trey! Nice to have you back," said a clean-cut brown skinned Puerto Rican boy with a friendly smile as Trey walked onto the soccer pitch.

"Thanks Phillipe."

"Yeah! Nice of you to return," Davis said with sly eyes.

Trey instantly recalled an interaction with Davis at Monday's practice.

"You had a good game last week," said a stocky brown headed kid with a crooked smile as Trey approached the south field where half of his teammates were waiting while others slowly pulled in. "That goal you set up for me was great. I keep telling coach to put me at striker so you can feed me more passes. I'm sure we'd dominate."

Trey sat looking up at the thick-headed kid. "We already

dominate this league, Davis. I think you'd do well in the position, though. I'll do whatever coach wants me to do."

"Don't be full of yourself, Trey. You'd cry like a little baby if Rafiq placed you anywhere else on the field or worse took you out of the game."

"It would suck, but the only way he'd do that is if I stop trying." Trey said rising to his feet, facing Davis. "And I'm not gonna do that," he finished coldly.

"Yeah. Whatever Trey," Davis said stalking off to the other end of the bench.

Phillipe the center midfielder said to Trey, "Don't let that guy get to you. He just wishes he was half as good as you."

Trey smiled and returned to his seat as coach Rafiq approached the now full bench.

Trey returned from his memory to Davis gloating, "And by the way, you're looking at your new striker, moron. I look forward to receiving lots of passes from you!" he said laughing, then walked away.

"Don't listen to him. We're gonna rock the pitch together!" encouraged Phillipe.

Phillipe was Trey's favorite teammate. He always encouraged Trey to be a smarter player and is one of the friendliest people he knows.

"That's right," Trey said happily, but it's been a long time since I've played midfield. I'm so used to you telling me where to go and what to do I may have forgotten."

"Come on out, we can work on a few things before practice starts."

Rafiq addressed the squad of teenagers after they all regained the bench. "Ok team!" he said in his typical intentional Spanish accented speech. He rested his hands on his hips. "We have our biggest match of the season tomorrow against Ridgeview. Remember, they are a very aggressive team – they will be on constant attack. We have been working on a new formation that provides a good transition from our normal 4-3-3. This should challenge them enough for us to have many opportunities to score." He glanced in Trey's direction. "However, the key to winning this match is proper and effective communication." He resumed addressing the entire team. "I only want to hear soccer related communication, not how many points you scored in the mindless video game you played last night. You understand?"

"Yes Sir!" resounded the team.

"As you all can see, Trey is back so let's get out there and settle him in to his new role. On three! One, Two, Three!"

"Pirates!"

After practice Trey said, "Can I have a word with you, Coach?"

"Sure, Trey."

Trey looked uncomfortable to Rafiq, but he spoke strongly, "Davis was having a hard time making enough space for us to send him decent passes. I'm concerned if he isn't able to get open, we will struggle to put points on the board tomorrow."

"He had a tough day today. He has been doing better." Rafiq regarded him knowingly. "I know it's hard for you to see someone else in your position, but Davis is our striker tomorrow. We'll have to see later about where to put you for the rest of the season."

"No. That's not it. I'm not trying to get my position back," Trey said discouraged about how his coach took his request. "I just want you to help him be a better striker. He won't listen to me."

"I'll have a word with him. Go on home and get

some rest. You did good today but seemed a little unfocused. Let's leave whatever is bothering you at home tomorrow. Ok?"

"Ok, Coach."

"I'm glad to have you back."

"I'm glad to be back. See you tomorrow, Coach!"

~ ~

"Hey Mom!" Trey yelled as he bowled into the kitchen from the garage door. "Mom?" He called again receiving no response. Trey's mind sizzled as he imagined the worst. He rushed to her room thinking she may be in the shower – but no, the water wasn't running, and she wasn't in the back of the house.

"Mom!" he yelled more desperately.

He bolted through the sliding glass door to the back yard.

"Mom!"

"Hey Sweet T," she said with a smile that changed to concern when she turned from the garden to him. He looked disheveled and worried. "Are you ok?"

"Mom! You're here. Thank goodness," he said with a deep exhale.

"Yeeeah," she replied inquisitively. "Where else should I be?"

"Oh," Trey realized how panicked he must have looked and sounded to her. He instantly forced a relaxed position with a hand on a hip and twisted his face into an awkward smile. "No – Nowhere," he said in a higher voice than normal. "You, uh, shouldn't be anywhere else. I'm ok. Don't worry about me." He then returned to the house leaving his mom in a confused stupor.

She followed him in to find him sitting in a chair in his room staring at a dresser drawer when she asked again, "Are you ok? You're acting very strange."

"Yeah, uh. I'm ok. I'm just having a hard time at soccer," he said raising his eyes to the wall so she wouldn't suspect anything in the drawer.

"You want to talk about it?" she asked as she sat on the bed next to him.

"No. Not really," he said still looking away.

"Well if you –" she began before he turned to her and blurted rapidly.

"Coach moved me to midfield and I don't really remember how to play and Davis is no good at striker Phillipe thinks it'll be ok but I think we'll have a hard time against Ridgeview in our current formation but coach won't move me back but I don't want to be moved back I just want coach to help Davis be better so we don't lose the game tomorrow and I'm hungry.

"O-k," she said with a raised eyebrow and a caring mama voice. "How about we have dinner and talk about it then. "

"That's a good idea. Thanks."

She hugged him with one arm around his back then left the room. His attention drifted to the drawer again when she popped her head back into the room, "We're having BBQ chicken tonight. Is that ok?"

Startled, he quickly drew his attention away from the drawer containing the artifacts and said, "Yeah. BBQ would be great. How about some butter toast with it?"

"If you want butter toast, you can make it yourself."

"Ok. I'll make some for you too."

"No. Thanks. I'm watching my carbs," she said as she pressed her tight tummy.

"What do you need to watch carbs for? You're

already skinny."

"Thank you, Trey," she said appreciating his compliment. "Now let's get dinner ready."

"Ok. I'll be there in a minute."

Over dinner Trey told her about the position change and his challenges with Davis. When she asked why Rafiq made the decision, he stumbled but convinced her it was related to the formation change rather than his recent excursions considering she thought he was at Marcus Bouer's working on a school project that for some strange reason required a real sword.

He finished the evening in his room working on homework. He fell asleep amid conflicting thoughts about Sarah and Leslie.

Looking over the desolate cliff, the flaming sword became alive in the evil demon's grasp. Now standing beside the demon he felt deathly heat from the dispassionate weapon. The sword lowered – Trey became the flame, driving violently toward the village. Blurred landscape in reds, blues and whites passed his peripherals. The impact of the attack jolted his sleeping body askew. The missile of plasma now engulfed him head on while he kneeled ahead of a woman and child who screamed helplessly as the fire ravaged everything around him. An image of a sun separated into three pieces by a thin line emerged in the sand at his feet while attempting to duck from the blast. HAHAHAHAHA!

Trey awoke to the haunting laugh – gasping for breath and rolling around snuffing out imaginary flames. "Holy crap, what a dream!"

"Ready for your match today, Honey?" Trey's mom asked as he stumbled into the kitchen for breakfast. She wore jeans and a white tee shirt.

He rubbed his scruffy hair patted the disk in his pocket and said, "Yeah, I guess so."

"Well don't seem so enthusiastic about it," she said as she turned from the sink with a warm bowl of cinnamon oatmeal.

He slumped into a chair at the kitchen table. "It's not that. I'm just ... tired. I haven't been seeping well lately."

"Does it have anything to do with that Sarah girl?"

"Sarah?" He instantly woke and sat upright. "How do you know about her?"

"I'm your mother. It's my job to know about you," she said smiling.

"No. it's not about her. She's just a friend. Besides," he scratched at the worn wooden table, "she likes a high school kid."

She looked off into the distance, "I remember when I was in middle school. Those high school boys just seemed so much cooler ... and sexier (she said as an afterthought) than the kids my age."

Trey's teenage sarcasm took over, "Thanks, mom. You're really comforting."

"Sorry Hun. Looks like it's just as true today as it was back then. Don't worry about it. High school boys are dumb. She'll figure it out."

"Thanks. I guess."

"Well, eat and get your stuff ready. We have Ridgeview to beat!"

He smiled and continued his oatmeal.

After breakfast back in his room, he took the sword from under his mattresses. He spent the next hour watching and mimicking the actions from online sword play videos on his phone. Jabbing and thrusting, a smile crossed his face as he worked harder and thrusted stronger with each move. After his self-motivated training session, he replaced the sword and went outside to work on dribbling in the backyard. The disk, while incredibly light, bounced annoyingly in his pocket. He reentered the house found an elastic band that fit perfectly around the disk and his upper thigh while hidden under his shorts, keeping it secure and out of the way during activities.

Trey changed into sneakers. He looked toward the road as he left his soccer gear in a neat pile by the front door. He grabbed his bike from the side of the house then slowly peddled by a car with tinted windows he hadn't noticed in the neighborhood before. The engine started as he passed. He approached a similar car parked at the entrance of the neighborhood.

I wonder if these are the people Lyza said would be watching me and my family. He looked back periodically at the slowly trailing vehicles. He briefly considered cutting through a wooded lot in an attempt to ditch the lurking watch, but fear crept into his spine and opted for the added security.

He rode to the park to meet Donald. The temperature was mild. Flimsy clouds battled in the blue sky. One of the tinted windowed cars stopped on the far side of the park.

Trey jumped the curb with his bike, crossed the open space toward Donald who was passively swinging in the swing set. Trey then skidded to a stop sending woodchips flying onto the adjacent slide.

"Hey, Trey! Thanks for coming," Donald said as he jumped from the swing. "Thanks again for bringing dad home."

"No problem. He's an amazing man, your dad – very smart," he replied as he set the bike down.

"Yeah. Yeah, he is. I've missed his witty humor and ability to build stuff."

"Haha! I bet you did. I'm glad he's back."

Trey intended to wait for a good opportunity to ask his questions but became too anxious and spouted it right out. "Did he, by any chance, say how he knows my dad?"

"No. Sorry. We didn't talk much about him."

Trey looked down in disappointment then he perked up as the comment registered. "Much? So, he did get mentioned?"

"Yeah. Dad said he worked with him on a project in Atlanta. Said he needed his expertise on a device."

"What kind of device?"

"He said something about it stopping portal access."

"Really? He said it would stop someone from using a portal?"

Donald misunderstood Trey's motivation for asking the question and tried to avoid the embarrassment of Trey thinking he believed his dad's crazy stories. "I think so. I don't believe it either. He said a lot of really weird stuff. I think he lost it while he was away."

"I don't know," Trey said unsure of how to address the uncomfortable topic. "Did he say exactly where they worked in Atlanta?"

"He said they used a physics lab at a university in the city."

"That was all?"

"Maybe not, but that's all I remember."

Trey kicked at the woodchips then asked, "What exactly did he tell you about what happened?"

"Everything," Donald said with wide unbelieving eyes.

"What do you mean by everything?" Trey further inquired, not believing Don would be entirely forthcoming about his line of work.

"Everything, Trey," he said as he leaned in closer and lowered his voice as if someone were spying in on their conversation. "He told me about his office in China, his work with ancient artifacts and that some were," he looked away then back with a serious expression, "magical."

"And you believed him?"

"Not really," he said in a way that Trey felt he was unsure about what he believed. "But he was convincing. He said a bunch of stuff about a group of whacked monsters and the end of the world."

"And you don't believe any of that?" Trey said trying not to give up his position on the matter.

"Uh. Of course not," he stumbled with the response. "I'm not that gullible. What I do believe is that you went out of your way to convince the lady to bring him home."

"That's what he said happened?"

"No. He said something ridiculous about you, a dragon and teleporting with Mr. Hampton."

Trey looked away and said distantly, "Yeah. That is a ridiculous story."

"Do you think my dad's crazy?" he said directly. "Do you think all that time alone made him lose his mind?"

"I - I don't know about that. I think your dad is very rational. I'm not sure why he said all that other stuff."

"He said I needed to know so that I would be prepared when they come again."

"When who comes again, the monsters?"

"Yeah. He's crazy, isn't he?"

"I, uh – " Trey noticed an elderly woman with a cane slowly approaching. She entered the playground area from the road about half a football field away. "Something looks strange about that woman," he said to Donald.

"What do you mean? It's just an old woman," Donald responded while looking over his shoulder behind him.

"No. Something isn't right. Do you think she knows us? She's coming right at us and…" he thought for a minute, "there's something about how she's walking."

"Dude. You're freaking me out. I don't recognize her. It's just an old woman with a cane."

"That's it! She has a cane but isn't using it! It's just dragging behind her like a limp tail."

"Run! Donald! Run!"

Just as Trey turned to run, the old woman leaped into the air and landed ten feet in front of them.

"What the heck!" Donald shouted.

Its face withered into a gruesome mass. Donald screamed like a little girl as it morphed into a rogglet.

The two boys dashed across the grassy park, away from the creature.

"I'm sorry Trey!" Donald said as they hurdled a large plastic pipe designed as a playground obstacle.

"What could you possibly be sorry for!" Trey screamed as the rogglet launched after them.

"For chasing you and your friend the other day!" He looked back and screamed again.

"Not the time, Dude!"

Donald suddenly stopped and turned toward the approaching rogglet."

Trey screamed as he fell down trying to catch his friend, "Donald! No!"

BAM! BAM! Sounded shots diagonal to them. Donald flopped onto the ground holding his hands over his head as if he were hiding.

The rogglet's head exploded, sending chunks of greyish-green ooze everywhere. The remaining body toppled awkwardly to the ground with a thud. A leg continued to twitch for several seconds scattering pieces of chipped wood while it dug a lifeless hole. Two men holding pistols rushed toward them from the direction of the tinted windowed car.

"Trey! What is that thing! Trey! What is it!" Donald shrieked as he sat up facing the decimated creature. He began hyperventilating.

"Hey buddy," one of the men wearing a red baseball cap said as he holstered his weapon. "Let's have a seat over here," he continued as he helped Donald off the ground and ushered him toward a bench away from the mess.

The other, with a buzz cut rapidly scanned the area. He said to his partner, "It looks clear." He then approached Trey. Trey noticed the shield symbol tattooed on his forearm. "Trey," he said with a friendly French accent. "My name is Charlie." Which sounded like Sharlie to Trey. "I'm with the Order of Hsehk. That was close. We were informed they can take the shape of humans, but that one looked so real."

"You didn't know it was a rogglett?" Trey asked worriedly.

Charlie replied evasively, "I, uh, we haven't yet seen one of this kind." He redirected the attention toward Trey's efforts, "We might have experienced a gravely different outcome if you hadn't been so quick to notice its inability to use the cane properly."

"Yeah. I guess I'm lucky," Trey responded gloomily.

Charlie replied with an upbeat tone that hinted of defensiveness, "Hey. Don't be so down. We're here to help."

"I know. Thanks for getting here on time."

"I promise we'll do better next time."

Trey winced at the comment. "Next time?"

"We didn't expect them to be onto you so soon after returning. Where's the sword?"

"I hid it."

"You may need to keep it on you at all times."

"I don't think that's possible. It's a big sword and I'm a small kid and if you haven't noticed, normal people don't carry swords these days."

"I suppose you're right. Just hide it well and we'll be nearby when you need us."

"Ok. Thanks, Charlie."

Trey sat next to Donald who regained his composure and gazed far away.

"It's all real isn't it? Everything my dad said is true."

"I'm afraid so." Trey flicked a glop of goo from Donald's shoulder.

"He's really not crazy then?" He looked at Trey with an empty expression.

Trey smiled, "Nope."

"So, you really did battle a dragon to help rescue my dad."

"Yeah."

"And teleportation is real?"

"That too."

"Holy crap."

"Exactly. But these guys are here to help," he motioned to the two guys that wasted the rogglet.

"They'll keep you and your family safe."

"Ok," Donald responded still in shock.

"Trey. We should go," said Charlie.

"Ok. Can you take him home? I have my bike. I'll be fine."

Charlie looked as if he were texting someone on his phone then replied, "Another unit just showed up. We'll carry your friend home. You're free to take the bike."

Trey thought to himself, *Free? I'm free to go?* He didn't like the sound of that. He instantly felt claustrophobic and infringed upon.

"Hey, Donald." Donald slowly looked into Trey's dark hazel eyes. "You gonna be ok, buddy?"

Donald didn't respond.

"These guys will take you home. They'll sort it all out with your dad. Ok?"

Donald nodded in agreement then followed the red-capped guy to the car.

Trey then said, "Thanks," to Charlie and peddled away with an unassuming car following close behind.

He felt like he should be a little more freaked out about the attack. He was concerned that maybe he was becoming too accustomed to life threatening situations.

He dropped the bike in the yard as the car pulled to an adjacent curb. The adrenalin from the playground was gone while the shocking reality of the event creeped in.

His mom stood in the kitchen when he entered the house wide eyed and thoughtless. "Where were you? We'll be late. Grab your stuff and let's go."

Trey was instantly plucked from the darkness and didn't understand. "What? What do you mean late? Late for what?" He came around and realized he had plenty of time to get to the soccer fields. He pushed away the playground attack and said, "But Mom, It's only noon."

"I know. I have to run by the museum, and we should probably eat some lunch."

"Oh. Yeah. I am hungry. Can we do the Indian place set up like a sandwich shop?"

"That sounds like a good idea and it's near the Metro Station we'll need to take to get to the museum."

After Trey and his mom put away lunch, they boarded the Metrorail heading east toward Washington D.C. Trey noticed the man with a buzz cut enter the train right behind him. They exchanged nods of acknowledgement.

Regardless of the added protection from his personal security escort, Trey was instantly nervous entering the train. It was full and the lively Saturday crowd was suffocating. Flashbacks to the Shanghai incident with the shape shifting rogglet on the train passed his mind as well as the recent one with Donald.

Trey stood while his mom took a seat next to him. He scanned the crowd looking for anyone odd, trying not to single out older people considering that's been his only experience with the new breed of rogglet that could be anyone. He breathed a little easier when he didn't notice anyone that wasn't engaged in a conversation or staring mindlessly into an electronic device. The uneventful ride ended when they exited at the L'Enfant station which emptied onto a busy glass shaded sidewalk lined with newspaper kiosks and food trucks.

They turned right onto Maryland. Trey eyed the domed capital building in the distance. They passed several white buildings of similar construction as they neared the National Mall.

Walking through the museum, a canopy of stars

greeted them with a moody and reflective atmosphere. As they walked, the halls told a story of the native American's relationship with nature, seasonal observances, ancestral wisdom, and beliefs about the order of the world in vivid color and detail. Further in the museum, depictions describing the complicated history between Indian Nations and the United States were arranged in artistic formations. Treaties, diplomacy, armed conflict, and forced removal were etched on every boarder. Trey felt that the exhibits were deficient in accurately describing the injustices and horrific treatment of Native Americans by the U.S. government, something he hoped his mom could convey in her exhibit.

They entered a restricted area leaving Trey's personal guard behind. He followed her down a brightly lit hall to turn right into a key carded room. On a desk sat a large box addressed to Janet Boatright.

"Oh, Trey! It's here!" She sounded like a teenage girl who was just approached by the most popular guy in school.

"What is it?"

She opened the box, scraped away layers of biodegradable packaging peanuts then removed a plain wooden box. She opened the housing to reveal something protected by layers of bubble wrap.

She looked at Trey like it was her birthday and about to open the best gift.

She carefully removed several pieces of tape then unwound an oval object with an inscription carved into the face.

"What's that say?" Trey asked.

"I don't know," she replied inspecting the intricate letters.

"It looks like a warning," Trey said ominously.

"Yeah. It does."

She rested the dark stained wooden piece onto the bubble wrap and said, "This came to me from the chieftainess of a native tribe in Utah. Her family passed it down for over two thousand years. She reached out to me over a month ago wanting to protect it. She doesn't have any other family to pass it down to."

"What is it?"

"I don't know. Let's open it to find out," she said excitedly.

She began to carefully pry open the object.

"You're gonna open it?" Trey said worriedly.

She looked at him curiously, "Of course. Why wouldn't I?"

"The warning," Trey stated.

"We don't really know that's a warning, plus, I'll be very careful.

Trey looked at his mom cautiously as she rolled the wooden egg shape until she found the spot she was looking for. She then carefully pried the pieces apart revealing a stunning headdress made of gold and jewels. It was designed to wrap around the wearers head which would then prominently display wide bands of feather-shaped gold strips slightly layered side by side. Each feather was encrusted with red and green jewels. The golden feathers tapered in size from about seven inches in the middle front to one inch in the back. Raised shapes of familiar animals made of differing colors of metal decorated a thin band circumferencing the base. It looked as if it were used as a crown.

"That doesn't look like it was made by anyone in ancient America," Trey said insinuating his mom may have been scammed.

"I know. Isn't it beautiful?" she said disregarding his doubtful tone. "I think it came from Egypt."

"What makes you think that?"

"I'll have to look, but I think these are ostrich feathers. See how wide and bowed they are?"

"Yeah. They don't look like the ones in your collection. But how? How did a family in Utah thousands of years ago come across a headdress such as this?"

"I don't know. I didn't ask those questions. I just said yes and had it shipped here rather than the office across town considering most of my time is spent here with my exhibition."

Trey inspected it further and noticed a striking feature. A small thin piece of metal shaped into a fist holding a single rose. It was placed precisely in sync with the rest of the design. He wouldn't have noticed had he not seen that color of metal before. It wasn't gold, but another metal that was copper in color but nearly blended in perfectly.

Is that a – He looked closer – a portal key? He was so surprised he nearly said it out loud. *But it looks different than Lyza's.* He dared to lean in closer. He reached his hand to caress the intricately constructed feathers. As his finger came into contact with the piece a heart-stopping pulse rocketed through him. The pulse forced him to a knee like he'd been punched in the stomach. He coughed several times before catching his breath.

"You ok, honey?" Mom said as she looked over a paper.

"Yeah. I just uh –" He noticed his mom wasn't paying attention, so he didn't finish his excuse.

He peered at the artifact and dared to touch it another time. As his finger pressed against the cold metal, nothing happened. He pressed it several more times finally picking up the piece.

"No! No! Trey. Don't touch it. It says here that we shouldn't touch it. Tarnish and such I suppose."

He gently set it down. His mom quickly went over it with metal cleaner and specialized utensils.

With urgency in his voice he said, "What do you intend to do with it? You can't display it considering it isn't Native American."

"Easy, T. You're right. I can't display it and I don't know what to do with it. I'll probably get the curator of the National Museum of History to take it."

"No!"

She looked at him strongly.

He backed off and said in a less forceful but equally urgent tone, "I mean, no. I don't think you need to tell anyone about it yet. Let's do some research first. Maybe we can find something online. It looks very important. I don't think anyone needs to know we have it."

"Why do you have such interest in ancient artifacts today?"

"Well, uh, Kathy," He thought quickly. Aunt Kathy was talking about Grandpa and got me interested in his work. I guess I just have that side in me," he gave an uneasy smile and shrug.

She regarded him another second or so, smiled an enthusiastic mama smile then said cheerfully, "Ok. Let's do some research and see what we can come up with. It'll be a fun thing we can do together."

Trey took a picture of it with his phone then said, "You need to put this somewhere no one can find it."

"There are lockers near the cleaning lab. I can put it there anonymously."

"That's a good idea. Thanks, Mom," he said then hugged her. "We have to go now...my game."

"Ok. Let me take this to the locker.

She rewrapped the case placed it back in the box then carried it away. A few minutes later she returned with only a locker key in her hand.

"Ready to go?"

"Yep."

Trey's heart pounded. His mind struggled with questions about how this could have possibly found its way to his mom by chance. It was too circumstantial she received it knowing what he was currently facing and his family's history with such artifacts.

They reentered L'Enfant Metro Station and took a west bound train back to Tyson's Corner where they previously left the car. He didn't notice the security detail following nor did he consider rogglets on this trip while his mind raced over the discovery of the headdress.

~ ~

They drove to the soccer complex where he began to prepare his mind for the match against Ridgeview and pushed away the revelation of the artifact for the next ninety minutes. His mom wished him luck and gave him another hug. He then ran off to the sidelines to meet his team.

Coach Rafiq addressed the boys, "Ok team! Ridgeview is a formidable opponent. They haven't yet been defeated. Today that changes! Let's stay focused out there, play your positions and most importantly communicate! One, Two, Three!"

"Pirates!"

"Good luck," Trey said to Davis as they took the field. Davis simply returned a nervous smile.

Trey causally waived to Don and Donald in the stands then gave a smile and salute to Leslie who sat on the front row.

"Pop, Pop, Snap," on his shoulder alerted Trey of Tessie's presence.

"Thanks Tessie!" he whispered. "Now get out of here before someone sees you!"

Tessie popped away as Trey smiled at his fan support.

Trey walked the slightly dampened pitch toward his position at right midfield repeating a mantra under his breath, "I move the ball well. I pass the ball well. I shoot the ball well. I move the ball well. I pass the ball well. I shoot the ball well." Over and over.

His boots gripped firmly in the grass. The significance of the day's previous excitement – a distant memory. His intense focus was solely to perform the job at hand to the best of his ability.

"I move the ball well..."

The sidelines were packed – everyone eager to see the battle between two undefeated teams. Trey took his position. Shortly after, the whistle blew indicating the start of the match.

Ridgeview launched aggressively with several successful passes, then turned the ball over to the Pirates right defender. He passed back to the keeper who booted it down the left field.

Several change of possessions later Ridgeview's center midfielder sent the ball to the right forward who placed a perfectly lofted ball into the path of their striker's head leading to the first score of the game, prompting glorious cheers from the Ridgeview supporters.

A few change of possessions later, Trey received

the ball from a defender then one-touched to Robbie, the right forward.

"Get open, Davis!" yelled Robbie.

He dropped it back to Trey who placed a target leading pass back to Robbie who caught his fullback on the wrong foot. Robbie attempted to center the ball, but the center fullback punted it away from Davis.

"You have to make space, Davis. Otherwise, the defender or keeper will get the ball every time."

"Shut up Trey and do your job!" Davis spouted.

After several more possessions, Phillipe sent the ball to Trey who dribbled past a midfielder with a shoulder feint, then a defender with a stepover. He continued toward the left side of the field before passing it off to the left winger. Trey moved forward into open space toward the goal. The left winger centered it. Trey had a nice shot but let it go to the better positioned Davis. Davis missed the pass completely, watching it exit the back of the field.

"That was your ball, Trey! Why didn't you score!" yelled Davis.

Trey and Phillipe shared a concerned glance, then moved back into position to defend the goal kick.

After a few more possessions the whistle blew twice indicating half time.

"Dude," Phillipe said to Trey as they walked toward the sideline. "We're gonna lose this game if Davis keeps hacking. We have to do something about it."

"I know! He's killing us." He looked toward the bench. "I'll talk to Coach. I'll see if he'll rearrange the positions for the second half."

Coach Rafiq addressed the team, "Guys, you're doing well but we're not finding many open shots on the goal." Trey and Phillipe looked at each other. "Robbie, you as right forward need to move more center to draw the defense away from Davis. Trey, you and Phillipe keep doing what you are doing. Defense, you are outstanding let's give them a hand. Keep it up and we will come out of this with a win!"

"Coach," Trey said in private as he followed Rafiq away from the team.

"What is it, Trey?"

"Davis isn't getting open. Put me at striker and we'll win this game."

"I won't change it now. Give him the opportunities he needs. Help him get open."

"I can't play the game for him, Coach," Trey said emphatically.

"No, you can't. You'll just have to do the best you can in your position."

Trey looked out onto the field then said, "The best I can...in my position."

Rafiq gave a questioning look in response to Trey's comment.

"Ok! I'll do the best I can!" Trey said with a big smile running out onto the field.

Startled at Trey's instant change in demeanor he yelled, "Play your position, Trey! Play your position!"

Back on the pitch, Trey gave Phillipe a straight-faced nod. Understanding what to do he nodded back. He did the same to Robbie the right forward. Davis dropped the ball back to Phillipe, the center midfielder, to start the second half. Phillipe passed to Trey who passed forward to Robbie. Trey darted into open space past Davis separating the defenders. Robbie quickly sent it back to Trey who nailed an upper left corner goal. The home crowd cheered wildly at the quick score.

"Yeah!" shouted Rafiq. "Nice goal, Trey! Play your

position!"

"Why didn't you center it! I was wide open!" hollered Davis at Robbie.

"Davis, try slowly drawing your defenders away from the goal then quickly turning back to your right. That should give you enough space to receive a lead from me," Robbie said. "Then all you have is the keeper to beat."

"Who's the striker here, huh? I know what I'm doing!"

They returned to their positions. Trey, Robbie and Phillipe shared a confident nod.

Ridgeview kicked off the ball to continue the game. Several possessions later Trey won the ball from a Ridgeview forward near the penalty arc after a blocked corner kick. Way out of position he had no one to pass to. He drove the ball with quick precise movements. He spun around a midfielder, sprinted, stopped the ball short with the inside of his left foot then redirected the ball with his right to avoid another midfielder. He passed to Phillipe who caught up with the drive. Phillipe immediately one-two'd it back to Trey. Trey stepped over, then shot it through the legs of a defender to continue the run which drew various shouts from the crowd, "Meg!" He glanced at Davis breaking out to his left with an arm up and a defender on his heels. Trey chose to ignore the incompetent striker. He snaked past the last defender, then powered a shot over the keeper to put the Pirates ahead by one. The crowd rose to their feet cheering at the change in momentum. Ro-berts, Ro-berts, Ro-berts they chanted.

"Coach! They're completely ignoring me out there," whined Davis holding his arms wide.

"Trey! Robbie! Phillipe! Use your striker! This is a

team effort!"

"Ok, Coach!" Trey said as the three players smiled at each other. "Phillipe! Coach says we need to use our striker!" Trey yelled with adrenalin saturated veins.

"Ok Trey! Let's do it!"

Ridgeview kicked off again, Phillipe intercepted an errant pass to the center midfielder. He dribbled past a defender toward Davis at a left angle to the goal. Trey dashed into the open no more than seven yards to the right of Davis. Phillipe quickly passed to Trey who boomed the ball off the angled back of Davis propelling it into the net. Davis plummeted to the ground face first from the force of the strike. The crowd cheered wildly at the goal.

"Congratulations Davis!" Trey said happily to the downed boy. "You scored your first goal as striker!" He ran off to give Phillipe a high-five before settling into his position at right midfield.

Trey made one more impressive goal by streaking through the defense to place a well faded left footed shot into the bottom left corner of the goal to complete the hat-trick. Three whistles followed to give the Pirates a firm victory over Ridgeview. Cheers from all around as the champions left the field.

After Rafiq dismissed the team, Trey replaced his soccer boots with athletic shoes then heard from a familiar voice, "That was a brilliant game you played!" He looked up to find Lyza from the other side of the fence. "I've never seen a right midfielder make so many goals in one game."

Trey's elation faded into worry, "You! What are you doing here?"

"What? I can't watch a sports match in my free time? That striker of yours sure is a nasty kid," she said smiling.

"Yeah. He's not very nice. But I feel bad for what I did. I should have included him in the second half. I didn't have to embarrass him."

"He was embarrassing himself. He deserved it. Plus, he got credit for the goal which will look good on his record," she replied.

"I suppose so. But no one deserves to be treated poorly."

"He'll get over it."

"That was a good game you played today," said Coach Rafiq from behind as he joined the conversation. "I'm disappointed you didn't play your position, but you helped us come out with a win and I appreciate that. You have your position back."

"Thanks, Coach! I won't let you down again."

"I know you won't," he said with a fatherly smile. "I just wanted to teach you about commitment and communication. Clearly you didn't learn the latter."

"I have now." Trey hung his head seemingly ending the conversation.

There was a momentary pause before Trey said guardedly, "Hey, Coach." Rafiq regarded him with tender concern. "I feel really bad about today...you know...how I treated Davis."

"I know you do. You're a good kid. Don't let it eat you up inside. You have to let those things go. It also wouldn't hurt to let Davis know how you feel."

"Yeah. You're probably right. I'm sure he's super angry with me. I'll try to catch him at morning break Monday."

"The sooner the better. You two have a long season together."

Rafiq then took a significant interest in Lyza.

"Who's your lady friend? Do I need to be concerned?" he said in such a rich romantic voice that Vicente Fernandez's legs would've quivered.

"No Coach," he said giving the man a strange look. "She's a friend...of my mom's. This is Lyza."

"Oh, if only my beautiful mother, rest her soul, had friend's as fine as yours," he said continuing to pour it on while staring into Lyza's big blue eyes. "Carlos Rafiq," he said holding out his hand. "It is very nice to meet such a lovely person as you, Ms. Lyza."

"Thank you for your generous complement. I am likewise pleased to meet you," she said taking his hand with a charming smile.

Focusing his attention back on Trey he said in his former coach's voice, "Remember, Coach Wood next week."

"Ok, Coach."

"It has been a pleasure, hermosa dama," he said passionately regarding her one last time while walking away – gently sliding her hand out of his.

"That's some coach you have there. He must be very popular with the ladies," she said affectionately.

"I suppose," he replied watching Rafiq walk away. "Why are you here again?"

"I'm just checking up on you. You know. Making sure you're ok after the past few days."

"You heard about what happened today?"

"Yeah. How are you doing?"

"I'm fine. How's Donald?"

"He was shaken up, but I think he'll be ok. He's a tough kid."

"I hate that he was thrown into it like this."

"It was bound to happen sooner or later considering his father is back."

"I guess you're right."

"Anything else going on with you since our little adventure?"

"Uh, No. Nothing new with me," he said as he thought about the dreams and the key discovery. "I'm still concerned something will jump from out of nowhere to get me and my mom. What about my friends? What if they try to use my friends against me?"

"Don't worry. As you've seen, there are many protective eyes on you and your family as well as Marcus."

"Dang! What don't you know about me?"

"You don't have anything to worry about. Commerand is only after the eye."

"Have you found it yet?"

"No. Clievan is still MIA so the eye should be safe."

"What about that creeper today? Why'd it attack us? How did it know where I was?"

"I don't know. We're still looking into it."

"Ok. I guess I have to trust you on that one. By the way, this disk, I can't seem to lose it. I leave it somewhere and it appears later in my pocket. What's the deal?"

"I'm not familiar with the disk. All I know is that it's a magical artifact created by Master Olerand. Khaitu only used it for destruction. Maybe one day you can find more peaceful uses for it. But let's just keep it undercover for now. Magic is unbiased. It doesn't know the difference between good and bad. It just is what it is and does what it does. The user is the differentiator. Do you understand? You don't want anything to happen to you or anyone else because of a tragic accident."

"I understand."

"You coming, Trey?" Phillipe shouted from his mom's van.

"Go on and celebrate with your friends. I know where to find you."

"Thanks, Lyza. I'll see ya later."

The team celebrated the win with a boisterous pizza celebration.

Disk Play

Later that evening, Trey sat in his room staring at the disk on the dresser waiting for it to move. Thirty seconds. Two minutes. Nothing happened. He placed it in a sock in the sock drawer, then began counting.

"One, two, three,..." he counted until he reached twenty.

He felt something in his pocket. He reached in, then pulled out the disk.

"This doesn't make any sense."

He put it back in the drawer inside the sock.

"One, two,..." then pulled the disk from his pocket again once he reached the count of twenty.

He put it on the bed and watched.

"One, two,.."

He counted to one hundred and thirty. It remained on the bed.

"I don't get it," he said to himself, then left to get some water.

Pouring the water, he felt the disk fill his pocket. "What the heck?"

He set the disk on the counter, then turned around and began counting.

The disk appeared into his pocket after twenty seconds.

So, if I watch it, it stays but if I take my eyes off of it, it comes back to me after twenty seconds.

He went to his room, placed the disk into his empty backpack on the floor then counted. After twenty seconds the disk was in his pocket. He replaced the disk into the backpack, but this time put the backpack on. The disk remained in the backpack after twenty seconds.

"That's good. I don't have to keep it in my pocket forever."

He then changed into pocketless shorts. He removed the backpack and placed it on the bed. After twenty seconds, he found his hand clutching the disk.

This is going to be a big problem come summertime.

He had a brilliant thought. He set the disk on the bed and on top of the disk he placed the gold coin Karim gave him. He turned around and after twenty seconds he looked in his hand to find the disk and the golden coin.

"Unbelievable." His excitement nearly overwhelmed him.

He set it back on the bed, then laid a large encyclopedia on the disk. After twenty seconds, BAM! The book fell to the floor next to him while the disk occupied his hand.

He then placed the disk, encyclopedia and the coin in his backpack on the bed. After twenty seconds the disk and coin were in his hand while the book rested at his side.

Even more excited now, he went out to the garage.

He set the disk on the ground, then on top of it he placed the edge of a fifty-pound weight. He ran to the front yard counting down from twenty. Seconds later the disk was in his hand and the weight instantly appeared at his feet.

As a final test, he took the disk to the back yard, then set it on the trampoline. He ran to the far side of the back yard, leaving plenty of space for the trampoline. After twenty seconds the disk was in his hand, but the trampoline remained where it was. Confused, he ran back to the trampoline. Looking for a moment, he remembered the disk on the bed and in the drawer. The disk in the drawer was inside a sock but didn't bring the sock. It was inside the drawer and backpack but not under it. It was also on the bed.

So maybe it only transports items if the thing is on top but not under or if the items are inside something like a backpack?

He placed a leg of the trampoline on top of the disk, then ran to the front yard, for good measure. Seconds passed, then Trey found the disk in his hand and the trampoline at his side.

"This is so awesome!"

He returned the trampoline and weight to their original places – using the disk of course.

He fell asleep that night with the disk in his hand.

Flying high above a vast desert, Trey watched as if at the cinema. Quick looks, left, right down as wind rushed past revealing little of consequence. Higher and higher he flew in a swooping gait. Terrain, so far away, was displayed in the clearest detail. Three camels with riders traveling west came and went with a rapid glance. Smaller movement – a desert fox. Banking ever so slightly to the right, he darted through a wispy cloud revealing a small village several miles in the distance. Constant changes in view brought the landscape into perspective. To the west of the small village was the desert. To the southeast lay a larger village. To the East, a thriving metropolis bordering an immense river that had no end. He sailed toward the destination at a constant altitude. His view turned down when he approached the western perimeter. Rapidly falling, gaining speed, hurtling from the sky at a blistering pace toward a tiny wooded area to the west of the small village. Trees and ground grow closer and larger and closer until....

He stood at the edge of the thicket looking upon the town as if he were there all day. He turned toward a high-pitched call in the tree above. A grand brown and white eagle rested on a low limb. The eagle leapt from the branch transforming into a small grey and black wolf the size of a border collie. It trotted up to Trey, stopped to take a look then scurried off toward the town. The bright afternoon sun fell behind him at a nine O-Clock position to his left – the temperature mild.

The town thrived with activity. The wolf led him past shoeless brown skinned children kicking a craggy ball. They wore only a single wrap around their waist. Trey resisted the urge to play with them. He followed the guide around a corner, then down a street through a bazaar where people of various shapes, sizes and genders sold vegetables on a wooden rack, live chickens, and various clothing items that were different shades of brown. A man laughed to his right. A woman engaged in an argument over the price of a bag of grains to his left. The wolf paused next to an old woman selling three pieces of pottery intricately engraved with a symbol of a sun separated by three thin lines. The furry guide looked toward Trey before it turned left continuing the tour. It turned, then sat next to a sitting woman singing a disturbing lullaby to an infant with dark black hair wrapped in a soft brown cloth.

Beyond the river you will see
Miles of heaven past the tree
The sun has set on you my dear
The time has come for all to fear

On this day the beast alights
On our doorsteps with flames of fright
We must await for one in prayer
For he alone is our true sav-ior.

Urgency laced the wolf's demeanor, tail alert, mouth opened and closed quickly as if attempting to whine. When Trey approached, the wolf scurried toward the eastern boarder of the town, barking furiously. As Trey passed the woman, the infant focused a concentrated stare on Trey leaving him disconcerted. Trey ran to the dog, but before he could reach it, a blinding light engulfed him.

Trey woke with his arms crossed protectively over his face.

He caught his breath and said to himself, "What does it mean?"

After breakfast, Trey practiced with the sword for an hour then continued experiments with the disk. He concluded he could keep it in something like his backpack as long as he was wearing it. Otherwise, it would appear in his pocket or his hand along with all the other stuff in the pack. It would also transport anything he placed on top of it but not anything under or the thing it is inside. It always took twenty seconds to happen.

He decided he needed more information on the disk and hopefully, his father. He tossed the disk into a buttoned pocket then rode his bike to Donald's apartment, contrary to his mom's permission. The complex looked much less scary in the daytime. He recognized a man standing on the corner sidewalk. It was Lamar, the guy Nick befriended when they brought Don home.

"What's up, Cool Dude!" he said to Trey while holding out a hand.

Trey stopped to greet the man with a few quick hand slaps.

"Good to see you again, Lamar."

"Right on! You remembered my name!" He leaned closer and said in a friendly voice, "You ever need anything, you know where to find me, aight?"

Trey was confused by the offer but agreed anyway, "Sure. Thanks." He then rode off wondering what he could possibly need from Lamar. *There's something strange about that guy,* Trey thought. *I wish I could read his mind to find out.*

The man in the car following Trey tipped his hat to Lamar as he drove by. The scrawny black man responded with an affirmative head nod and a serious face much different from the jovial one presented to the young boy.

Trey dropped his bike by the steps of Don's building. A passing thought occurred of whether it would be there when he returned.

Donald's mom, Clara, greeted him at the door. "You must be Trey," she said.

"Yes, Mrs. Smith."

"Please come in. Donald will be happy to see you."

She walked him into the tiny apartment that

smelled of mold and cigarettes.

"Donald was shaken up yesterday after the attempted mugging. You two were lucky to have police nearby."

"Mugging?" Trey responded.

"Yeah," Don interrupted. "The officer that brought Little Don home explained it all," he said with an inconspicuous wink.

Trey caught on quickly that Clara was not in on the truth.

"Yeah. It was, er, very scary," Trey added nervously. Trey hated lying about anything but understood the nature of this truth necessitated some discretion.

"You know," she said embarrassingly, "we're used to that sort of thing in this neighborhood." She looked around at her shabby apartment. "But we didn't expect it on your side of town."

"I'm sure it can happen anywhere, Mrs. Smith. Mr. Smith, will you join me in Donald's room? I have some, uh, guy questions to ask you."

"Sure, Trey. I'll be right there." He leaned toward Clara and whispered, "His dad left him years ago. I better go see what's going on."

"Oh. Ok. I understand. No girls allowed," she said charmingly.

Don kissed her cheek lightly then led Trey to Donald's room where he was playing a game on his phone.

"Trey! I'm glad to see you." Donald rushed to hug him. "Yesterday was so crazy!" He looked at his dad in a loving way, "Dad explained to me what that thing was." His face then became white. "Do you think they'll try to get me again?"

"No. I think you're ok. I don't think they were after you."

"That's what dad said, but I felt it was after me,

like it was calling me toward it." He looked down, his face flushed, "I was so scared. That's why I froze. I'm so weak. I've never been so scared." He turned as Don stepped close to comfort him.

"Called to you? Did you really hear something? I didn't hear anything."

"I don't remember it actually saying anything, it was more like a pull, like I knew it wanted me." Donald sniffed a bit then continued, "I knew it wanted to eat me and I, uh, think I, umm, wanted it to."

"What?" Trey said hoping he didn't say what he thought he said.

Donald continued to whimper, "I wanted it to eat me. It seemed like the most important thing to do at the time. It seemed wonderful. I can still feel the euphoria of the possibility."

Trey looked at Don. "Have you ever...."

"No. I've never heard of them having any mind control or powers of any nature. This new breed is advanced and unstudied."

"Or maybe Commerand just has more control over them than before and he can use them in ways previously unheard of?"

"That's a good hypothesis," Don replied. "This isn't why you came today, is it Trey?"

"No, Sir. Will you tell me what you know about my dad?"

"Ah yes. Wallace Roberts, Jr. You have his name as well as your grandfather. You are the third, right? That's why we call you Trey?"

"Yes, Sir. But my grandfather uses our middle name, Patrick"

"Not to be morbid but you mean used, right?"

Trey looked away but wasn't upset, "Uh, yeah. I guess he's not really around anymore."

"I miss Patrick so much. He was such a character – and sharp. He was always quick witted and never ceased to find solutions to difficult problems." He looked away while he waited for his eyes to dry. When he returned his attention to Trey, he continued on the topic of his dad. "Wally is a brilliant physicist. He was able to quickly solve several mysteries surrounding the portals. In our studies at the physics lab in Atlanta, he discovered and created a device that would render the portals useless."

"What do you mean useless?"

"When we placed the device on the Atlanta portal, Lyza was unable to access any of the other portals around the world."

"Rendering it useless, as you said," Trey added.

"Not just it. All of them. We think all of the portals became depowered. Aside from the amazingness that there are actual teleportation portals around the world, developing a device that makes them useless is equally amazing," Don remarked.

Trey thought about the information Don just shared. He was concentrating so hard his face shrugged like a pug dog. It then softened then frowned.

Don knew the next question by reading Trey's emotional expression. "Trey. Your dad, he had to do what he did. Commerand found out about the device. Wally had to secure it. It may be our only weapon against Khaitu if he were to escape."

"He left to protect us." Trey said in a slow low voice.

"Yes."

"And why you two disappeared around the same time?"

"I believe so."

"Where's he today?"

"Trey, I've been out of the picture for a long time.

His intention was to disappear. Someone close to him informed Commerand about the device."

"Who would have told Commerand?"

"Someone with the information and would benefit from the disclosure. I have my suspicions who that might be and will dig into it deeper but won't divulge that information to you at this time."

"I understand, Mr. Smith. Please let me know when you find out."

"I will. Your father said he couldn't trust anyone, then just disappeared without a trace. Shortly after, I was sent to the Etherios. Your father is smart and very cunning. I'm sure when he decided to disappear, it was forever and no one will be able to find him, especially Commerand and his goons."

"That's why I could never call him back."

"What's that?" Don asked.

"He used to call mom - always from different numbers. Every time I tried to call back, of course without my mom knowing, I would always get a disconnected number message."

"Like I said, he will remain gone until he chooses to reveal himself. I'm very surprised he risked calling your mom."

"He hasn't called in nearly three years. I think he might be in trouble, like you were."

Don sighed. "I'm sure he's just fine."

Trey was quiet for nearly a minute then said, "I'm going to find him."

"Whoa now, Trey. I know you want him back, but he doesn't want to be found. Besides, if Commerand can't find him, the likelihood of you succeeding is exponentially small."

"I don't care. I'm going to find him, eventually," Trey said faintly.

Don took that as an indication Trey wasn't about to set out today on the quest.

Trey looked at his watch which brought him from his concentration. "I have to go. Thank you for talking with me about my father. Is there anything else you can tell me?"

"Nothing that will help you find him, I'm afraid."

"Ok. I appreciate your help. I'll see you at school tomorrow," he said holding out a hand to Donald of which Donald slapped in a friendly manner.

"Yeah. See you tomorrow," Donald replied with a smile.

Trey paused at the door turned and said, "Do you know Lamar? I think he lives in the complex. He's really skinny and wears baggy pants that hang low."

"No. I don't recall seeing a guy that fits that description," Don replied.

"Really? I've seen him both times I've been here – actually shaken his hand three times. Are you sure? His head is shaved almost bald."

"Nope. I don't know anyone by that description, but then again, I've only been here a few days."

"Oh. True. Well, I'll see you both later."

He walked through the apartment to Donald's mom.

"Mrs. Smith, do you know the skinny black man named Lamar? He sometimes hangs around this building."

"You know, Trey. I try not to look at anyone when I come and go. I might have seen him, but I wouldn't know him. I'm sorry."

"It's ok," Trey replied in a low disappointed voice.

"Trey. It's so good of you to come today. Little Don has so few friends, you know, because he's much bigger and kids get intimidated easily."

No. It's because he was a mean bully, Trey thought

but kept it to himself. *Donald is not the same as he once was.*

"No problem, Mrs. Smith. I'm glad he and I have finally become friends."

"It's so nice. Thanks for stopping by," she said again as she led him to the door.

He found his bike undisturbed at the bottom of the steps. He thought about what Lamar said and decided to confront him. He pulled his bike to a stop next to the skinny man on the corner.

"What's happening, Cool Dude!" Lamar said happily.

"Nothing much. Just visiting my friend."

"That's cool," he said shaking his head approvingly.

"Hey, Lamar," Trey asked as he looked away trying to think of how to structure the question. "What did you mean when you said if I need anything? Were you just being friendly, or did you mean it?"

Lamar looked at him questioningly then replied with a subdued voice as he leaned forward, "I meant it literally. When you rolled in here with Mr. Smith, I thought you might be someone who may need a hand every now and again."

Trey's eyes brightened. "So, you know Mr. Smith and knew he was missing."

"Sure. Everyone knew."

"That's not what I meant."

"I just know of him from this neighborhood."

Trey thought he wasn't being forthcoming but didn't press him.

"Do you know my dad?"

"No. I barely know you." Again, Trey thought he wasn't telling the truth. "Why do you ask?"

Trey thought for a second then said, "He's missing,

and I need help finding him."

"I feel for ya, but I can't take on a project like that yet." He looked toward Donald's apartment building and then back to Trey, "I have something else that should be concluding soon. After that, we can talk about finding your dad."

"Ok. Thanks, Lamar." Trey was disappointed but accepted the reality that Lamar was most likely just talking and not actually helpful.

"No problem, Cool Dude," he said with his usual smile and head bob.

"Yeah. See ya later."

Trey placed a foot on a pedal then Lamar said, "What's your dad's name?"

Trey looked at him questioningly and said, "Wallace Patrick Roberts, Jr."

Lamar with a thumb and finger on his chin, looked up then asked, "Where was he last seen?"

Trey became more curious, "Atlanta, three or four years ago."

"That's cool. I'll let you know if I hear anything."

"Thanks!" Trey tried to make it sound enthusiastic but was even more sure that Lamar was full of it and was just pretending to be helpful.

He pedaled a minute to the curb and looked back to find Lamar was no longer there. "What's the deal with this guy?" Trey said aloud.

He stopped by his house for a rest and a sandwich before heading out to meet Marcus at the four PM movie.

~ ~

"Hey Marcus!"

"Trey! What's up" Marcus said coolly.

They exchanged a series of hand slaps that ended in a chest bump.

"I heard about the game yesterday. I wish I could have seen you give it to old Dumb Davis."

"How'd you find out so quickly?"

"Kid, please. It was yesterday. I found out from Tyrone before the game was over. He texted me from the sidelines."

"Of course. His twin brother's on the team."

While standing in line to get tickets Marcus said seriously as he looked out into the parking lot, "Dude. I'm sorry."

"What are you sorry for?"

Trey turned around to see Sarah and Kenny walking to the ticket booth – hand in hand.

His face paled as his smile faded to a forced version of acceptance, "What? That? That doesn't bother me. It's...It's not like we were dating or anything."

"Yo! Trey! What an awesome match yesterday!" Kenny said.

"Thanks, Kenny," Trey said unenthusiastically.

"You made that Davis kid look like a doaf! That was the funniest thing I've seen in years! There's even an online video of the play with clown music and everything! It might even go viral, yo. You could make bank with that!"

Trey looked away, embarrassed by the memory of his actions.

"Hey Trey," Sarah said shyly.

"Hey Sarah," Trey said trying not to look into her mesmerizing eyes.

Kenny continued, "I hear you'll be practicing with

us next week. Stepping up with the big boys, huh? We'll show you what soccer's all about. What are you guys watching today?"

"We're gonna see Tim Crosby Goes to Hollywood," Marcus blurted.

Trey cut him an angry eye.

"I heard it was lit! We'll do that one too."

"I'm really in the mood for something more adventurous," Sarah said.

"Na girl. We'll do that next week," he smiled, winked then hugged her with one arm.

Trey cringed in dismay.

Trey and Marcus followed the couple into the lobby. Sarah and Kenny targeted the counter. Trey took that opportunity to diverge from the arduous path.

"What? No popcorn today?" Marcus questioned.

Trey thought up a quick excuse. "Nah. You go ahead. I'll run to the restroom and will meet you in there."

"I'll get an extra-large so we can share."

"Ok. Thanks."

Trey turned into the restroom and stopped at the mirror. He looked at the moping sob of a person he'd become over the past ten minutes and said to himself as he rubbed a newly forming pimple, "This is stupid. Why do I care what they do? All she and I did was walk home together. We've hardly spoken since then and never spoke before that day. I'm delusional to think she'd like me. That dude's older, has a car and is probably a better soccer player than me. Just forget about her and get on with your life."

A stall door unlocked surprising Trey from his depressing pep talk. He started toward the door when he heard a familiar voice say, "Having girl trouble, Trey?"

"Oh. Hey, Mr. Johnson," he said in an embarrassed tone to his next-door neighbor that helped he and Lyza by slaughtering several rogglets outside of his house earlier that week. He turned toward the aged man and said, "You heard all of that?"

"Yeah. I reckon I got most of it. Sorry to hear but if it helps, everyone goes through this sort of thing."

"Really? Because right now it seems specific to me."

"No, Son. It's pretty common. I think it's good to remember that girls come and go and then sometimes, if you're lucky, the good ones come back around again."

"So how does that help me today?"

"It doesn't but should give you hope for the future."

"Yeah. I guess I can see that. By the way, what are you doing here? Are you following me too?"

"What do you mean? I like movies."

"You know what I mean."

"Ha ha!" He chuckled. "Lyza keeps me updated on you and I think I'd just get in the way of the guys watching over you."

"So, does that mean you are or are not following me?"

"I keep my eye on you. I don't always trust everyone."

"I feel that same way, Mr. Johnson."

"Hope you enjoy the movie, Trey."

"You too," he said then opened the door. He stopped and turned back to his white-headed lanky neighbor, "Mr. Johnson?"

"What is it, Trey?"

"Thanks."

Mr. Johnson smiled a warm wrinkly smile and said, "You're welcome."

Trey felt better when he joined Marcus several rows in front of Sarah and Kenny but he barely paid attention to the film. He tried not to think about them holding hands, talking about interesting stuff ... kissing.

Marcus was in hysterics next to him. Trey didn't find the film humorous but laughed several times at his friend's reactions, one of which involved a stream of soda blasting from his nose.

Afterward Marcus asked, "Want to get some ice cream?"

Mounting depression of the Sarah event returned, "No. I'm not feeling well. I'll just go on home." He grabbed his bike and peddled off.

"Hey! Wait up!" Marcus yelled following behind.

That night Trey laid in bed wishing his life were back to normal. No creepy creatures after him, no sorcerers trying to free a crazy evil ancient king, no magical artifacts. None of that. Just me and Sarah, walking home together hand in hand.

The woman and child scream. He held them tightly closing his eyes to shield the fiery assault. Feeling the brightness diminish he opened his eyes to reveal the destruction from outside the perimeter of the village. A Long faced trim bearded man appeared behind him, ushering with his arms for Trey to follow. Trey walked slowly toward the apparition. The man vanished into a thicket. Trey ran after. He dashed through finding on the other side a large wall made of thick grey smoke. Instantly it poofed into the shape of a sun broken into three pieces by thin lines before it slowly faded.

Trey woke that morning tired and heartbroken. The remnants of the dream barely registered as he spooned cereal into his mouth.

On his walk to school, a red convertible slowed

next to him. "Yo, Trey!" It was Kenny and Sarah.

"Need a ride?" Kenny hollered.

His skin boiled. He secretly wanted to deface the beautiful paint. He was too hurt to understand the source of his anger.

"No Thanks," he snapped.

"Ok, Dude. See you at practice."

Trey winced at the comment. *Practice with Coach Wood today*, he thought. *Practice with the varsity team.* He shuttered at the thought.

"See ya in History class," Sarah said sweetly.

He simmered down at the sound of her voice. For some reason, he couldn't remember why he was so angry. He and Sarah were nothing and probably would never be ... anything. "It's completely ok that she's with Kenny," he convinced himself.

They drove away leaving Trey to his lonely walk down the sidewalk.

When he finally arrived on school grounds, he stopped by the science lab.

"Mr. H!"

Nick Hampton stood near his desk wearing khakis and a blue button up long sleeve shirt with the top two buttons unbuttoned. His face was tan with a day's stubble. "Hey Trey. See any goblins last night? Just kidding. That's nothing to joke about. Seriously though. What's up?

Startled at the comment he replied, "How'd you know?"

"How'd I know what?"

"So, you don't know?"

"I don't know what?"

"Are you messing with me?"

"I'm confused. What are we talking about?"

"The rogglet that attacked me and Donald

Saturday. Did you know about it?"

"No! Really? You look ok. Are you ok?"

"Yeah. I'm fine. Donald's fine too."

"Jeez. I thought Lyza said you'd be safe?"

"I was. A couple guys blasted it before it got too close. It was really gross."

"So, they really are watching you closely?"

"It looks that way. They've been following me everywhere I go."

"That's good."

"Speaking of Lyza, she came to my game Saturday."

"She did?" he said clearly startled. "What did she want?"

"Nothing really. Just said she had people watching us, which I found out earlier, and that she still can't find Clievan. Seemed like she was just checking in." He ran his fingers through his bushy hair and continued, "I hate this waiting around stuff. It's unbearable thinking something insane could happen at any moment."

"I know what you mean, Trey. Just know that I'm here for you. If you need anything, please don't hesitate."

"Thanks Mr. H. I appreciate it."

Trey glanced in the back corner, "What are you gonna to do with the portal?"

"I'll disassemble it, then move it to my house. I started it here because I thought I'd need to use school resources. But there isn't anything to it. It seems to use the electromagnetic energy from the earth to function. The key is some sort of metal resembling copper. The connection the key makes opens some sort of gaping energy vacuum that is somehow controlled by the shape of the key."

"That sounds like a good scientific explanation."

"Well what do *you* call it?"

"Magic, Mr. H. It's magic."

"I believe in science. All so-called 'magic' has a scientific explanation."

"So, you have a scientific explanation for everything you witnessed last week?"

"Sure. I just partially explained the portal. What else was there?"

"What about Seth and Clievan? What about Commerand's wandy wavy thingy? And don't forget about the dragon."

"Well, uh, they were, um. Ok. I don't have an explanation for everything but I'm sure there's a scientific rationale for how Commerand was able to manipulate physical things."

"Yeah. It's called magic. The sooner you believe in it the more sense all this makes."

"Ok. Fine. We'll call it magic until I can prove otherwise. Deal?"

"I guess that's as good as I'll get for now," Trey said smiling.

"Today's your first day with the high schoolers? Are you nervous?"

"Not really." Trey hid his true feelings of incompetence and lack of confidence. "I've played pickup games with some of them. Kids my age never show up so most of the guys there are older. Some even in retirement age like you!"

"Ha. Ha. You just won't let it go, will you?"

"Nope."

"Well. I hope you do well. Don't let them intimidate you. You're just as good as any of them and probably better than most."

"Thanks Mr. H. I appreciate your encouragement. Catch you later!"

"Later, Trey."

At lunch Trey was startled when Leslie, the auburn-haired girl with green eyes slammed her lunchbox onto the table in front of him.

"Hey, Leslie," he said nicely. She seemed disturbed or maybe angry. Trey couldn't really tell. She just sat there, looking at her lunch box, like she was trying to make it explode with her mind. As she opened the box Trey finally asked, "Are you ok?"

"I don't like how you treated Davis," she said sternly.

"Ok." He set his fork down. "I don't either."

"That was his first time at striker. You could have - " She looked at him curiously. "What? What did you say?"

"I don't like how I treated him either."

"Oh."

"I feel really bad about it. Thanks for reminding me and for making it worse."

"Worse?" she said disturbed at how he put it on her. "How could I make it worse by just mentioning it?"

"Oh, you did more than mention it with your lunchbox slamming and accusational overtones. Why do you care anyway? Davis is a jerk to everyone."

"That may be so, but he's a person just like you...and all people should be treated with respect."

"Even a rich spoiled brat like Davis?" he added.

Her eyes widened. He said before she wailed at him again, "Just kidding! I'm just kidding."

She threw a small biscuit at him and said, "You be nice!"

"Ok. Point taken. I'll try to catch him after lunch to apologize."

She seemed to lighten up. "I think that's a good idea," she replied seemingly satisfied with the outcome of the conversation. "I'm sorry I accused you of being mean."

"It's ok. I was...and I regret it. How was your game

Saturday? Did you get to play?"

"I played the last half of the second half," she said excitedly. "I was really nervous but made a few good passes. One set up a shot on the goal." She smiled a big smile and softly clapped tiny claps really close to her nose.

"That's wonderful! I'm glad you got to play. I'm sorry I couldn't make it. I was with my mom in D.C. It's something else to be out on the field isn't it?"

"Like nothing I've done before. It was great. I was wondering, do you think, maybe sometime..." she seemed really nervous, "...that maybe you could, um, teach me, only if you want, to do that snake move you did for your second goal?"

"Snake? I did the snake? Oh yeah. I didn't even know I did it. It's also called Elastico."

"Ooo. That's much more fun to say." She smiled and over enunciated, "E-las-ti-co."

"Sure. I'll teach you. But I'm training with the varsity team this week, so maybe next week sometime?"

"The varsity team? Really? That's awesome!"

He became defensive. He put space between he and Leslie. "No. It isn't. I don't belong with that group. They're way too aggressive. I don't think I'll do well."

"What? Get out of here. Your good enough to play with those guys. Heck you're only a year or so younger. Stop psyching yourself out."

He relaxed a little and thanked her for her confidence in him. *If only he could somehow find that sort of confidence in himself*, he thought.

"That's ok that you can't meet me." She seemed agreeable but disappointed.

Trey thought for a second, "Wait. You have recess with me, don't you?"

She nodded in agreement. Her sparkling green eyes and raised eyebrows indicated she seemed happy that he remembered – possibly so that she wouldn't have to ask.

"We could work on it then."

"Ok," she happily agreed. "I'll meet you in the open space between the basketball court and swing sets."

The bell rang.

"Sure. See you then."

"Don't forget Davis," she said as she trotted off.

Trey thought she had that planned all along. "Davis," he said to himself as he turned in his tray.

Trey approached Davis in the atrium. He was laughing with a couple boys when Trey said, "Davis."

Davis' smile faded into a vicious frown upon turning to see who called his name. He immediately without saying a word, shoved Trey to the ground. He stood above Trey – his round red face pulsed. "Don't you *ever* talk to me again!" He then turned and stormed away from Trey and his friends without saying another word.

Trey picked himself off the floor as the other two boys laughed and walked in Davis' direction. He straightened his shirt glanced at Davis down the hall then entered the playground.

Trey walked the playground toward Leslie, who was juggling quite poorly, he thought. Trey picked up an errant kick and juggled it back to Leslie while at the same time shaking off the incident with Davis.

"Try using your hands to keep it going and if you can, put a little backspin on the ball to keep it coming back to you," he said demonstrating the instructions. He then bounced the ball off his knee in her direction. She caught it with a knee then kicked it awkwardly with her foot, sending the ball away again. He ran to retrieve the ball then bounced it back to her.

"I don't think I'll ever get juggling," she said then screeched as the ball shot away.

They kicked the ball around a bit before jumping into the lesson.

"Ok Leslie. Get ready. I'm going to come at you and try to do the snake on you."

"You mean, E-las-ti-co, don't you?"

He laughed and said, "Yeah."

"What do you mean by try?"

"Well, I can't do it every time. It's super hard to perfect. Maybe I get it sixty or seventy percent of the time."

She registered the comment then said, "Ok. Come at me."

She hunkered down in a strong aggressive stance. Her pretty heart-shaped face became a vicious snarl that caused Trey to pause and smile.

She relaxed slightly and said with a questioning look but forceful tone, "Well? What are you waiting for?"

Trey shook off the comical scenario and said, "Nothing. You ready?"

"Yeah!" she snarled.

He smiled a big smile just before he launched at her. He stuttered a few steps then rolled the ball with his right foot slightly right which drew Leslie to his right. He then snapped it back to the left, easily pushing past her.

"That was fast," she said.

"I can't believe I got it the first time," he smiled.

"You stop your show," she said pushing him in the chest. He blushed slightly.

"Now. This is how you do it. Use the outside of your foot with your toe pointed down. It's not an outside kick then an inside kick." He demonstrated what not to do. "You want to maintain contact with the ball by sort of rolling the ball around your foot. Lean to the outside then snap your ankle back across then explode."

"Yeah. That's what you just did to me," she said paying serious attention to his instructions.

"Ok. Now that I've shown you and told you, you try."

"What? Now?"

"Yeah. You won't get it until you do it."

"Ok," she said nervously as she slowly dribbled the ball a small distance away.

She paused, took in a deep breath, put on her aggressive face which made Trey smile again. She darted at him. Trey thought she growled but it all happened so fast that he wasn't sure. She dribbled a couple times with her left then switched to her right. *Very good footwork*, he thought. It was all going well until she went for the snake. She made one too many dribbles which put her too close to Trey. When she tried to roll the ball, she accidently put too much pressure on it and tripped, toppling right onto Trey, sending them both to the ground.

It wasn't one of those sweet Oh no! I fell into you so we should kiss sort of falls. This one was ugly and wild. They first bumped heads causing each to reflexively arch backwards, one of her feet became entangled in his causing him to try to jump away to save a sprain. He then went flaying awkwardly in the air while she continued to fall forward with her knee bent in a precarious way. Trey saw her fall under him so he turned himself sideways the best he could to avoid smashing onto her with all his weight. She curled into a ball just as his legs bashed into her side propelling his upper body forcefully into the ground on his left shoulder.

Leslie laughed hysterically.

"Oww. What's so funny?" Trey said rolling onto his back.

She continued laughing. Heaving to catch her breath. He sat up to find her sitting and holding her head, laughing wildly. He rubbed his head then massaged his shoulder.

She calmed down a bit until he said, "That did not go well. I think the lesson is over." She busted out laughing again.

"Y...You," she said amid hysterics. "You said...you said you try." She held her belly. Her face looked painful. "Oooh, my stomach hurts," she said as the laughing subsided. "You said you try." She laughed again. Trey didn't think it would ever stop. She calmed a bit and said, "I don't think that could have gone any worse."

Trey smiled and said, "No. That was quite possibly the worst snake I've ever seen." Her eyes widened and then they both shared a hearty laugh together.

"Hey Trey,"

Trey looked up and was startled to see who was standing there. His joyful laughter turned into an eager smile. He instantly stood and brushed off the dirt from his shirt and pants. "Sarah." He looked down at Leslie still sitting in the grass then turned to again face Sarah. "Wha...what are you doing here? You don't have recess now," he said nervously.

"Hey Leslie," Sarah said in a friendly non-threatening voice and genuine smile. Leslie raised a hand to acknowledge the greeting but didn't say anything or stand. "Mr. Peterson loves me. He lets me leave class whenever I want. I usually go to the library, but I need your help."

He eagerly replied, "Yeah! Sure. Whatever you need." His eyes were bright and hopeful.

"You have practice with Kenny today, right?"

"Yeah. Thanks for reminding me." As hope faded,

he slouched in disappointment wishing he could sink into the ground away from this uncomfortable interaction.

"Do you think you could give him this? It's the address to my uncle's house where he'll pick me up tomorrow. I totally forgot and my mom doesn't let me bring my phone to school."

He replied in a lower less jovial tone, "Yeah. I'll give it to him." He looked at the folded piece of paper like it was a death sentence.

"Thanks, Trey! I hope you do well today." He watched her skip away without looking back.

"You like her don't you," Leslie said.

"What? No. Who? Me? No."

"You're terrible at hiding it."

Trey didn't reply. He looked away and placed the paper in a pocket.

"She's very pretty and popular. The popular thing doesn't seem to fit with you though. Is it just that she's pretty?"

"No. She's smart too and likes science."

"So, you do like her," she said smiling.

"It's really none of your business you know."

"Yeah, but now I'm making it my business. I don't just smash into anyone without getting to know them better."

He smiled at her remark then said evenly, "Keep working on that snake. You'll pick it up soon. There's the bell. We have to get to class." He helped her up and she didn't lose eye contact until they said bye to walk toward separate entrances to the building.

His confidence was at an all-time low as he sat in Mr. Hampton's science class moping over lost opportunity and perilous dangers.

Playing with the Big Boys

That afternoon Trey walked onto practice field four for the first time – the varsity field.

"Yo, Trey! Over here! This is the kid in the video!" said Kenny to a few guys sitting on the bleachers. "This is Trey Roberts, the middle schooler coach said would practice with us this week," he announced to the group.

"Dude! That move on your weak striker was sick AF!" a medium sized pimple faced boy said.

"Yeah! I bet I've watched it a hundred times! You were awesome!" another said.

"You won't be able to pull that crap on this field," a tall well-muscled senior said. "We aren't little middle schoolers here. I don't know why coach thinks you can play with us, but I'll make sure he learns why you belong on the playground rather than a real pitch."

"Stop giving him a hard time, Tucker. He's cool.

I've played with him at the Sunday pickup game. He's pretty good and can probably out dribble you!" said a tall lanky defender.

"Ooooooo!" the other players said.

"Really? You think so, Art? We'll have to test that theory." He turned to Trey with an overly serious face, "See you on the field, Roberts."

"Don't listen to him," said Art. "You always juke me out. Just do what you do and show him you belong on the team."

"What do you mean, belong on the team?"

"That's why you're here, right? To be assessed for the team?" Art replied.

"No!" Trey said disturbed. "Coach Rafiq just said I was practicing with you this week. I thought he wanted me to play with better players than what I get in my league so that I'd be more challenged."

"No Dude. You're trying out today," said Kenny with a laugh.

"Good luck!" said Art.

"Mr. Roberts!"

"Yeah, Coach Wood?" Trey said weakly, still in shock from the news. He ran to the dark-skinned man with a stubble beard and Caribbean accent. He looked to be in his late fourties.

"Thank you for working with us this week. I'm not expecting you to keep up with the speed or strength of these older kids. All I want from you is your best. Coach Rafiq recommended you work with us at left winger because you're fast and good with both feet. I look forward to seeing what you can do."

"Coach, but I –," Trey started feebly before Coach Wood turned from him to address the entire team. Trey sulked to the front row to hear the speech.

"Listen up!" Coach Wood commanded. "Today we have Mr. Roberts here to fill our open left winger position. He's a little smaller than most of you but he's fast. We'll have a friendly scrimmage today to see how we all work together. A team vs B team. Trey, you'll file in with B Team over there. Let's all put some pressure on him to see what he's made of."

Whispers from the others echoed in his head. Trey hated being singled out and today that uncomfortableness was in addition to a significant lack of confidence and feeling he didn't belong. He received many wayward eyes as the older kids left the bench.

The field was damp that day from an early afternoon shower. Trey walked wide eyed to his position breathing in humid air as his boots lightly squished the grass.

"Let's see some hustle, Trey! There's no walking on this team!" Coach Wood yelled.

Trey sprinted the rest of the way. Just as soon as he neared his position the striker, Josef, kicked off to Trey while is back was turned.

"The ball, Trey!" he yelled.

Trey turned to find the ball speeding toward him. He awkwardly received it, then was painfully bulldozed to the ground by Tucker. He let out an audible, Ooomph, at the apex of the collision.

"Keep your head up, Roberts!" Tucker said running off after passing the ball forward.

Trey jumped right up, then ran to open space near the midway line. He received a bullet from a defender controlling it nicely by accurately turning to the left in mid-air slowing the speeding ball while maintaining forward momentum. He dribbled past Art but was slide tackled by the pimply kid. Trey went down hard. In pain but not injured, he popped up, then sprinted into position.

Trey found it difficult to move the ball or find open passes. Often times two and sometimes three players were blocking or knocking him down. Each time he fell, he immediately jumped up to continue the game.

Josef kicked off to the center midfielder, Kenny, which sent it to Trey who found space between two defending midfielders. They closed on him as he darted through. He scissored past Tucker, then passed to Josef. After the pass, he broke out into open space between Art and the pimply kid. Just before he received the pass after cutting back toward the ball, Tucker stepped in front of him smashing his muscular shoulder into Trey's chest and face, pounding him to the turf. Tucker passed the ball up field, then said, "Stay down, Roberts. You don't belong here."

Trey laid on the ground longer than any time since stepping onto his first pitch. He got up much slower than the other times, then trotted into position. He gave Coach Wood a thumbs up indicating he was good to continue. The rest of practice was just as difficult...and painful.

After practice, Trey sat alone on the grass by the bench. He leaned back on one hand while rubbing out a bruise on his thigh. Kenny walked up and said, "You took a beating out there. You ok?"

"Yeah. I'll be fine." He winced as he labored to stand. Kenny offered a hand to help but Trey declined the assistance.

"You know you don't have to show up tomorrow. This is completely voluntary."

"What? Quit now and let that muscle head win? No way. I'll be back tomorrow."

"That's the spirit," Kenny said with a pleasant smile.

"Oh yeah. I almost forgot." Trey rummaged through his school pants to retrieve the paper Sarah gave him. "Sarah said this is the address to her uncle's house."

"Thanks, Trey. See you tomorrow." He began to walk away before Trey stopped him.

"Kenny," Trey said with an uncomfortable stance as if he were trying to get out of asking the upcoming question.

"Yeah?"

"Who has the video?"

"Video?"

"You know. The one with me and Davis."

"Oh Yeah! Lenny."

Trey's look indicated he had no idea who Lenny was. Kenny continued, "Lenny, the slide tackler."

"Oh. That's Lenny?" Trey said rubbing his hip as he remembered the painful moment.

"Why?"

"He can't keep the video online. I'm going to ask him to take it down."

"Yeah, that's probably for the best," Kenny said with a caring smile. "Good luck with that. Lenny's pretty tied to the video right now."

"I have to try."

"That's cool. See ya tomorrow, Trey."

"See ya," Trey said to Kenny's back as the winner of Sarah's affection walked away from the pensive boy.

Trey grabbed his bag, tapped the disk strapped to his thigh and wished he could teleport straight to his bed rather than asking Lenny to remove the online video. He ran across the field and hollered to the pimply kid walking through the gate, "Hey Lenny! Wait up!"

Lenny didn't stop.

"Lenny! Hey man, wait up!"

Lenny turned and said as he continued to walk, "Hey, uh...Kid. I have to hurry home. I'll catch you tomorrow." He opened the door to an aged sedan and nearly closed it on Trey who caught up to him in the parking lot.

"Hey, just wait a second," Trey said surprised at Lenny's insolence. He then stepped back but maintained a hand on the door as Lenny fired up the tired engine.

"What is it. I'm in a hurry," Lenny said with a scowl.

"I need you to take the video down. It's not –" Trey began just before Lenny said, "No Way," with an unpleasant smile then sped off.

Trey was tired, beat up and disillusioned but he knew Davis was out there in a different kind of pain than what he experienced on the soccer field today – and it was increasingly unlikely Trey would be able to do anything about it.

Trey walked with a slight limp to the entrance of the complex. He dreaded the walk home in his current condition. He then had the best idea of the day – significantly better than showing up at practice. He walked to the tinted windowed car in the parking lot facing the soccer fields. The window lowered revealing a stocky bearded bald guy who didn't say anything.

"Can you give me a ride home?" Trey asked the stranger assigned to protect him.

Baldy motioned with his eyes and a slight tilt of his head for Trey to get in the back as the locks sounded the acceptance of his request. Trey crumpled into the car, nearly passing out from exhaustion.

Trey eased into bed that night, favoring his right thigh. Large dark bruises seeped to the surface of his arms and legs. His right ankle was especially sore where Tucker stomped it. He thought he'd never sleep as he tossed and turned attempting to find a less painful position.

Trey woke the next morning thankful for a dreamless night. The bruises from the day before were gone and he felt no pain in his ankle. It was as if yesterday's pounding never happened. He thought of what Tanny the dragon said when he was burned so badly in the fight with her in the Highlands. "Maybe there's something to this fairy healing thing after all."

He jumped out of bed, full of energy. He whistled to the bathroom as he readied himself for the day.

~ ~

"Hey Kid," Marcus said guardedly has Trey danced into the hall. "How was practice yesterday?"

Trey smiled and said, "What's the deal? Your sources not on top of the outcome of my practice with the high school team?"

"You're funny, Kid. I don't have close contacts in high school."

"It was awful," Trey replied happily.

"Really? You sure don't seem down about it."

"They really had it out for me. I thought a few times they would hurt me so badly that I'd be out for the season."

"But you seem fine. Not even a limp."

Trey became evasive, "Yeah. I soaked and did some

other stuff. I bounce back pretty well."

Marcus replied jokingly with wide eyes and a mocking voice, "Maybe it wasn't as hard as you thought it was?"

Relieved Marcus was letting it go he said, "Maybe so, but dude, it was one of the hardest things I've done." He looked distantly after the comment as he mentally compared the previous day to all the days related to the relics. He then felt better about soccer and longed for it to be the most difficult challenge he would face from now on. However, he knew that dream wouldn't become fulfilled for some time to come and that the greatest challenge of his life was closer than he realized.

"Hey Trey," Leslie said yanking him from the contemplation. He said hey in return as she walked by.

Marcus looked at Leslie then at Trey questioningly. "You sure do seem to be hitting it with the girls lately."

"What'd ya mean?"

"What I mean, Kid, is that it can't be coincidence that Sarah, forget she's seeing that high school dork, is now talking to you after all these years of not knowing you existed and now you have random girls saying hey to you in the hallway. What's your secret?"

"I don't have a secret. I guess I just fall into these weird situations and then we become friends." He smiled as he briefly relived the disastrous soccer lesson with Leslie.

"Friends? Is that it?"

"Evidently. Sarah is seeing someone else and I barely know Leslie."

"Well, whatever you're doing you should keep doing. It seems to be working. Maybe I'll accidently trip into Jenny Jacobson today in third period," he said dramatically.

"Ha! Yeah. Let me know how that works out!"

"Sure. Oh yeah! Did you hear?" Marcus asked.

"Hear what?"

"So, you don't know about Davis?"

"No. I haven't spoken to any of the others since Saturday. What happened?"

"He quit the team."

Trey nearly dropped his books as his face paled. "Please tell me you're kidding."

"No. I heard from Conner that Phillipe was asking Coach Rafiq who would be playing striker if you got on the varsity team."

Trey's heart doubled. His stomach churned. "Oh no! That's terrible! It's because of the game last weekend. Dang! I'm such an idiot! Why couldn't I just play nice? He's really good at soccer, not a good striker but he makes for a great winger and mid-fielder. I have to talk to him. I have to try to make it better."

Marcus just looked at his friend reeling from the ramifications of his actions at the game.

"Do you know what class he has after home room?" Trey asked.

"I think Science with Mr. Hampton."

"That's great! I can make it there before History."

"See ya." Marcus said as Trey ran down the hallway.

Trey met Davis just before he entered the science lab.

With a worried look Trey grabbed Davis' arm and said, "Davis. I need to talk to you."

The scowling boy quickly snatched away from Trey's grasp. Trey slipped to the side to avoid Davis' attempted shove. Davis caught his footing, turned and nearly screamed with serious emotion, "What do you want!"

Several curious students turned toward the commotion.

"I just want to talk," Trey said calmly with considerate concern on his face.

"I already told you! Don't ever talk to me again."

"I know," Trey looked down then back up to the blustering teenager. "I want to talk about the team. You are – ".

"I'm done with soccer! It's a stupid game."

"No. It's not, and you're very good at it. The team needs you. No one is as good at floating from winger to mid-fielder as you."

"He's right," Phillipe said joining the conversation. "You're very fast and are an excellent passer."

"But you have what most players don't have," Trey added. "You're tough. No one else can handle those big defenders like you. They can't push you around like they do me and Robbie."

Davis regarded them both individually. His red face showed a hot temper. "I'm finished with soccer. You two will have to figure it out on your own." He then stormed into science class.

Trey and Phillipe looked at each other sullenly.

Phillipe looked worried when he said, "What will we do without you *and* Davis on the team?"

"You'll be fine. Plus, it's not going well with the high schoolers. I'll be back next week."

Phillipe smiled and said, "That's the best news I've heard all day!" His smile instantly faded, "I mean, I'm sorry about varsity and all but I'm glad to know you'll be with us for at least the rest of the season."

"Me too, Phillipe," he said hitting him lightly on the shoulder.

"What was all that about?" Mr. Hampton said entering the hallway from the lab.

"Nothing," Trey replied without looking Nick in the eyes.

Phillipe walked away waiving bye to Trey.

"You and Davis still at it?"

"No," he said looking away from his teacher friend. "Davis quit the soccer team because of what I did last weekend."

Nick's face softened, "You can't blame yourself for that."

Trey quickly replied blasting Nick with troubled hazel eyes, "Of course I can! I embarrassed him and now he quit a sport he loves. It's my fault."

The bell rang.

"I have to get to class," Trey said then sulked away.

Nick watched the boy until he exited the hallway.

~ ~

"Hey Leslie," Trey said unenthusiastically as she skipped over to take a place across from him at lunch. Her ponytail bopped to the side as she sat.

"Hey Trey," she said in her usual chipper demeanor. "Alone for lunch today? Where's Marcus?"

"He had a band thing. Is this going to be a normal thing?" he asked with a raised eyebrow.

"A normal what?" she replied with a curious smile.

"Us sitting together at lunch."

Her eyes brightened as she turned her head slightly and gave him a smug smile, "I don't know." She then added with raised eyebrows, "Do you want it to be?"

"I haven't decided yet," he said with an equally

smug smile.

"Fine. I'll go sit with Tracy," she made a motion to grab her lunchbox.

"No! No. Sit," He smiled. "I like your company."

She smiled and settled into the seat. "That's what I thought," she said raising the intonation of the I to make her point.

"Ohhhh," Trey said. "Is that right? Maybe you should go sit with Tracy."

She gave him a sour look then smiled, "So. Tell me. How'd it go with Davis yesterday?"

Trey's smile became a deep frown. His eyes leered sideways and down.

"It was bad, huh?" she added.

He looked up into gentle light green eyes, unlike the deep green of when they first met. He wondered if her eye color shifted based on her mood. He then dismissed the thought and said, "He quit the team."

"What? He quit the team?" She replied, clearly caught off guard with the revelation.

"Yeah. I just found out today. I tried to talk to him about it this morning. Even Phillipe was encouraging, and he can't stand the guy. But Davis was adamant. I don't think he's coming back."

"Oh my. I can't believe he quit."

"Me either. I feel terrible."

"I'm sure you do," she said in a comforting sort of way.

Trey reeled like she caught him with a left hook then said, "Dang. Ok. Thanks for the encouragement. I'll try to talk to him again soon."

"Today?"

"No. I'll give it a rest today."

"That's probably best."

Small talk dominated the remainder of their

conversation as Trey continued to struggle with what to do about Davis and Lenny's video.

Later that beautiful Tuesday afternoon at soccer practice, Trey continued to have a difficult time. The scrimmage was just as brutal as the previous day. Trey seriously questioned his commitment to prove himself worthy to Coach Wood as well as his commitment to preserve himself from severe harm – regardless of how well or quickly the fairy magic healed him.

After practice, Trey sat next to Lenny who was changing out of his soccer shoes.

"Lenny, man," Trey pleaded. "You have to take down the video. Davis, the kid I hit with the ball," Lenny snickered as Trey continued, "he's having a hard time."

"He should, the little sh..."

"I know he's not a nice kid, but he doesn't deserve to be ridiculed. It's been long enough. Take it down please."

Lenny looked at Trey. Trey noticed a whitehead poking out from the boy's cheek. He thought it might blow at any moment. He lurched his eyes away from the bulging pimple and back to Lenny which seemed to genuinely consider Trey's appeal.

"No."

"But why?" Trey asked infuriated at the boy's consistent stance.

"It's the best video I've ever had but it's not getting the views I think it should. I'll promote it and see if I can reach a wider audience."

"No! You can't!" Trey exclaimed and stood to face the taller boy who remained sitting on the bench. "You must take it down. That kid that you don't care about just quit the soccer team because of what I did, and he was good. So many of the kids at school have seen the video. It needs to go away so they can have a chance to forget about it and I can convince him to rejoin the team. Think about Davis and how he feels. What if it were you?"

"You're right. I don't care about the dumb kid. I won't take it down."

"But you have to!"

Lenny stood and looked angrily down at Trey. He bowed his bird chest to where it nearly touched Trey. "I don't have to do anything – especially nothing a stupid middle school kid says." He then pushed Trey with both hands. Trey nearly fell down but caught himself with a few quick steps backward. "Now stop bothering me about the video!" Lenny said harshly. "I'm leaving it up." Lenny then left him standing at the edge of the soccer field unconcerned about the crushing guilt building in Trey's core.

After the unsuccessful attempt at getting Lenny to remove the video. Trey sat on the bench alone while everyone else filed out of the soccer complex. Coach Wood regarded him with a hat brim salute then shuffled on his way leaving Trey completely alone inside the complex.

Trey rubbed his calf where Tucker kicked on an errant play for the ball. A large bruise had already appeared. He could barely flex it.

Just as tears of pain welled, a charming metallic voice with a hint of a British accent resonated over his shoulder. "Hello," his eyes widened, and he stopped rubbing his leg, "Fire Tamer."

A shrewd chill coursed through his body. He quickly turned to find an elegant slender woman standing several feet away.

"Tanny! How did you...? I didn't even hear you. What are you doing here? How did you get past my guard?"

"It's nice to see you too," she smiled as she gracefully drifted toward him. Her draping green dress glittered in the fading sunlight. Her hair, the color of autumn leaves, flowed effortlessly behind like a stream of dandelion puff caught in the gale from a soft breath.

Trey felt he should be frightened at the sudden appearance of the humanized dragon but was pleasantly surprised after the initial shock of her instantaneous presence quickly wore off. "I'm sorry. It's good to see you. I guess I'm not...."

"It is quite alright, Fire Tamer. First impressions are persistent. Your watch is asleep. I will wake him upon my leave."

"I suppose if you wanted to eat me, one guy with a gun couldn't stop you. Why are you here?"

She smiled softly at his comment then said, "I came to talk."

"But can't you just do that anytime? You know, mind to mind?"

"Sure. But I thought it would be pleasant to see you again."

"Ok." Trey said leery of her reason for the visit. "Let's talk. So um, how's your newfound freedom from prisoner guarding going?"

While she was striking as a woman, her reptilic yellow eyes served as a constant reminder of what she was hiding.

She smiled at his choice of topics relating to her four-year watch over Don Smith in the Highlands. "Very calmly, until a few days ago."

"Oh yeah? You decide you want to give Don another shot?"

"No. Silly." She smiled.

"Well? What then? Clearly it has something to do with me or you wouldn't be here. So out with it."

She responded to his bluntness with a probing statement. "You found something recently. Something that has been hidden for many years."

Trey looked at her curiously.

She continued, "A powerful demon knows. He will come for it."

"Another demon?"

She returned a serious tone, "Nafarl is no Ragnistant. He is wicked and cruel. There will be no bargaining with him."

"I haven't found anything. I've been here the whole time getting my butt kicked on this pitch."

"Of course, you found it, Fire Tamer. Its radiance is on you." She waived the backside of her hand from Trey's head to just below his knees in a snake-like movement. "Do you see?"

Trey observed his hands and lower body. A yellowish orange sheen emanated several inches from his skin then quickly faded.

"How'd you do that?"

"Dragons descend from wizards. Several of us who chose to maintain our human form retain magical powers. Others have become wholly dragon – wild, unmagical and uncontrollable."

"Why would you choose to lose your powers? I think it's awesome how you change, and magic, that's an added benefit."

"Being a dragon is exhilarating," she said looking far away. "It's like riding a rollercoaster, eating cake and falling in love all at the same time. It takes a tremendous effort to retain this dull human form."

"I do like cake," he said sarcastically. "What's he

after?"

"A golden crown. He'll stop at nothing to get it back."

"Mom! He's coming for mom! I have to go!" He darted toward the gate. She easily cut him off. "But how?" he said confused at how she moved so fast.

"Your mum. What does she have to do with it?" she said. Trey thought she was genuinely concerned.

"She found it in Utah. She hid it at the museum where she works."

"If that's true, how did *you* get the radiance?"

"I was with her last Saturday."

"And you touched it?" Trey felt her become more agitated as the conversation drew on.

"Yes."

"Didn't you see the warning?" she nearly yelled.

"Yeah. But we didn't know it was really a warning."

"Uggg! Do you go around touching everything you see?" Now she sounded more like an elementary school teacher.

"No. But it looked –"

"What? What did it look like?" she said looking down upon him with blazing yellow eyes.

"Shiny." Trey thought instantly but was too slow to keep it from exiting his mouth. "It looked shiny and I wanted to touch it," he finished in a voice as if he were a five-year-old admitting to hiding his sister's favorite doll.

She rolled her giant eyes and looked toward the sky. "Humans. Why didn't we just eat them all before there were so many." She then said in a high-pitched sing song voice as Trey's eyes grew to the size of teacups, "Kidding! I'm just kidding. But seriously, when you touched the crown, it sent out a pulse that awoke Nafarl. We have to get it out of the museum before he finds it.

We must go now. I can remove the radiance and quell the crown's call once it's secure. I will then take it to where he cannot reach it."

"That won't work. We can't get into the museum."

"Fire Tamer," she said in a matter-of-fact tone. "There's very little I can't get into."

"I'm sure you're right, but we can't just go busting up the museum. There has to be a better way. How much time do you think we have?"

"It could be any day."

"Do you think you can find out? I think I know a way to get the crown, but it'll be tricky, take a day or so and I'll have to lie to my mom which I hate doing."

"I'll see what I can do. I'll be in touch." She then lept into the air and twisted into a dragon. She hovered with a few beats of her gigantic forest swathed wings. She regarded him another moment then disappeared.

"Whoa," Trey said out loud as he felt the torrent of wind from her launch higher. "She cloaks like a Klingon ship." He watched another few seconds then said to himself, "I think I can get back into the museum, but I have no idea how I'll get the crown out without anyone noticing. I wonder if she's there now?"

Trey sent a text to his mom, "Hey Mom. Are you at the house?"

He waited a minute or so before the phone pinged her response, "At the museum for another hour. You need me?"

Tanny, Trey thought. *Are you still near?*

"I'm right here," Tanny the woman said behind him.

"Oh my god!" Trey yelled. "How are you so quiet? I mean, you're so loud leaving but eerily silent arriving."

She smiled then said, "It's a special trick I developed just for you, Fire Tamer. Your mum is at the museum. Will she help us?"

"Not intentionally, but I have an idea. Can you get us there?"

"Sure,"

"Ok. Hold on. Let me send this text so she'll expect me."

I'll be there in a few. I want to take another look at the crown.

He looked up from his phone and pleaded to Tanny, "Please don't throw me this time."

She smiled and as she twisted into a majestic green and grey dragon, she lifted Trey up with a steady root-shaped clawed foot and gently placed him onto the trough of her neck ahead of her wings. She then cloaked their short journey to the National Mall where on average sixty-five thousand people visit each day.

The rush of the wind was exhilarating. He freed his hands from a protruding spine and held them out to each side as if he were the one flying. "There's Arlington Cemetery!" he said as they flew over hundreds of rows of white markers spread across the grounds. "My great uncle is buried there.

"Do you know how much trouble you could get into for flying over the Pentagon?" Trey said disapprovingly as they flew over. She cut him a nonchalant glance from a large golden-yellow eye.

A crosswind hit him as they crossed the wide Potomac River. He watched dozens of cars navigate the Rochambeau Memorial Bridge to his right.

They flew over the circular pavilion of the George Mason Memorial then dove low to the water past the statue of Thomas Jefferson standing proudly in the center of the rotunda dedicated to his service.

She cut to the left past the Holocaust Museum,

made a loop around the tall white obelisk built to commemorate the first president of the United States, then proceeded down the eight grassy fields leading to the Grant Memorial of which Trey indicated she stop short of.

She transformed into a woman as she landed them in the midst of dozens of people in the grassy open space.

"Are we still cloaked?" he said as she held a firm grip on his hand.

"As long as you are in contact with me."

"Maybe you take us somewhere less conspicuous?"

"No! Run with me!" she said enthusiastically as she pulled him with her.

They sprinted toward the museum, avoiding a well thrown frisbee intended for a long-haired college aged ultimate player. They crossed the road avoiding a bus, entered a thin wooded area then casually emerged from the other side. Tanny trailed off to the left as Trey approached the door where his mom was waiting with a sour look.

"What are you doing coming here on your own. We talked about this already," she said looking into his eyes with her hands on his shoulders.

"I know." He looked at her sweetly. "But I don't have a lot of time and this evening seemed like a good time since you're already here. Besides, it's perfectly safe. There were a ton of people on the Metro and it's still daylight. Don't worry so much."

"I know I shouldn't but you're all I have. I don't want you getting hurt." She recognized stress in his demeanor and asked, "Are you ok?"

"Yeah, sure." He hoped she didn't see the forthcoming deception in his ruse. "Why do you ask?"

"You've just been acting funny since last week."

He attempted to avoid the probing. "I'm ok, Mom. There's nothing to worry about."

"You know you can talk to me about anything, right?"

"I know, Mom. I love you," he said staring into her concerned coffee eyes.

"I love you too." She smiled then said as she walked him into the museum, "Have you found out anything else about it?"

"Uh, yeah. The feathers are definitely ostrich. I want to take a closer look at that rose on the front."

She smiled at her enthusiastic son, used her key card to enter a restricted area then proceeded them toward the locker that held Nafarl's crown.

"I'm really proud of how you're taking to studying the history of this artifact," his mom said. "It's all pretty exciting when you think about it."

Trey was too lost in thoughts concerning the dragon waiting outside to pay close attention to what his mom was saying. "Think about what?" he said distantly.

She looked at him more closely. He glanced and gave her a quick fake smile before refocusing on the corridor.

"You know...what we may find. Nobody knows anything about the crown – not even the woman who entrusted it to us."

"Yeah. Yeah. The woman. She didn't have anyone to give it to," he blindly responded while maintaining a quick pace.

"You sure are in a hurry."

"Yeah. I just want to see it."

"Why did it have to be today? We could have come this weekend."

"I, uh, I just wanted to, you know – I, um, think I saw something similar in my history book today and really wanted to compare before I forgot."

"I don't think there will be anything in your history book like this," she said with a chuckle.

"Yeah, sure," he said faintly. He perked up. "It's there right? In those lockers?" He pointed toward an adjacent hallway with a row of white lockers for staff to keep personal items.

"Yes," she said enthusiastically. "I haven't opened it since we first put it there. I'm also very excited to see it again."

He looked at his mom with a genuine smile then turned the corner and faced the lockers.

His mom seemed to shuffle for the key for a century. The anticipation of his forthcoming deceitful deed gnawed at his insides. He nervously pressed his hand against the disk in his left pocket.

She located the small insignificant key and carefully fit it inside the appropriate lock. With a twist it popped freeing the door from the latch.

The door slowly swung open – his mom's mouth dropped. "It's gone," she said in a whisper. Her shrill voice cracked, "Where could it have gone? I don't understand. No one knew it was here except you and me. I mean, no one."

"We're too late," he said to himself. "I have to go!"

"But where? Where're you going?" she said as Trey dashed toward the exit.

"I forgot. I forgot something," he yelled, "at home! See you at the house!" he finished.

"Trey! Wait! What do you mean we're too late?" she yelled to no avail. Trey already left the building in a huffing sprint.

He nearly tumbled down the staircase then crossed the road in leaping strides. "It's gone!" he said as he entered the lightly wooded area. "It's gone! He already has it!"

"Are you sure what you saw?" Tanny said appearing amid the trees. "I thought for sure we arrived in time."

"I'm sure." He looked at her funny. "Were you standing there the whole time?"

She disregarded the trifling question. "This is very disturbing."

"So, what happens now that he has the crown? What can he do with it?"

"The crown gives him power over fire."

"So, he's like a dragon?"

"No!" she said curtly. "With the crown, he can wield fire in extraordinary ways, much like the true owner of the sword you carry." She then looked beyond the horizon and held a hand to her heart, "He'll use it to conquer a peaceful people in a place I dearly love." She turned back to Trey, "Dragons do not wish to rule anyone."

"Is the place your home?"

"Not originally, but I did spend a great amount of time in Azuliposa. It is a wonderful place," she said with a large warm smile.

"How do we find him?"

She frowned, "We don't. You stay here and I'll do what I can."

"And you'll let me know what happens?"

She smiled, "Of course. You've been involved this far, how can I leave you out now?" She then looked worriedly at the darkening sky.

"What is it?" Trey asked.

"I don't know what direction he's gone."

"You think you can track him down?"

"Yes, if I can figure out which way to go before dark."

"Is he on foot?"

"Possibly. He doesn't fly or drive to my knowledge. At least he never did in the past."

"Can you track the crown? You know, the pulse?"

"No," she said distantly then looked curiously at Trey. "But maybe I can track its radiance. But I'll need your help with that. Care for another fly around the ci-y?" she asked really Britinizing the word city.

"Yeah! Let's go!"

"But first we need to strike a signal." She once more snaked the backside of her hand in front of Trey. He began to glow dimly in response.

She then threw Trey screaming into the air onto her back as she twisted into a giant tree like dragon before disappearing from sight. A barely perceptible light glow startled several people that looked above as she flew an ever-growing spiral overhead.

"It's not fading," Trey said.

"Yes. It will last longer than before."

"Will he glow like me? Is that what we are looking for?"

"I don't believe so. I think the spell will cause you to glow stronger the closer you come to the crown. So please let me know if you can tell a difference in your glow."

"Ok. Why will I glow more when we get close?" He looked at his hand but didn't notice a difference between now and the first time.

"It's how Nafarl designed it. He was paranoid for the crown's safety. When he crafted it, he inscribed in it an enchantment that would send the pulse that you felt as well as a visual signal so that recovering it would be easily achieved."

"But I've never touched it before. Why do I have the radiance?"

"That's easy. So, he would also be able to track down who stole it."

"Oh. Ok. He's after me?"

"Yes, Fire Tamer. You are not safe until we regain the crown. Only then will I be able to remove the radiance."

Tanny swooped between tall buildings and above busy streets. She flew past national monuments and historic landmarks. Trey was too caught up in the thrill of the ride to notice his fingers blazing orange.

Nafarl the Wise

Suddenly as they flew low over a neighborhood baseball field, a flaming blue lasso wrapped around Tanny's back tail. She crashed hard to the ground sending Trey rolling across the dusty red clay of the infield. Tanny, now uncloaked, righted herself and blasted a stream of fiery plasma at a tiny creature.

Nafarl emitted a ball of blue fire around himself that diverted Tanny's blast aside, scorching the neatly groomed grass of the ball field in a wide arc. It looked like a battle between a butane torch and plasma gun. Nafarl's laugh was high pitched but hearty within the protective sphere.

"Ha Ha Ha! Tanarkin the Green. I wasn't expecting you. Still quick to strike first, I see. It's been too long," he said in a jovial voice when she ended the inundation. He began, "You know violence isn't –".

Before he could finish the sentence, she engulfed

him in roaring flames as she launched into an arc above the diminutive demon. She landed between him and Trey, then settled in an aggressive crouch.

She regarded Trey for a moment who said, "He's a turtle? He doesn't seem like such a scary guy. You sure you have the right demon?"

Without acknowledging Trey's comment, Tanny returned her attention to the figure wearing pin striped pants. Nafarl stood on pudgy hind legs giving him an odd unsteady look as the encompassing checkerboard black and dark grey shell protruded from his back. He seemed unphased by Tanny's assault.

Nafarl's lion-like face shined an intelligent smile, "A tortoise to be exact young fella." He said through four protruding sharp teeth. He then regarded the dragon, "You know you can't hurt me with your tricks, old friend. I'm simply here to express properly my gratitude to the one who recovered my crown and liberated me from that awful somnolent prison. Let's just make this easy and we'll all be happier afterward."

She transformed into human form and approached Nafarl but remained at a distance.

"You know, young lad, are you sure you want to follow this wyrm? Her kind can't be trusted. Whatever she's told you is most likely in consideration of her own interests."

Trey didn't reply as he glanced quickly toward Tanny. Her facial expression after Nafarl's comment didn't give him confidence as to whether Nafarl was lying or not.

Tanny asked in a very polite voice as she slightly postured for an imminent attack, "What would you have me do? Just leave you with the crown?"

"Tanarkin, my dear friend. You haven't changed at all," he said calmly. "I care nothing for the crown itself."

He held the exquisite golden feathered crown in the palm of a glowing hand. "Gold and the status of the crown are meaningless," he said nonchalantly as the crown melted before them – oozing around his hand into a puddle of gold and jewels surrounded by burning grass at his feet. The orange glow diminished from Trey. "I care only for this," he held out in the palm of his dexterous hand, a metal fist holding a rose.

Trey's eyes widened. He paid close attention when Nafarl placed the object into a pant pocket.

Nafarl remained in a non-threatening position and retained a brilliant smile. He stood nearly half the size of his elegant counterpart. He opened his stubby tortoise arms with fingers stretched in a welcoming gesture, "Me leaving here with the Clutched Rose is our shared outcome regardless of your futile efforts."

"You will not leave here with it!" Tanny said firmly. Her eyes glowed a fierce gold. Her muscular legs tensed.

"Then we are at an impasse," he said as his eyes narrowed.

Nafarl continued to tranquilly smile as he rapidly closed his hands together releasing a deafening explosion of light and blue flame. Tanny defensively pushed her hands forward, one pointing up and one down, producing a green field which effectively deflected the demon's impromptu attack around and over her and Trey. It, however, did nothing to prevent the pain Trey experienced from the thunderous sound. He fell to the ground holding his ears.

Tanny retaliated with a wave of her hands sending Nafarl rolling toward third base. She rushed to check on Trey. "Are you ok?"

Blood stained his ear lobes. He huffed, "I'm ok. I can't hear well but I know what to do."

"What do you mean?" she asked.

"Just get him off of me when I say."

"No! I refuse to risk your life."

"This is the only way." He shifted his soccer shorts, stood then said eye to eye, "Trust me."

She glanced quickly to find Nafarl recouped and ready to attack. She glanced back to find Trey had passed behind her on his way to confront the tortoise shelled demon.

"Ok! You can thank me now!" Trey commanded as he continued to briskly walk forward not knowing whether his plan would work or if Nafarl would strike him dead before he could get close enough."

Trey noticed when he glanced back, Nafarl's surprised expression even seemed to surprise Tanny. *This is going to work*, he thought confidently.

She spoke to his mind, "What are you doing. He will kill you."

"On my mark, make sure you get him off of me so that I'm clear to run."

"What are you doing, Lad?" Nafarl said clearly confused at the turn of events. He took a step back as if Trey were attacking.

"You said you wanted to thank me for finding that thing for you. Now thank me oh wise Nafarl." Trey eased onto his knees as he nearly got into reach. "Thank me, Sir! Please!" Trey crawled on his knees toward the muddled lion-faced tortoise. Trey grasped at the demons clawed feet as if a desperate worshiper. Nafarl held his ground not sensing danger from the delusional child.

"Clearly your injuries from the blast have ogled your brains," Nafarl said.

Trey continued to gently clamor at the tortoise's feet and pants legs. "Please! Thank me!" he screamed as he aggressively grasped the demon's waist pushing him slightly off balance enough for Trey to roll to the side and sprint toward the bullpen. Tanny the Green dragon, then blasted the unwary opponent several feet away with a torrent of fire. Trey dashed through the gates and sprinted down the road.

A massive roar erupted along with a flurry of violet colored fiery explosions from the field behind.

"Trey!" someone called ahead.

Trey stopped in amazement.

"Trey! What's going on?" Nick yelled and ran toward the heaving boy.

"Mr. H? What the heck are you doing here?"

Nick's eyes shifted nervously, "I saw the fire while driving by and stopped to help."

"It's all crazy! Tanny's in there fighting a demon! But I think it's over now," he said as he opened his hand. In it were the disk he secretly planted in the demon's pocket and the Clutched Rose, the source of Nafarl's fiery power.

"You're lucky to be alive. Let me help. I'll keep the rose for you while you get out of here."

Trey dismissed his teacher's request, "I think we're ok. Let's go back and see what happened."

Trey turned back toward the ball field. Nick grabbed his shoulder harshly and turned him back.

Nick's eyes burned with intensity, "Seriously, Trey. You need to listen to me."

"We're ok now. Calm down will ya?" Trey felt uncomfortable with the confrontation. He scanned the parking lot and noticed something strange. "Mr. H. Where's your car?"

"What do you mean?"

"You said you were driving by. Where's your car?"

Nick replied with more sincerity, "That's not

important." He then continued the intensity, "Just give me the rose and we'll get you somewhere safe." A silver flash, barely noticeable in the darkness, unnaturally crossed Nick's eyes.

Trey tried to pull away, but Nick intensified his grip and said forcefully, "Give me the Clutched Rose!" His eyes became completely silver.

Trey secured the rose in his fist and closed his eyes. His hand erupted in a ball of fire causing Nick to fall away with a high-pitched screech. Trey quickly scurried backward as Nick regained his balance.

"The Clutched Rose, I will return it to Master," it screeched in an ear piercing shrill.

Nick launched into the air and exploded into a lanky thin black creature with tattered bat wings which seemed minimally useful as it surged up and down to maintain flight – like a mosquito bouncing toward its next meal.

The creature that looked like a skeleton wrapped in black plastic wrap up to a noseless face made a final push higher then dove toward Trey with strikingly accurate aim. Trey rolled to the left avoiding a swipe from a single claw tipped wing. It ran out of the dive on the ground, skidded to a halt and again faced Trey.

It launched again but this time met a burst of blue flame from Trey's reflexively outstretched fist. As it rolled in a smoking heap in the empty parking lot, Trey opened his hand to observe the glowing Clutched Rose which burned its impression into his palm. He quickly moved it to the other hand and prepared for another attack.

The creature slowly rose, settled into an unsteady attack posture then disappeared into the night sky with a leap.

Trey panicked. He looked all around but couldn't find the ghostly shape anywhere. He then sprinted back to the ball field to discover the outcome of his plan.

He found Tanny the woman standing above a charred but alive chimera tortoise.

"I was just attacked in the parking lot!"

"Attacked?" she exclaimed. "By who?"

"Not a who, a what! It was a flying black skeleton-like thing."

"A skylien," she said distantly. "How did you know what it was?"

"I told you. It looked like a skeleton in a tight black plastic bag."

"No. That's not what I meant. They never approach in their true form. What was it to begin with?"

"Oh yeah! That's the freaky part." He looked at her intensely. "It was disguised as Mr. H before it changed. I mean, it didn't just look like him. It sounded and moved like him also. It was really convincing. I almost gave him the rose."

"How did you know it wasn't Nick?"

"Nick's never asked me for any of the magical stuff I've acquired, and this guy seemed to be intent on getting it. And –"

"And what?"

"And I saw a flash in his eyes. It wasn't natural. I knew it wasn't Nick after that."

"You're very perceptive. I may have even missed that detail."

"It said it wanted to get the rose back to its master. I thought the rose belonged to him," he said referring to the decrepit demon at Tanny's feet

"He was referring to his master not the rose's."

"And that would be who? I'm guessing not Nafarl."

"It could be Nafarl, but also could be anyone else that successfully conscripted the Skylien. I assume it's

Nafarl's since it is so close to us."

"How can anyone ever control those things?"

"It's not so much control as it is giving it a task so it can complete its pledge to you."

He continued looking at her in disbelief.

"It's usually a trade for doing a specific thing."

He continued to listen and stare. He raised his eyebrows in acknowledgement of her comment and to insinuate her to continue.

"They will only accept something of great personal value for the conscription."

"Like hiring them to do something?"

"Yeah. That's it except they don't take money."

"Right. Something personal to the employer." Trey looked at the lump of Nafarl on the ground. "Will he live?"

"If you call being a demon living, then unfortunately, yes."

"What do we do with him?" Trey asked still looking at the heap on the burnt field.

"I'm not sure. I can't imprison him on my own."

Trey thought a minute. "What about the Etherios? Should he go there?"

"Yes. That's where he came from and where he belongs, but it's impossible."

"Ma'am," Trey said seriously. "I'm getting very good at impossible. Take me to my house and we'll see what we can do about getting this guy home."

Trey climbed onto her graceful neck and she clenched Nafarl's limp shelled body tight in a massive claw. She then launched into the air.

Upon arriving, he found he had beat his mom home. He ran through the screen door then returned shortly after. "I don't know if this will work but it's worth a try."

"What are you doing?"

"I'll be right back. I have to try something first."

"I don't understand?"

"You will in a moment." He then opened the bag holding the Etherios key then slipped it into his hand.

"Logos! I have returned!" Trey said in his energetic mind. He tried to make it sound powerful but couldn't tell if it worked.

"Logos! I will trade a Nafarl the demon for my grandfather, Wallace Patrick Roberts!

"Logos! What is your answer!"

"Certainly, you have returned."

Trey sensed the image of Logos. "I have Nafarl. I wish to trade him for my grandfather. Answer me now or I leave immediately."

"Certainly, you will."

"Agree to the trade or I leave."

"I cannot agree to your terms. Nafarl is not equal compensation for someone such as Patrick Roberts. Agree to stay along with the demon and I will consent."

Trey nearly said yes to Logos' counter-offer, but he then remembered his father saying, "Never take the first offer. Always find middle ground or walk away."

"I will not stay. We have no deal." Trey began to turn the key in his palm.

"Certainly, you will hear my next offer to revive your beloved grandfather?"

"Go on," Trey replied curiously.

"Bring to me the demon Koltek along with Nafarl and I will free your grandfather."

"Where do I find the demon?" Trey replied sternly.

"That, young human, will be the easy part. You are destined to meet."

Trey more confused than ever felt a strong pull of the Etherios on his spirit. He replied to Logos, "Agreed." Trey then turned the key and appeared before Tanny the woman.

"Where'd you go?" she said with piercing eyes. "Is that a key to the Etherios?"

He returned her mystified gaze with an affirmative sincere expression.

"But how is that possible? Who are you?"

He continued to hold her veneration, grabbed Nafarl's unresponsive left arm then turned the key disappearing from sight.

Trey returned to Logos.

"Certainly, you may be a very useful human, Mr. Roberts. We shall meet again."

Trey said nothing as he released Nafarl's arm and turned the key.

~ ~

Upon Trey's return, he said to Tanny while holding out the Clutched Rose in a palm, "This is not safe with me. Something this powerful belongs elsewhere. Do you know of a place?"

"Not safe with you, Fire Tamer? You seem to be harboring several items unsafe for a child your age."

Trey smiled humbly and replied, "I know. Plus, I seem to have trouble with creatures trying to get it all. It wouldn't be good for this to fall into the wrong hands."

"I fully agree. I will take it to the Azuliposians.

They will hide it, and no one will expect to find it there."

"Wonderful. What happens with the skylien now that Nafarl is gone? Will it go away or continue to hunt the rose?"

"I'm not sure how that works."

"Hopefully it'll go back to where it came from."

"Hopefully," she replied hoping to hide her disbelief.

"Before you go, can you first take me back to the soccer field so that my guard won't be suspicious about my disappearance?"

"Of course."

That night, after Tanny returned Trey to the soccer complex and revived his guard, Trey decided to contemplate the previous frightful events on a slow walk home. The watchful man in the car followed carefully at a distance unaware of the mayhem through which he slept.

"Trey! You scared me to death!" him mom said as he walked through the kitchen door. "Why on earth would you run out like that?"

On Earth. That's a good one mom, he thought. "I – I don't know. I guess I sort of freaked out when the crown wasn't there. I'm sorry."

"I'm just so disgusted with myself. I should have put it somewhere safer."

"Mom. It's not your fault. Think about it. No one knew you had it, and no one knew you put it in the anonymous locker. Whoever got it, had to have been following it and used some sneaky spy tactics to steal it without using the key."

"I don't know honey. That sounds kind of crazy. Why would that happen to me?"

Trey nervously said, "I – I don't know, Mom. It's

just a guess."

"I'm just so upset with myself. I know there's more I could have done. It was the most amazing thing I've ever had in my possession. I felt great knowing I was one of the few people in the entire world that knew of its existence."

"Probably exactly how Grandpa felt every time he discovered a new artifact."

She gave Trey a big smile and an even bigger hug. "I bet you're right, Sweet T. I bet you're right."

He hugged her again then went to his room feeling guilty for keeping such dangerous situations from her. "It's for her own good. She would freak out if she knew what was going on," he said as he looked at the drawer containing ancient artifacts and magical potions.

Dream Walker

He slept restlessly that night only to awake with renewed energy for the day. After discovering a way to save his grandfather, optimism and hope flowed like soda through a straw.

He visited Nick Hampton in the science lab before home room. "Mr. H! You have a second?"

"Yeah, Trey. What's going on?"

Trey slowed his approach toward his favorite teacher. He scrunched his brow and looked at Nick cautiously.

"You ok, Trey? Is something wrong?"

As if woken from a trance Trey said, "Oh. No. I'm ok. Tanny visited me yesterday."

"The dragon?" he said clearly alarmed.

"Yeah."

Nick turned to his desk and picked up a squeezy

ball. He crushed it several times before he said, "Why? What did she want?"

Trey detailed the previous night's events but replaced his visit to the Etherios with Tanny flying off with Nafarl.

"It looked like me?"

"No. It was exactly like you. I was totally fooled for a second."

"Geesh. Sorry about that."

"Nothing to be sorry for. It wasn't you."

"I saw a headline this morning about vandals at the ball fields. This is getting out of control," Nick said sternly. "But you seem to be taking it all well."

"I'm good today considering what happened last night but I'm not sure how well I'm taking it overall. I keep finding ways to stay alive so that's good," he said with an uncomfortable chuckle. "I want out. I don't know how much more of this I can take."

"Believe me, Trey. If I could make that happen I would."

"I know. I just wanted you to know what happened."

"Thanks."

"I'm gonna go to home room now."

"See you later, Trey. Hang in there."

Trey ushered a weak smile and left the lab.

School flew by like a dream and on a breezy Wednesday afternoon, Trey and Marcus sat under a big oak near the edge of school campus discussing Trey's upcoming third day of soccer practice with the high schoolers.

"I don't get it, Marcus. They pass to me when I'm covered, they slide tackle me, they smash me to the ground, and my squad intentionally hides behind the defenders, so I'm forced to move the ball. They clearly don't want me on the team. I don't know why I'm even there or why I continue to go. The only ones that seem to be rooting for me are Kenny of all people and Josef the striker."

"Oh. That's tough, Kid. They're just being stupid. Think about it this way, you're a thirteen-year-old who has a great chance to make a competitive varsity high school soccer team. That could do amazing things for your career."

"I suppose. I'm not gonna quit. I actually think I've figured them out a little. Art I already know. He's easy to avoid. Lenny the pimply kid is fast and an outstanding defender but often slide tackles. I just have to jump him to evade the tackle. Tucker is a great athlete but is out to destroy me. I just need to use a little judo on him...you know...use his anger toward me against him."

"I like where you're going with this," he said excitedly with overly large eyes behind round wire-framed glasses. Can I come watch today?"

"Sure! Come on!"

They both jumped up and made their way to the soccer complex.

"Look, Trey. It's Sarah," Marcus said approaching the stands at the soccer complex.

She wore tight fitting light blue jeans with a snug sapphire V-neck T-shirt.

"She must be here to see Kenny."

"She's walking this way," Marcus said excitedly under his breath.

"Hey, Sarah," Trey said.

"Hey, Trey. Hey Marcus."

"Very nice to see you Sarah," Marcus replied with a smile. "You're here to witness the carnage?" He looked at

Trey and continued, "Sorry, Trey."

"It's ok. I think today will be different."

"Kenny said you were trying out for the varsity team. That's really amazing."

Trey shuffled his feet and looked away before replying, "It hasn't been very amazing so far."

"Yeah. They've been kicking his butt out there," said Marcus.

"He said they weren't being very nice. Especially Tucker. But he's not nice to anyone."

"I would just like my squad to help a little rather than go along with it. It's hard to do it all by myself."

"It must be difficult for you to have to prove yourself with all those big guys against you."

"Yeah but that's life isn't it? Always having to prove yourself with grades, responsibilities or to fit in? I just play my game and we'll see how it comes out in the end."

"That's a good way to think about it," she replied. "Please try not to get hurt out there."

"I'll do my best."

Sarah and Marcus sat on the bench together, both hoping Trey wouldn't get hurt too badly.

During a grueling drills session, Trey was one on one with Lenny. As Trey dribbled up to Lenny, he said, "Take the video down, please."

"No way," Lenny replied with a smug smile.

"Trey then faked left drawing Lenny with him then megged him to the right to easily beat him.

In a three on three defensive drill, Lenny was driving toward Trey. Trey yelled, "Take the video down, please!"

"I said no!" Lenny said sternly.

Trey sprinted and slide tackled the ball away

causing Lenny to fall hard to the turf. Trey quickly regained his feet and passed the ball up field.

"What the heck, Trey!" Lenny screamed as he stood.

Trey didn't acknowledge the red-faced boy.

Trey received a pass from Josef to kick off the scrimmage. Trey one-touched it to the left midfielder just before he was slammed by Tucker's tackle.

Sarah and Marcus released audible oooo's and showed painful expressions.

Tucker chortled as he trotted off.

"This will not be like yesterday. I will be successful today," Trey told himself. He then said in a low voice as he returned to the midfield line, "I move the ball well, I pass the ball well, I shoot the ball well."

Josef dropped the ball back to Trey to begin the next drive. Trey made several spot-on one touch passes which moved the plays along nicely – putting solid pressure on the goal as well as leaving little to no time to be bullied by Tucker and his cronies.

Trey positioned past the halfway line into his squad's side which were defending a powerful offensive. Team A were playing four fullbacks and three midfielders when the ball was randomly kicked in Trey's direction. Trey stepped up to receive it when he heard 'Man On!' from Josef. He lofted the wild ball over his and the defending midfielder's head while quickly spinning around him to re-receive the airborne ball. He tapped it a couple times keeping it off the turf while continuing to move it forward. He passed to Josef who immediately sent it back to avoid a fullback.

Trey did a stop-and-go to fake out another defending midfielder. He cut quickly toward the left side of the field. Tucker rushed over to make the stop - violently if possible. Trey touched the top of the ball with one foot, turned causing Tucker to cut, used the other foot to drag the ball forward then turned again dashing past the charging Tucker who stumbled to the ground failing to find proper footing.

"Oh Snap! Did you see that!" yelled Marcus giving Sarah a high five. "That's my boy!" he hollered.

Two defenders working together slowed him down. He spied Tucker closing in quickly – sure to end Trey's mythic run. Doing a footwork session to briefly delay the defenders he timed his moment carefully. At the last second, he turned left, rolled the ball behind him to the right, then with an ever so light touch turning back to the right plus Tucker's momentum, Trey tossed the speeding muscle train into the unwary defenders sending them all sprawling to the ground. Trey continued the run as he approached Lenny.

"Take the video down, please," he said enthusiastically.

"No, Trey! No! I won't do it!" he said in a panicked screech. His eyes shifted rapidly. He rocked backward, unsure of what to do.

Trey confidently dribbled within a few yards of Lenny, lofted the ball into a perfectly executed rainbow just a foot over Lenny's head, darted past the pimply kid to re-receive the ball then easily defeated Art to finish with a left-footed blast to the upper right corner of the goal.

When he turned toward the other goal to return to his position, he found the entire team standing and clapping at the magnificent effort. Marcus was jumping up and down on the bleachers. For just a few seconds, he silently reveled in the recognition then ran back to his position ready for the next kickoff.

"In all my years, Trey, I've never seen anything like that," said Coach Wood who walked onto the field after the goal. "You have something special in you. I don't know if it's enough right now to make this team, but it is something truly amazing." He turned to the team and said, "Ok guys! We've spent enough time today letting this middle schooler teach us what it means to play this game. Let's get back to work!"

"Nice moves back there, Roberts," Tucker said before running back to position.

Kenny shot Trey a surprised glance of which Trey responded with a shy smile.

After practice, Marcus ran to Trey, then said, "That was pretty sweet how you demolished those big dudes!"

"Yeah Trey! You were great out there," said Sarah. She had an exuberant smile that hinted of holding back certain emotions which faded as Kenny put his arm around her.

"Good practice, Trey! See you tomorrow," said Kenny giving him a high-five.

He and Sarah walked away. She turned and said, "Bye Trey! See you at school tomorrow!"

"Yeah. See ya....Sarah" he said as his voice diminished.

Marcus slapped Trey on the back and said, "Don't worry about her. She'll come around."

"Thanks. How about that ice cream you wanted last week?" He gave Marcus a friendly smile.

"Yes! Chocolate fudge, here I come!"

They turned to leave the field when Trey heard someone call his name. He turned to find Lenny walking toward him.

"Hey Lenny –"

"I know. Take the video down, please." He smiled then laughed causing Trey to become uncomfortable. "You were pretty amazing today. I'd love to have you on the team. I hope Coach agrees with me."

"Thanks, Lenny. I appreciate it."

"Do you think you can teach me that rainbow later this week?"

"Yeah. I guess so." Trey wasn't sure he wanted to help the boy that caused him so much trouble and brought Davis to quit soccer all together.

"Thanks. I look forward to it," Lenny smiled. It was a nice smile. A friendly smile. One Trey didn't think the boy possessed.

Trey slunk in his stance when Lenny turned to walk away. He regretted every second of niceness he showed the foul boy. His anger turned his face cherry red.

Just as Trey was about to speak his mind, Lenny turned and said, "Oh yeah, Trey," Trey backed off his temper to hear the boy out, "I'll take the video down."

Trey's eyes popped and he released a thankful sigh. "Thank you, Lenny! Thank you so much!"

Lenny smiled, turned and walked away without another word.

"I can't believe he did that for you," Marcus said excitedly.

"I know. I've been asking him all week. We have to tell Davis. Maybe he'll get back on the team!"

"Hopefully so. But it can wait until tomorrow. Right now, is ice cream celebration time!"

Trey gathered his stuff and the two eager teenagers strolled to Danucci's ice cream shoppe.

"What are you getting?" Marcus asked Trey at

Danucci's.

"Vanilla."

"And what else?" he said smiling.

"Vanilla."

"That's all?" Marcus asked with a perplexed face.

"I like vanilla ice cream."

"No gummy bears? No chocolate pieces? Not even sprinkles?"

"Nope."

"Just vanilla." Marcus stared.

"Yep."

"Why am I even friends with you?"

"I don't know, Marcus," Trey replied snickering.

They sat outside the tiny shop in the cool fall day. Marcus unsuccessfully attempted to arrest a falling gummy worm before it reached the table. Trey nonchalantly tipped his head to the bald bearded guy sitting on a bench no more than thirty yards away – the same guy that drove him home the previous unpleasant night. Trey's personal guard offered no response.

Trey took a huge bite of his treat just as Leslie stopped at the table.

"Hey Trey! Hey Marcus."

"OOMMM. Goust a muinet," Trey tried to say pointing to a full mouth with a drip of vanilla flowing down his chin. Leslie giggled.

"Hey Leslie! What's up?" Trey said finally choking down the bite of frozen treat.

"Hey," Marcus said as he continued to struggle with his gummy worms.

"I saw you two sitting here and wanted to say hey."

"Go grab a cup and sit with us," Trey said as he pulled out a chair next to him.

She hopped and said with a large smile, "I'd love

to! Be right back!"

Trey watched her skip off into the store.

"You have a thing for Leslie?" Marcus asked.

"No. She's just nice ... and she plays soccer."

"And she's cute," Marcus countered with raised eyebrows and a goofy smile.

"Well, there's that too....but I wasn't noticing," Trey said, hoping to ward off Marcus' friendly assault.

"Sure, you weren't. You know her dad's into all that bizarre psycho mumbo jumbo stuff, right?"

"What do you mean?"

"He talks to spirits and does that freaky meditation stuff where he runs around everywhere. My mom went to one of his meditation sessions because she thought it would be relaxing. She was pretty wierded out."

"No. I don't know her family. She seems pretty cool though. I'm not worried about what her parents do."

"Just watch out. I don't want him stealing your soul or anything."

"Stop goofing. Here she comes."

"Strawberry and banana? Looks yummy," Trey said.

"Want a bite?"

"Sure."

She heaped out a scoop, then placed it softly into his mouth.

"Mmmm. Very good," he said looking into her eyes.

"You guys are making me sick with all this mushy stuff. I'm getting out'a here," Marcus said.

"Wait, Marcus! We just got here," Trey said.

"No. Really. You guys finish. I have to get to my homework anyway."

"Ok, dude. See you later."

"Bye Marcus!" she said sweetly.

Trey turned back to Leslie and said with a huge expression, "You'll never guess what happened today?"

"What?" She replied as if it were her birthday and someone brought her the biggest gift to open.

"The kid with video of me and Davis is taking it off the internet!"

"Oh gosh! That's great! You think he'll get back on the team?"

"I don't know. He was pretty mad about the whole ordeal. It'll most likely take more than just removing the video."

"You're probably right. But it's good that he did it."

"It's not down yet. We'll just have to see if he stays true to his word."

She replied with a full mouth of ice cream and an affirmative head nod.

"How's soccer going?" He asked.

"Really good. I love the team. I've also made a few new friends. Tina Lopez and I have become pretty close."

"Tina's very good. We played many seasons together in the rec league."

"How's it going with the high schoolers?"

"They're pretty tough. It's been really hard moving the ball. They're just so big and fast. I have to be really smart or they'll splat me."

"Sounds scary."

"It is scary. Some of those guys are twice my size."

"I heard about that Senior that was picking on you."

"Who Tucker? He's just making sure his team is sound. He didn't want some middle schooler messing up their progress this year. Hey!" Trey said abruptly.

"Hey," Leslie instantly replied with an open smile

before Trey could finish.

They both laughed.

"Hey," he said again with a big smile. "You want to finish up here, then go kick the ball around a little?"

"I'd love to, but it's getting dark and there's a full moon tonight. Plus, I'm still aching from last time," she bumped him in the shoulder with hers.

"Ha! That didn't go so well did it?"

"Nope," she said while spooning a dripping piece of banana.

"So, what's special about a full moon?"

"My father and I sit in every full moon."

"Why?"

"It's a great time to moon bathe. We breathe in allowing the moon to warm our hearts and expand the beauty of the present moment. We breathe out to release all that needs to go away in our lives. It also seems to give me delightful dreams."

"Dreams you say? I've been having some strange ones lately."

"Maybe my dad can help. He's very good at dream interpretation."

"Uh. Sure."

"Great! Let's go!"

"You mean now?"

"Yeah, silly. No time like the present!"

She jumped up, tossed her cup into the trash then turned around and said playfully, "Well? Come on."

Her smile was inviting like a warm cup of hot chocolate on a frosty winter day. Trey followed her unquestioningly – just like he would many times after.

Along the walk from the ice cream shop, they talked about school and soccer and missing old friends. They turned off of the sidewalk next to a multi-colored mailbox painted with small peace signs, a larger black and white yin yang and smiley faces. The driveway was long and edged with trees and robust bushes draped in colorful Clematis. They arrived at a front door decorated in markings along the frame, colorful stones at the base and were greeted by a small statue of a closed eye smiling man. Leslie removed her shoes, then entered the house. Trey followed her example.

"Daddy! Are you home?"

"Hey Leslie Bean! I missed you today," said a skinny middle-aged man with straight brown hair that draped past his ears. He spoke in a soft voice that Trey thought was intentionally acquired through time rather than natural.

"I missed you too daddy," she said as she hugged him tightly.

"Who's your friend?"

"Trey Roberts, Sir," he said holding out a hand. "It's nice to meet you, Mr. Taylor."

"Yes. Yes, it's nice to meet you too. Please call me Paul," he said displaying hands covered in dark muck. He gave an apologetic smile, then said excitedly, "Come look at what I'm making!" Trey noticed he felt instantly comfortable in Paul's presence.

Paul took them out back revealing a statue about the height of a fifth grader in the shape of a partially naked woman.

"I've made it completely out of stuff I found in the yard. It's shaped up nicely."

"That's putting it mildly. I don't see any tools. Did you make it by hand?" Trey asked.

"Yeah. Only my hands and the dirt, sticks and rocks I could find."

"It's amazing. Look at the detail on her face. Eyelashes and all. How did you ever get them to stick?"

"Those are pine needles. I thinned them with rocks. They turned out well."

"She's beautiful, daddy. Looks just like mom," she said shedding a single tear.

"I know sweetie. I also miss her tremendously."

They shared another heartfelt hug. Trey felt somewhat uncomfortable during their moment.

They turned to Trey and Paul said, "I'll go get washed up, then we'll sit for a chat."

Back in the house, Trey took a seat on the couch. Leslie sat comfortably next to him, shoulder to shoulder, touching her leg to his. She kicked her legs happily causing her to bounce a little as they waited on her father. He liked sitting next to her. She smelled of lavender and cucumber. Her smile was contagious. Mint green eyes mused of wonder and happiness. He felt at home in her presence.

Paul came in, taking a seat in a chair next to the couch.

"Tell me Trey, what brings you here today, besides my daughter of course?" he said with a small laugh.

"Trey's had some interesting dreams lately?" Leslie offered with a reverent smile.

"Dreams huh? Has it been the same dream?"

Trey started uncomfortably. He was nervous about sharing. He replied, "Sort of. It's in the same place but slightly different each time," Trey said.

"Honey. Please go fix us some tea."

"Yes. Daddy."

She gave Trey a sweet look, pushed on his leg to help herself off the couch, then trotted into the kitchen.

"Repeating dreams are typically the universe trying to tell us something. First off, how do you feel in the dream? Are you scared, happy, sad? What emotions do you feel?"

"I'm confused most of the time ... and anxious. I feel like I should be doing something, but I don't know what to do. I don't remember being scared. It feels more purposeful and I don't have time to feel much. I know it doesn't make any sense."

"No. It does make sense. It seems as if you have a mission. Have there been any animals in the dreams?"

"Yes, but only in one. There was an eagle and a wolf. Oh yeah, there was a tiny bird in the first one,"

"I'm not sure about the tiny bird," he said in a thoughtful manner. "In the dream were you the eagle or did you just see the eagle?"

"I was the eagle at one point then I saw it in a tree."

"Interesting." Paul sat back in his chair pondering Trey's response. "That could symbolize your awakening to a hidden strength. It may also represent a spiritual renewal. And the wolf?"

"The eagle turned into the wolf, then led me to various people in an old looking desert city."

"The wolf may be a spirit guide. It may also represent instructions to act using greater instinct. Wolves are also protectors. Was there any danger in the dream?"

"Yes. I think everyone died and the wolf was trying to warn me."

"Old city you say?"

"Yeah. Like an ancient civilization city or something. Everything looked really primitive. No cars or anything modern."

"That's very interesting. Not to freak you out or anything but dreams of events that occurred in the past are sometimes memories of past lives. Or," he mused, "they can be people living in their time, attempting to communicate with you in your time. This is a very rarely documented occurrence. However, the times it has been told, the people of old were reaching out for purposes of survival. If what you say are the events that took place, then it would seem that this city is in grave danger and whoever is reaching out has identified you as someone that can help."

"Me? How can I or anyone from my time help someone that is long gone?"

Paul leaned forward in the chair toward Trey and asked, "Why don't you ask that question to someone in the dream? Is there anyone that stands out?"

"Yeah. There's this old man that leads me to a cloudy image."

"What's the image of?" he asked curiously.

"It looks like a sun that is split into three pieces."

"Ok. Nothing rings a bell with that description. I suggest you make the intention of asking the man why he has summoned you there."

"Ok," he said as he built a modest level of skepticism regarding Paul's guidance. "And how do I do that?" he asked more out of politeness than actually desiring an answer.

"Before you lay down to sleep tonight sit on your bed, close your eyes, then say to yourself, I will awake in my dream. I will ask the man what I should do."

"That's it?"

"Yeah. I think that's all you can do at this point. Hopefully it will help you understand the meaning of the dream."

"Ok. Thanks, Mr...I mean Paul."

"Your welcome." Paul smiled and pushed a tuft of hair behind his ear.

Leslie came in with three cups of jasmine tea.

"Will you stay with us for the moonlight meditation?" Paul asked.

Thinking about what Marcus said Trey quickly responded, "Not tonight. I have to be getting home. Maybe next time."

"Very well then. It has been a pleasure getting to know you, Trey. I'll get back to my sculpture and leave you two alone."

"Thank you again, Paul."

"It's been my pleasure, Trey."

Paul left the room.

"So how did it go?" Leslie said taking a sip of warm tea with both hands wrapped around the tiny cup.

"Your dad is an amazing person. I'm not sure if what he told me will help but it certainly did put some perspective into the situation. And that statue! Oh my gah. I didn't know it was your mom. It's astounding that he made it by hand in the back yard!"

"That's wonderful about the talk. Thank you for your kind words about him. He really is the best dad ever. We lost my mom to cancer two years ago. I miss her terribly. Sometimes, I wish he wouldn't make things that remind me of her." A few tears streamed down her cheek. "But when I see the beauty of the creation and that it came from a tremendous place of love, I become so happy."

She looked around the room reminiscing on her mother then said, "She was a wonderful person. She painted the pictures on the walls."

"Really? She did those? They're beautiful."

"I know. Sometimes I sit here and cry looking at them."

"I'm sorry for your loss. My parents are divorced. I haven't seen my dad in over three years."

She lightly took his hand, looked him in the eyes caringly and said, "I think that would be harder than him dying. To know you are capable of seeing him, but not able to make it happen on your own."

"Yeah. I suppose I never thought of it that way."

They sat in silence for a few minutes her hand in his, beholding the stunning display of vivid colors splashed in various patterns on blankets of canvas.

"I need to be going. It's dark out. Thank you so much for bringing me to your father. I've really enjoyed this time with you," he said rising from the couch and turning to face her.

Still holding her hand, he pulled her up close to him. They looked into each other's eyes, then shared a soft innocent kiss.

She walked him to the front door, then he said, "I'll see you at school tomorrow."

"Yes, you will," she softly replied in his ear as she kissed his cheek. Her warm breath of jasmine gave him a pleasant chill.

He slowly walked out the door holding her gaze, her hand still in his until the bond was broken by distance. He looked over his shoulder only once as he proceeded down the drive to find her still standing in the doorway. He gave her a wave goodbye, then disappeared into the night.

That night his thoughts drifted to what Paul said earlier, thinking about the past week's craziness, thinking about soccer. He lay awake thinking about Leslie and the newfound flood of feelings he had for her. He rose, closed his eyes. He breathed in and breathed out slowly several times. A calmness settled upon him, then he said, "I will awake in my dreams tonight. I will ask the man what to do." He fell asleep almost as soon as his head hit the pillow.

Images of soccer balls darting past were interrupted by a skipping girl with bright green eyes looking back in a playful manner. "Come," she said waiving her arms. He ran to her, then grabbed her hand just as she transformed into a wolf with an eagle head and wings that flew him away. He soared through the air in a peaceful glide thoroughly enjoying the flight.

Flying is so wonderful. The wind in my hair, beautiful sky at my command. Wait. This is a dream and I'm still flying.

Realizing the impossibility, he began to fall. Streaking through the clouds at a breakneck pace he plummeted to the ground. He stopped upright just before impact. The trim-bearded man faced him.

"What do you want me to do?" Trey asked calmly.

"I want you to see," replied the man without moving his lips.

Trey followed him through the thicket revealing a cloudy sun shaped wall. The man pointed. Trey turned to find the woman and child behind him. Trey approached the infant who delivered a penetrating stare. Maintaining the gaze, the child slowly grew, transforming to a boy of Trey's size. As if looking into a mirror, Trey peered into his own eyes.

Trey turned back to the old man who said, "Do you now understand?"

"Yes. But how?"

The man crouched into a back legged lunge; his front leg slowly extended toward Trey. He circled his arms in a rhythmic pattern, shifted his body forward, then suddenly pushed his hands toward Trey releasing a massive soul penetrating light. Trey awoke.

"I know what I have to do."

The Key

Trey gathered a change of clothes, the cloaking potion and left the remaining artifacts in the drawer. He placed several other items into his school pack, the disk into a zipped pocket, hesitated, then picked up the gold coin Karim gave him in Egypt. He flipped it into the air, caught it then put it in another zipped pocket. He then looked at the sword.

"There's no way I'll make it into school with that. But it can't stay here."

He took the sword into the back yard and buried it under a row of bushes near the fence. He then went into the kitchen to add a few bars and other non-perishable food items to his kit.

"You're up early," his mom said joining him in the kitchen.

He continued to fidget with his bag as he said, "I

need to ask Mr. Hampton a few things before school starts. He's always there early." He looked at her and said, "I love you mom." He held back tears as he hugged her tightly.

"I love you too, Trey. Is everything ok? You're acting weird."

"I'm fine. We just haven't hugged lately."

"You sweet boy. I love you so much. I hope you have a wonderful day today."

"You too, Mom," he said releasing her from the embrace.

"Hey, um, Mom?" He fidgeted with his fingers. "Do you ever talk to dad?"

"Oh honey. I hardly ever hear from him. He's always travelling and doesn't stay in contact very long."

"Oh. Ok." He looked at her sadly. "Well. If you talk to him again, will you tell him I miss him?"

Her eyes swelled – a few tears streaked down her face. She grabbed him, then hugged him tightly with her head on top of his.

"I will, Sweetie. I'll tell him."

"Thank you, Mom," he said hugging her back.

She released him, then said, "I'll be at the museum late tonight, so you'll have to fend for yourself for dinner."

He couldn't look her in the eyes when he said, "I'll be at Marcus' for a couple days working on the project so don't worry about me."

"Oh Great! Judy sure does get to see a lot of you."

"Yeah, his mom is great. See you later. Love you!" he said walking out the front door not knowing if he'll ever get to hug her again.

"Love you too!" she replied standing in the doorway.

He glanced back one last time before turning the corner and out of sight.

He walked up the drive, then knocked on Marcus' door.

When it opened, he said, "Hey, Mrs. Bouer. Can I speak to Marcus for a second?"

"Sure, Trey. Come on in."

"Dude! What are you doing here before school?" Marcus said sitting in front of a big bowl of cereal when Trey entered the kitchen. His hair was disheveled, and he still had on PJ's with decorations of various African wildlife.

"Can we talk in your room?"

"Yeah sure. Let's go," Marcus replied with obvious concern in his voice.

Trey followed the boy with a lion printed across his back side. A bubble caption with the word Roar! protruded from the image's mouth.

Once in the room with the door closed Trey said, "I have to go away for a little while and just wanted you to know." Trey couldn't help but make an opportunistic jab at his friend's attire. "Nice PJ's by the way."

"What are you talking about?" Marcus replied disregarding Trey's jab.

"Remember? I didn't tell you last time? Well, I'm telling you now."

"Oh. Ok. I get it. Thanks. Where are you going?"

"I don't really know and don't know how to explain it."

"What? How do you know you're going somewhere but don't know where you're going?"

"I know. It doesn't make sense and I'm not even sure why I'm here telling you. A lot has happened over the past couple weeks. I'm in big trouble and have to go handle it now."

"Trouble? Like what?"

"You wouldn't believe me if I told you and plus it might put you in danger."

"Danger? What've you gotten yourself into? I'm your best friend. I'll believe anything you say."

"You won't believe me. You'll think I'm crazy and making it up."

"Try me," Marcus said sincerely.

"Fine. I'll tell you. But you have to know that it's all true and I'm not insane."

Trey then began from the day Lyza showed up to his house and finished with Tanny in the ballpark.

"So that's what happened," Marcus said astonished. "It was all over the news. Are you sure you haven't gotten mixed up with the stoners?"

"I'm not crazy and I'd never do drugs. It's all true. Look here's the disk. Watch what happens when I put it on the dresser."

After twenty seconds Trey pulled the disk from his pocket and Marcus exclaimed, "That's an amazing trick! How'd you do it?"

"I told you. The story is true."

"The portals, flying cat and the snake? They're all real?"

"Yes."

"And people are watching me too?"

"Yes. Just in case they try to get to me through you."

"And Donald knows all of this?"

"I'm not sure what all his dad told him, but yes, he's involved now."

"Ok. I believe you."

"Really?"

"Yeah. You said it so it must be true."

"You're the only person I trust enough to tell. Mr.

Hampton knows a little but not all that I just told you. He doesn't fully believe it. He's still trying to find a scientific explanation for it all."

"Seth's the flying cat, right?"

"Yep."

"And the dragon. You have to introduce me."

"No way. I'm keeping you as far from this as I can. I shouldn't even be here now. You have to keep this a secret. You can't tell anyone."

"You can trust me, but if you want to keep me as your friend, you have to show me the dragon."

"Dude!" Trey said seriously.

"I know. You can't put me in danger. Whatever," he said rolling his eyes.

"I know I can trust you. You're a good friend."

"Thanks, Trey. Please don't die."

"I'll do the best I can."

"I also told my mom I'd be staying with you for a few days. Please respond to her texts like you were me," Trey said handing Marcus his phone.

"Sure."

"And....will you tell Leslie I won't be at school today?"

"Leslie? Why her? Ohhhhh. Ok. You and her are a thing now?"

"No. I just told her I'd see her today. I don't want her to worry."

"Yeah. Sure. I'll tell her."

"Thanks, Marcus."

"Don't sweat it, Kid."

"No. Really. I'm glad you're my friend."

"I get it. I love you too. Now get out of here and go do what you have to do."

"I'll let you know as soon as I'm back."

"I'll be waiting."

"Thanks, Marcus," he said as he hugged his best friend goodbye.

Trey walked the lonely sidewalk toward Lownes Middle School spinning thoughts in his head. *I hope Nick isn't there. He'll do everything he can to stop me. This is nuts. I don't even know if it'll work. Like Marcus said, I have to do what I have to do. I am the only one that knows what to do, but what is it really that I'm doing? I still only have pieces of the puzzle. I'll have to figure the rest out as I go. What if it's a trap? This is too dangerous. Maybe I just go to school and forget all this ever happened. Maybe it'll all go away. Arggg! I'm only thirteen. Kids are supposed to worry about girls and what's cool, not goblins and magic portals!*

He climbed the steps to the school and stopped before the double doors. "Communication is the key to fútbol as well as life," he said, reminiscing on the words of his soccer coach.

He jumped off the steps and sprinted to the gym where he found Coach Rafiq shooting free throws on the basketball court.

"Hey, uh, Coach. I see planning for your history class is going well."

"Trey! Nice to see you! I like to come in here before school starts. It puts my mind in a state that prepares me for all the wonderful minds I get to impact."

He passed a ball to Trey who bounced a proper jump shot off the rim. He let it bounce away as he lied, "Coach. You think you can tell Coach Wood I won't be a practice today or tomorrow?"

"Yeah. Sure. What's going on?"

"I'm, um, going to my grandmother's house for the weekend. I'm leaving right after school today."

"To your grandmother's, huh?" he said taking in the young boy's demeanor.

Trey didn't dare say anything else. He knew he was a terrible liar.

"Sure. I'll tell him. Good thing we have a bye week this weekend."

"Yeah. I thought it worked out well."

"Thanks for telling me."

"See, Coach. I did learn from your communication lesson," he said then uncomfortably chuckled.

"Yeah you did, Trey." He smiled at Trey like a proud father and also frowned at the kid's lie but while he didn't know the reason for Trey's deception, he didn't let on that he knew.

"I have to go now, Coach." He turned to walk out before Rafiq called him back.

"Trey," He said tenderly.

"Yeah, Coach?"

"Is everything ok? Is there anything I can help with?"

"I, I'm fine coach," Trey stumbled. "I'm good. Thanks for asking."

"Ok, Trey. I'm here if you need me. I'll see you next week!"

"Yeah, sure. Thanks." Trey quickly turned and left the gym before Rafiq could try to get the truth from him.

Hearing his coach's words chilled him. He wasn't sure he would see Rafiq next week, or anyone for that matter. He had no idea what he was doing or what was in store for him. For all he knew only instant death awaited his next actions. He shook off the thought and pressed on with his loose plan.

He entered the double door on the right. Turning down two halls he arrived at the science lab to find Nick reading at his desk.

"Mr. H! You're here," he said anxiously.

"Yeah. Where else should I be? I am a science teacher, or did you forget?" he replied playfully.

"Right. Um…" Trey was nervous. He didn't know how he would accomplish his task with Nick in the room.

"What's going on, Trey? Why are you here and at school so early?"

Trey walked to the desk, noticing the ceramic box of which he picked up as he sat in a chair.

"You still have the key and portal in the lab?" Trey said opening the box and removing the key.

"Yeah. I haven't moved it yet. Are you here because of the portal?"

"No," he replied quickly. "No. Well, maybe," he said as he slowly folded one end of the key to where it touched about a third of the way down. The malleable metal was surprisingly easy to shape. It felt more like bending stiffened putty than metal. It held strongly after the initial bend.

"I've been having these dreams lately. In each one there's an old dark-skinned man with a trim beard. Was there a man of that description in any of your dreams?" he asked as he folded the other end of the key to touch a third of the way down the other side.

"No. None of the dreams that led me to build the portal had any people in them. Just locations, cities, and images. What else was in the dreams?"

"There was this old looking town and a woman and her baby. I think the village is destroyed and they all die. And an image continues to appear," he said as he stood from the chair, then walked toward the window observing the constructed portal with his back to Nick.

"A town and everyone dies? That's intense."

"It was. I think the man was asking me to save them. I think if I don't, I'll die," he said as he touched the previously bent ends together forming a circle. Trey's eyes widened in astonishment as the key became animated in his hand and eliminated the imperfections from his manual bending.

"It wasn't a sun; it was an image of the key!" he mumbled quietly.

"What was that you said, Trey? You're acting really strange," Nick said with significant worry in his voice. "Maybe you've been under too much stress. Besides, I'm not sure how you would go about saving a town from destruction, or how it could possibly relate to your life, but it is very interesting. What was the symbol? Maybe it's something we can look up."

"It was a circle with two lines that separated it into three pieces," Trey said as he turned around holding up the perfectly formed key. His heart raced. The confused teacher saw terror in the young boy's eyes as he watched him reach for the stone portal.

"Trey! Wait! You don't know what you're doing! Don't touch that!"

Nick leaped toward Trey but was too late as he watched the frightened boy disappear with the connection of the key to the stone.

"Noooooooooo!" screamed Nick.

The Librarian

Whomp, Whomp, Whomp presaged a drop in Trey's personal atmospheric pressure. His body twisted in the vortex. His mind merged with his stomach. Everything became clear then faded into confusion. He felt himself rushed forward then promptly stilled.

Trey found himself minimally nauseous in a naturally lit room. A perfume of old paper and wood polish tickled his nose. He raised his hand off the stone which was flush with the floor. He rubbed his finger across the circular image on the face of the cold stone portal.

"It worked. I actually made it. But where am I? More importantly, what do I do now?"

He stood finding rows of neatly indexed books on stained wood shelves.

"This must be some sort of library," he said to himself.

Tall wide windows on the front wall illuminated the charming area with warm sunlight. He slowly walked down a row toward an exit, unwary of beady eyes watching his every move.

He pushed out into a bustling town where several people wearing long coats and top hats shuffled about their day. A woman in a poofy white dress passed staring at him with curious eyes. The buildings were made of intricately carved wood and stone. Shaggy haired horses with a single upward curved horn pulled carts down dirt and brick roads. Several nicely dressed people rode bicycles; dodging holes, people and other objects in their path.

"What is this place? It's straight out of the 1800's," Trey said to himself in amazement.

He strolled down a busy street lined with carts and displays full of trinkets, foods and medicines. He turned on a side road, then after a brisk walk, arrived at a park.

"This looks just like Lake Hapawak. The old tree! It's even here. It's all the same, except back home there's a playground just on the other side of that hill. Well, the same except for the big city that surrounds it," he said as he turned around taking in the lively metropolis.

He stood a few minutes watching a black bird with yellow wingtips swim in the calm water. He began making his way back to the city center drawing eyes of several passerby's.

A small child approached and asked in an unmistakable proper English accent, "Excuse me, Sir. Could you possibly spare a few pence?" The boy reminded Trey of Tiny Tim with a soft English voice but moved around without a cane and iron frame.

"What? What do you want?" Trey responded kindly to the small child.

"Money, Sir. Do you have any to spare?"

"Oh. Oh, Yeah." Trey reached into his pocket and pulled out a few dollars. When he handed them to the boy the boy replied angrily, "What is this, Sir. I don't need paper. I need money for food. I'm staaaavin!" He threw the bills to the ground and stormed off.

Trey brushed away the vagrant's attitude toward his generosity and continued walking after picking up the money. He glanced once more in the boy's direction then accidently bumped into a man who sported a rounded reddish-brown beard and no moustache. He wore a brown hat and a casual buttoned coat.

"Excuse me, I wasn't looking where I was going?" Trey said apologetically.

The man gave Trey an odd look, then kindly said in an accent that reminded Trey of a crazy Australian zookeeper he used to watch on TV, "What brings you to Roberton, Mate? Are ya lost?"

"Yes. I mean, no Sir."

"Well are you lost or not?" the man asked again leaning back with his thumbs folded into the front of a thick black belt.

"No. I know where I'm going. Thanks for your help."

Trey scurried away from the inquiring man back toward the library. He glanced over his shoulder to find the man still looking his way.

"Maybe there's something in the library that can help. There has to be a reason the dream sent me here."

Upon entering the building, he looked through the books filling the shelves.

"The Rise and Fall of Halviticus. Who or what is that? The Ronodanian Empire? The wars of 2098 through 3047. What is this place?"

"May I help you?" said a short, slightly plump light skinned attendant with long ears and a long skinny nose. He wore a black silver buttoned coat with olive pants. His smile was inviting as his small wise eyes were fixed on Trey's.

"I'm not sure."

He fingered a chain protruding from a pocket (most likely connected to a hidden watch). "Yes. Of course. I am Cierden, the librarian," he said in a light and proper voice one would expect from a butler for a wealthy family. "How shall I address you, Sir?"

"What? Oh. Trey. My name is Trey Roberts."

"It is a pleasure to finally meet you, Mr. Trey Roberts," he said purposefully. "Let's get you out of those clothes. If you will, this way please."

Hesitantly, Trey followed the odd librarian. They crossed the center floor engraved with a large image of a long shield with wavy horizontal lines and a center stone depicted in brightly colored brick. *The symbol of the Order,* Trey thought.

He was led into a back room where Cierden laid out a pair of gray pants, beige shirt and dark brown coat. "These will help you avoid questioning looks from the locals."

Trey put on the shirt and coat. "Not wanting to reveal the items he previously stored in his pockets Trey said, "My pants seem to match well with the rest of the outfit."

"Very well," replied Cierden after giving him a discerning look-over.

"But how did you know...that I'm not from here?"

He raised thin eyebrows humorously, "Besides your ridiculous brightly colored outfit?" His tone became more sincere, "I saw you enter through the stone. To my knowledge, no one has ever used it."

"No one? Why?"

"Dimensioners are uncommon. There hasn't been one in this land for ages. Also, this is a very special portal. I wasn't aware anyone alive today, other than myself of course, knew of its existence. I would very much like to know how you came upon it."

"Special? In what way?"

"This place is a library of history and ancient myths. My family has watched over these texts and this stone for millennia. We preserve the ancient knowledge and secure the stone from destruction. It was predicted by Master Olerand himself that one of great power and wisdom would appear in this location. We have been waiting a long time for the one to arrive. Tell me Mr. Roberts, is that person you?"

"I'm afraid not, Cierden. I have no powers and don't feel very wise at the moment. I'm also fairly certain that I'm here by mistake."

"Yes. Perhaps. But there are no mistakes."

"I guess we'll see about that. History and myths, huh? What can you tell me about a king....a king named....Khaitu?"

"King Khaitu!" he replied in astonishment. Lowering his voice, then looking around he said, "Why would you desire to learn of him?" the elvish librarian said with increased excitement.

"It's a long story that I don't have time to explain."

"I understand. Come with me," he said leading Trey to an obscure door in the far corner of the library. He produced a long copper key from his pocket.

"You may not enter this room," he said disappearing into the darkness.

Moments later, the librarian returned with a large black leather-bound book with cracks in the binding. There were no words printed on any part of the cover.

"In this volume is all we know about the dreaded king."

Trey looked at the book in awe. Until now, he had only heard of rumors of Khaitu. Granted, he was attacked several times by demons and ghouls associated with the guy, but this book was clear evidence of his actual existence – a history of what is known of his actions and deeds. Trey ran a finger down its spine which triggered a tremor in his own. He flipped it open to a random page which displayed intricate writing.

"Look here, it says he conquered a peaceful world called Namjai."

Cierden's eyes brightened as he regarded him. "Interesting," he said.

Trey kept reading. "He nearly killed everyone. Why? Why would he conquer a peaceful world just to want everyone gone?"

"If you were to keep reading, you would find they didn't agree with his rule. They all joined in a peaceful protest of which Khaitu had no tolerance."

"So, he just wiped them out rather than leaving or finding a better solution," Trey said in a disgusted manner.

"There is no logic to his madness. Tell me Mr. Roberts," Cierden paused regarding Trey intensely then said as if singing a hymn, "Orelath omag loritni comparl a getalo nara?"

"Script of the Kings? You mean this book?" Trey replied.

Cierden nodded without removing eye contact.

"No. I don't have any trouble at all reading it. The writing is exceptionally neat. I've never seen anything like it, almost as if it were typed in a fancy cursive font. Tell me more of what you know."

"Very interesting." Cierden's amazement faded

back to his former reasonable demeanor as he continued, "To summarize the story, he came from the land of kings. He was the sorcerer of King Ronodan, a mighty and benevolent king. Khaitu had a tremendous thirst for power and made a deal with an ancient demon named Gorgemon who granted him conditional immortality. He rose to power, then forced Ronodan to flee to another land, yours I believe."

"Conditional?"

"Yes. The condition was that he would stay immortal as long as he drank the essence of others. Otherwise, he would die."

"What do you mean, Drink the essence?"

"That part is vague, but it is believed that through dark magic granted to him, he would consume their souls, leaving the victim's bodies undead."

"You mean like zombies?"

"If that is your word. Yes. It is believed that he has an army of these zombies, as you would say, waiting for his return."

"An army? Where would he keep an army of zombies?"

"Everywhere. Khaitu travelled the multiverse for centuries claiming the souls of thousands. We were all very fortunate for the Order and their effort to imprison him."

"I didn't know about the zombies. I only thought there was just the one bad dude. Does it say in there how he can be killed?"

"Killed? No. He cannot be killed by mortal means. However, he can be eternally imprisoned which is where he is today."

"Does it say in the book how to do it? How to imprison him?"

"Yes. It says with the power of the seven relics, one's soul can be confined to an eighth relic only to be freed in the same way."

"Ok, and the relics are where the seven's essences are stored from the ceremony intended to give Khaitu immortality?"

"That is correct."

"But Khaitu wasn't completely bound to the eighth relic. Couldn't there be another way for him to escape?"

"Possibly, but he probably would not survive the Etherios in the physical form he needs to rule worlds. But even if he were to survive, he would require assistance leaving the spirit realm."

"He has assistance."

"Commerand?"

"Yes."

"Of course. He is under the curse."

"How do you not know about Commerand? You seem to know everything else."

"He must be confined to your world. He cannot gain possession of a key or the eye."

"Yes. I am aware of that warning. The eye was recovered and, well, sort of re-hidden. I, of course, have a key and there is one other that I know of that seems safe."

"Commerand will find the eye. It calls to him like a siren to a lonely sailor. Safe is relative when it comes to the cursed sorcerer. Having two keys available to Commerand is too risky. You must let me protect this one for you," he said urgently.

"No!" Trey panicked. "I need it to return home."

"I see. You cannot return through this portal. It was designed one way."

"That's not very useful, now is it?"

"It was designed in a way that if the wrong people passed through, they would not have the ability to easily escape."

"Oh. Ok. Where do I find another?"

"You will find it north past Mount Klipping, across the wide river and at the base of a waterfall feeding Lake Oshugar."

"Will I have trouble making it that far?"

"Yes. Leaving the city is not recommended. Mount Klipping is very dangerous. You must never go on or through the mountain. You must go around to reach the river which is swift and unpassable by swimming and the lake is home to a water beast."

"Water beast? Really?" Trey said in a disbelieving voice.

"I don't know. That's what I was told. I've never been out of this library. I think it was just made up to scare people away."

"You've never left?"

"Like I said, I am the librarian. I made a vow to never leave this place unprotected."

"I'm not trying to be disrespectful, but you are just a little dude all by yourself and these are just books. What could you possibly do to protect any of this and why is it worth protecting?"

"If the world were to forget it's past, it would be destined to repeat it. Look at how many titles include the words war, empire, massacre and destruction. Without these teachings we would be locked in the cycle, constantly repeating our miserable mistakes. We must continue to move forward in wisdom, cooperation and love. Also, If the portal were destroyed, you would not have been able to arrive to provide whatever it is you will bring to us." He gave Trey a forceful look. "I know I seem meek to you, but I have a few useful tricks up my sleeve," he said finishing with a wink.

"I see," Trey said now understanding the little guy's purpose.

"What kind of tricks?" Trey said excitedly.

"Let's just move on shall we," Cierden said clearly avoiding the inquisition.

"Fine," Trey said disappointed he wouldn't get to know Cierden's secrets. "What can you tell me about the seven sorcerers?"

"We have very little on them before Khaitu summoned them from prima-dimensional space. It is believed they were given specific powers by Khaitu himself. It was they who created the portals as well as wrote this book."

"How did he become in control of them?"

"The seven, before becoming mortal, were not individually conscious beings. They were a collective conscious and creators of ways to improve life. The power Gorgemon gave Khaitu allowed him to force mortality onto the seven therefore controlling their existence."

"This Gorgemon demon seems like the ultimate bad guy. Why would he give a mortal power over the seven? What could he gain from it?"

"We don't know anything about him other than his name and what he did. Olerand didn't mention anything else in the book."

"Olerand wrote this?"

"Yes. Shortly before the imprisonment ceremony."

"And about these powers, what were the seven capable of doing?"

"Commerand has the power over physical things."

"Yes. I'm aware of his staff."

Cierden's face lit up, his voice cracked as he said, "You have met Commerand?"

"Briefly. I narrowly escaped," Trey said indifferently.

Cierden's voice changed and hinted of accusation, "You say you are here by accident?"

"Just keep going, please," Trey said dismissively.

"Moridon has the power of time."

"What do you mean time?"

"His purpose was to introduce into Khaitu a timeless state in the living world. The time ring is thought to grant vision of and communication with the past."

"Could he also use it to travel through time?"

"That was not in our teachings, so I do not believe it to be so. Satiran, Cholitar, and Teniua had the powers over wind, water and fire respectively."

"Fire?" Trey interrupted. "What could he do with fire?"

"I'm not sure. It just says here they have control over these elements. If I may continue, Barbudo had the power to heal. These were all to be combined through Master Olerand who would wield each to grant Khaitu power over the elements, heal from any wound and become unaffected by time."

Trey's mind raced. Could it be? Could the Clutched Rose be Teniua's relic?

"Sir?" Cierden asked to regain Trey's attention.

Trey drew his attention back and said, "Does it have in there what these relics look like?"

"No. The order did not want them found."

"Ok. I think I now understand. When he was bound, the relics containing the seven, well I suppose six, were scattered all over. Were any hidden here?"

"Yes. But that information was not written. I only know of its existence through rumors spread over time."

"Rumors?"

"Supposedly the protector of a relic came to this place thousands of years ago. Rumors of where they hid it remain today."

"Do you know where it is?"

"It is unwise to seek the relics, Mr. Roberts."

Trey smirked, "I told you I wasn't feeling very

smart."

"Very well. Visit a collector by the name of Karl Ropping in Hoppsburg. He can be found on Sharpe Street. It is a town directly east and a half day walk from here. He may be able to help. Do what you can to find yourself in town by nightfall. You don't want to be out when the sun goes down."

"What happens after dark?"

"You don't want to know. Just be in town before that happens."

"Warning noted. I'll be fast."

"Also, if by some miracle you actually find where the relic is hidden, know the protector would not have left it unguarded. You must be very careful."

"I'm not sure that's what I'm doing here, but it's all I have to go on so far."

"I have something for you before you go."

The librarian shuffled to a back room, then removed something from his desk. He returned with a small green draw string bag.

"Place the key in here before you put it in your pack, then say the word, aroushidium.

"Aroundushidum?"

"Aroushidium," Cierden repeated.

"That's what I said, Ashrouditum."

"Ah-roush-idium," he slowly enunciated.

Trey placed the key in the bag, cinched it up, then said the word properly.

"Now open it."

Trey opened the bag, then said in a panic, "Where'd it go! What'd you do with the key!"

Cierden raised his bony fingered hands and said, "Calm down, calm down. Close it, then say the word again."

Trey did as instructed, then quickly opened the

bag to find the key safely inside.

"A magic bag! Sweet!"

"The bag will provide you a simple level of security. If you lose the key, you will be stuck here. If you lose the key to the wrong people, we may all be doomed. You must protect it with your life."

"I understand. Thank you Cierden."

"You need to be on your way if you want to make it by sundown."

Cierden walked him to the door, then said, "Follow that road out of town, keep the sun at your back and you should be just fine."

"Thanks, and I hope to see you again."

"I don't. Because if I do, it means something went wrong. Remember, be inside the city limits by sundown."

"Right. Well, take care, Cierden."

"Bye Mr. Roberts. It has been my honor to aid in your endeavors."

Trey crossed the road fronting the library. He tripped on an uneven brick, nearly falling face first into the street. He looked back to find Cierden still standing in the doorway. Trey gave him an embarrassed wave, then continued along the perpendicular street adjoining the one he tripped on. No one looked his way as he left town through a massive gate connected to a high stone wall.

A New Friend

Trey traveled down a rocky dirt road. Mt. Klipping loomed to the North across a grassy landscape of sparse green and brown trees. Three black and red butterflies flittered across the path. An old man with a fishing pole stood as Trey walked past a small pond. He gave Trey a conspicuous look before settling back to his lonesome activity.

He walked nearly two hours with the sun high above his head before coming across another traveler.

"Hello there!" said a skinny elderly man with a big smile behind the reins of a two-horse wagon. He was missing a few teeth and had a scruffy beard.

"Hi," Trey said as he continued walking.

"Ya ain't from 'round 'ere are ya?" he said through a pair of large rimmed brown glasses.

"No. How'd you know?"

"I'm on this 'ere road every day hauling

rodobingers to Hoppston. I know nearly ever'one from ere to thar and never seen you before. What brings ya to Hoppston?"

"Just visiting a friend."

"A friend? D' yourn friend have a name?"

"I apologize, sir. I've been walking a long time and am pretty tired. I'm not really up to answer a bunch of questions. If you want to be friendly, you could give me a ride into town."

"Well, why didn'ya say so? Hop on in back thar but watch out for Cedric. He keeps the freight safe. It'll be best if you don' look eem in'd eye."

"Thanks!" he said. He noticed a large grey rabbit dash across the road in the distance as he cautiously climbed into the back of the wagon.

"Name's Porter."

"Trey. Thanks for the ride."

"No prob'lm, Trey. It bees my pleasure."

He sat between cartons of blue fruit similar in size and texture to oranges. Casually scanning the wagon his eyes met those of another crouched in the shadow under the eave supporting Porter's seat. Sharp teeth and a piercing stare forced Trey to quickly look away.

"Easy, Cedric," Porter said without looking back.

Porter prodded the horses into a trot. The cart bounced and jarred smashing Trey's head into the side more than once. Every so often, Trey's eyes would venture toward Cedric's direction noticing the menacing eyes always staring back.

"What's the deal with your dog?"

"Wha'd ya mean?"

"It won't stop looking at me."

"Cedric's a Wollybrougher. Most of'm are wild, untrainable and viciously fierce. Musta been ten yearn'ago when I found'm mos'ly dead in'a bush. Ya see, I stopped t' pee when I seen'm. Had I not already been peein, I surely would've. Looked like ee'd been trampled. People round here been killin'm off for years. Ev'n his poor condition ee nearly tore m'arm off when I tried to help'm. Took eem home and healed eem up, I did. Ee's been ridin wit me ever since. Ee's saved m'load more'n once. Ee don' trust no'n else."

Trey glanced at Cedric again before looking out the back of the cart. Warm wind ruffled his hair as they bounced along the road. He drifted off a moment thinking of an auburn-haired girl before being startled back to reality by a wild scream.

"Bandits!" yelled Porter as he whipped the horses into action.

Trey looked over the side of the accelerating wagon at six men gaining on horseback. Cedric growled fiercely but didn't move from under the eave. The riders gained and were nearly on top of them. Trey could see they brandished some sort of hand-held firearm.

"Get 'em Cedric!" Porter yelled.

Cedric jumped to his feet standing as tall as an adult brown bear and roar to match. Bulging muscular legs propelled the thick furred, shark-toothed, dog-like beast past Trey, then out the back of the wagon.

"It's a wollybrougher!" one screamed. The pursuer's scattered without attempting to use their weapons. Cedric touched the ground from his leap out of the wagon, then instantly launched himself into one of the fleeing men, crushing his chest with massive jaws before his victim could release a sound. He slammed the lifeless body down upon landing, then dashed after another. He bulldozed over the rider's horse flinging the screaming man into the air. Cedric caught the man by a leg. Bone protruded from the man's skin as Cedric slung him into a roadside field. Cedric leaped onto the crippled bandit, ending his days in a flurry of claws and teeth. The man's horse regained its feet and raced away. Cedric targeted another, then disappeared into a nearby wooded area. Porter never turned around.

Trey couldn't believe the horrifying scene and became sick to his stomach. Holding back vomit he concentrated on breathing. Breathe in breath out. Breathe in breath out.

"Oh my god, he just killed those men. He killed them." Trey was on the verge of hysteria. He heard a growl then a scream in the trees knowing another met his demise. It was like a scene from a horror movie except this was no movie. He heard the screams of the men as well as the dull sound of crushing bones. He closed his eyes wishing away the images but to no avail; they were all too clear – all too real.

He regained his composure, then asked shakily, "Aren't you worried about Cedric?"

"Na. Ee can handle m'self."

"Will you get in trouble for hurting those men?"

"Na. Bandits are despised roun here. I prob'ly be thank'd."

"Why are they after this fruit anyway? It doesn't look very valuable."

"Th'ain't after the rodobingers. They after th'a gold in this ere box," he said tapping his foot on a large unassuming wooden box.

"Gold? Really?"

"Yeah. Word got out I ride wit a wollybrougher, then before I know'd it I'sa haulin gold for th'a bank."

"That's pretty cool. I had no idea."

"No, ya would't. But thos'n bandits did."

"Good thing you have Cedric."

"Yes sir'e. He's good at what ee does."

"Clearly," Trey said to himself.

Trey closed his eyes with his head on crossed arms over his knees trying to forget about what just happened. He dosed off after a while.

"Trey. Trey. Wake up boy," Trey could hear Porter saying softly from a distance.

Trey picked his head up, then opened his eyes to find Cedric standing over him nearly six inches from his face. His dark eyes peered into Trey's. Hot breath puffed down his chest. Immobilizing fear over-came him.

"Na take it easy, Trey. Don' ya move a muscle," Porter said cautiously as the cart slowly rambled on.

"Uhh, Mr. Porter, I'm not comfortable with this. Can you do something, please?" Trey said with a shaky voice.

"Ee don' seem to be agitated so let's just see what he wants wit ya."

"What he wants with me? He wants to eat me!"

"Naw. Ee'da done that by now."

Trey wanted to close his eyes but couldn't disconnect from the beast's gaze. He felt as if the creature was inside pulling at his soul.

A twinkle sparked in Cedric's eyes. The hound raised its head, then let out a wild howl. Trey recoiled defensively. Cedric moved in closer as he brought his eyes back to Trey's. Trey shrieked when it wrapped its long tongue around his neck. It pulled the massive appendage back leaving a think sticky film. Cedric held Trey's frightened gaze for another minute before turning to settle back under the eave.

"Well woooohoooo! Look'a that!"

Trey slumped back against the wagon letting out a huge sigh of relief, then said, "What - was - that! I thought I was dead!"

"Ole Ced, likes ya! Wollybrougher's are parti'clar

bout who they snuffle. I ain't never seen one take to some'un so quickly."

"Snuffle? What's that mean?"

"Means you one of em now, like me. Cain't figure out why tho. Ee musta seen some'n in ya."

"Yeah, like I was full of sausage! He just wanted a taste."

"Wooowee, today just keeps gettin better!"

Still in shock, Trey slouched over in a fetal position and closed his eyes. He wished he were anywhere but here, but mostly wished he were at home with his mom.

After a while, Trey pushed himself up when he felt the wagon come to a stop. He regarded Cedric under the eave, then shook off a dreadful chill. After a good stretch he sat at the back of the wagon, looking at the city before him.

"Can I help you unload all this stuff?" Trey asked.

"Na. They'll come git the box shortly and then I av'ta d'liver tha fruit. Where's it you need ta go?"

"I need to get to Sharpe Street. I'm looking for a man named Karl Ropping."

"Ropping! Wha'dya need that good for nutin bum for?"

"I was told he had information for me. That he could help me find something."

"Well, I suppos'n ee could be helpful wit dat. I hear ee's good at findin stuff. Sharpe's roun tha corner there," he said pointing in the direction of the wagon. "Turn right, then you'll find his shop fifty-three steps down on tha left."

"Thanks for the ride, Mr. Porter. Now I've got plenty of time before sundown."

"Yep! My pleasure, Trey. Hope ya find what evr'n

it is you're lookin for."

Trey hopped onto the cobblestone road. He glanced at the furry animal under the eve. Cedric's head was alert with a fat tongue hanging limply. His wise eyes were set on Trey's. Not a trace of the earlier carnage remained. Trey frowned, broke the stare then walked past the wagon toward Sharpe Street.

The quiet street was narrow, maybe only wide enough for two carriages to pass. The walls of buildings, although no higher than two stories, obstructed Trey's wider view of the city. A couple emerged from what looked to be a clothing store. The woman carried a wide smile and playfully adjusted a feather decorated hat.

He thought it might rain soon as he walked down a spacious sidewalk past what may have been a barber shop and a restaurant that smelled of garlic and oregano. Trey's stomach gurgled, signaling him to dig out a bar from his pack – wishing it was a slice of Papparino's from back home.

While chewing on the crunchy granola of a bar from his pack, he observed a dirty man in a sackcloth standing on the corner. The man quickly approached Trey and said, "Beware! The end! It is foretold the great terror is upon us!"

Trey tried to ignore the spirited man. The destitute grabbed Trey's shoulder as he tried to pass and said, "You! Boy!" The man's eyes were hollow as if Trey were staring into an abyss. Had the man not been screaming and merely remained silent, Trey would have guessed he were mentally incapacitated in some way. "The end!" he continued.

Trey forcefully pulled away and hurried to the corner, leaving the man shouting to the air. "Repent! You must! Or be damned forever! He cannot be stopped!" The man's voice ended low and gravelly, "All will perish under the almighty sword!"

Trey released a breath then made the turn on Sharpe Street. He looked back at the corner as he passed a charcoal grey cat that rolled onto its back exposing a fat belly. He continued down the sidewalk passing an elderly man that gave him the shivers. He finally arrived at an antiques store on his left.

"Well how about that. Fifty-three steps exactly."

He paused a moment outside the beaten wood framed store, took a deep breath, then turned the doorknob. A hanging bell jingled as the door gently swung open. Loose papers on a wooden desk ruffled with the accompanying breeze.

He stepped into the naturally lit establishment and sneezed twice before a rusty voice said, "About damn time you showed up. Get over here so I can see you."

The Map

"Come on over here!"

Trey walked slowly past rows of pottery, swords, and other dusty old objects. He turned toward the counter to find a man sitting in a recliner. A pair of crutches leaned against the wall next to him and a wheelchair was parked on the other side.

"No! No!" he grumbled. "You won't do at all. I said I needed someone that can lift things. Someone taller. Not a kid. Uuuggg. This is what I get for trusting Malcolm. What's your name, boy?"

"Trey. I think you have me confused with someone else."

"What are you talking about. Aren't you here for the job?" the man said angrily.

"No sir. I'm looking for something. Something old."

"Good. You're useless to me as a helper.

Something old you say? I've got plenty of old stuff here. What is it you're looking for specifically?"

"Well you see, Cierden from Roberton said you might could help me find something."

"Get out of here! Leave! There's nothing here for you!"

Trey jumped back. He nearly turned to leave but stopped himself. *There's a reason I'm here. I have to find out. This man knows something, and I have to make him help me.*

Trey faced the crippled man again. "I need you to help me and I won't leave until you do."

"Boy! Don't make me get out of this chair and whoop you! You get on, now!"

"No," Trey said firmly and calmly. "I'm here for a reason. Cierden wouldn't have sent me if he didn't think you could help. I've come along way and have been nearly killed nine, no ten times and actually died once in the past two weeks by things you couldn't even imagine. I'm not going to let some crippled old man stop me know."

Karl looked at the confident teen making a stand in his dusty shop. "What have you gotten yourself into, boy?" he said inquisitively.

Trey remained standing and didn't answer.

"There's only one reason he would have sent you and I can't help. All that fairytale stuff is phony. It doesn't exist," he said looking away.

Trey's confident stature waned. "What do you mean it doesn't exist?"

"You dumb or something? They don't exist. I've been chasing rumors my whole life only to nearly die trying. Do yourself a favor and leave it all behind."

"Don't worry about me. Just tell me what you know about the relic that was hidden here, then I'll be on my way."

"So, you are after the relic. There's no way a boy

would be able to retrieve it. I was almost killed, and I didn't get close. How do you even know about it? And what is more surprising is that you know it's here." He looked at Trey for a moment, tapping his right fingers on the arm rest then said, "Tell me what you know about the prophecy."

"I don't know anything about a prophecy."

Karl looked at him closer, then said, "You're lying."

"I really don't know what it is. I over-heard people talking about it...well, some of them were people. They think I am part of it but I'm not. Just tell me what you know, then I'll get on with it."

"Of course, you're a part of it. You may even be the one to fulfill it. There's more to you than what I see. Tell me, Trey Roberts, why are you searching for Moridon's relic?"

Moridon! He held the power of time!

"Until now, I didn't even know that's what I was looking for." Trey paused then said, "I've seen some crazy stuff and believe the story's you've heard are true. If you'll help me, when I get it, I'll bring it back to show you it's real. Plus, you can't get it yourself, so I may be your only chance."

"So, it is true," Karl said in quiet astonishment. He whispered to himself, "From the line, one will become a savior of his forefathers." He then said to Trey, "You will surely die trying but that is your decision to make. Help me into my chair." He then held out a hand.

Trey grasped his thick hairy hand, leaned back, then pivoted Karl into the wheelchair. Karl swiftly rolled across the shop through a door in the back that opened into small living quarters. He pulled up to a desk, then shuffled through a messy drawer.

"What I have gathered about the relic is that it is

located in the Grey Swamp and this."

He pulled out a leather scroll, unbound it, then laid it upon the desk.

"It's a map," said Trey.

"Yes, it would seem. But I wasn't able to find the relic with it. There must be something I'm missing. I deciphered from rumors the relic would be located here, near this small pond," he said pointing to a specific spot on the map. "You can see how the map sort of leads you that way. But I looked everywhere and never found a clue. I also explored this southern area and these narrow valleys to the west. I spent six weeks straight in that cursed swamp and found nothing but the boggers."

"What's a bogger?"

"It's a sickness that turns your appendages black and smelly. If not treated quickly it gets worse and requires amputation – and oftentimes, death. It's why I left in the first place. Otherwise, I would have continued looking for the relic."

"This is all you have?"

"Yeah. That's it."

"What do those symbols mean? They're hieroglyphs, right?"

"Yes, they are. Very good. I had them roughly translated a few years ago."

"This one means 'sit'. That one, 'don't believe' and the last is 'rock'."

"Really? That doesn't help at all."

"No. It doesn't, but it must be the piece of the puzzle I couldn't solve."

"So, it could be anywhere or not there at all," Trey said in a frustrated tone.

"You got it, but everything I have found has led me to the swamp. That's why I live so close today."

"When were you last there?"

"About sixteen years ago."

"You haven't heard anything different since?"

"No. But I haven't asked either. I gave up shortly after I was injured."

"You mean your legs?"

"Yeah."

"What happened? Was it the boggers?"

"No. Not the boggers. I wasn't messing around with that. I thought it might have been a possibility after I nearly submerged in a mud bog that I wouldn't have made it out of had it not been for a random vine laying nearby. I took special medicine afterward that delayed its effects, then promptly left the swamp. It still nearly killed me. I was bad sick for weeks. While I was recovering from the boggers, I heard there was a large diamond deep in a cave in Mt. Klipping. So naturally, I went after it once I was capable. I took an obscure trail about midway up to a wide pass. I entered the mountain through a large crack, then was attacked by a mountain troll. I should have died but I was quick back then. I leapt from the crack just as the troll landed a blow to my backside. I tumbled awkwardly down the mountain, settling in a crevasse. I came to shortly after, then crawled with my arms to the base of the mountain where a trader picked me up when he passed by. I haven't felt my legs since."

"Sounds like you're lucky to be alive."

"Sometimes I don't feel so lucky. But I guess you're right."

"Well, if all I have is a swamp and an ambiguous map, then I guess that's all I need. Is there anything else I should know about the swamp?"

"Not really, but you'll need a few things. Follow me."

Karl led him to a wooden storage shed in back situated in the corner of a vegetable garden.

"You'll need a tarp for shelter, rope and some kindling for a fire." Trey put these in his pack.

Karl wheeled back into the living quarters.

"You'll also need matches, some food and take this jacket – it'll keep you warm and dry."

He tossed a pack of matches and bread looking items mixed with dried fruit and nuts to Trey.

"I'm giving you my last vile of medicine for the boggers. Take it only if you get wet."

"What happens when I get wet?"

"That's when the boggers worm burrows into your skin. Otherwise, don't take the medicine. It'll make you violently nauseous."

"Ok. Stay dry and don't take the medicine. Got it. Anything else?"

"Yeah, take these waders. They'll keep you dry in water crossings. You'll be plenty hot, but it'll be better than the boggers. And this knife. You may need it for a variety of things," he looked at him solemnly, "including protection."

Karl handed Trey a smooth black handled knife with an eight-inch steel blade."

"Now that's a knife!" Trey said with excitement. "What's this intricately carved symbol in the handle mean?"

"It's my family crest. You bring this back to me. It was given to me by my father."

"I'll take good care of it."

"I know you will. You must be off now if you want to make it by sundown. You'll take Dolly. The swamp is a few hours ride east of here. Let her loose when you get to the entrance of the swamp. She'll find her way back. You don't want to be in the open at night. While the swamp isn't the coziest place, at least you'll have some shelter and security from the night."

Karl led him out the back again to the stable on the other side of the shed. It smelled of manure and wood shavings.

"This is Dolly. I've had her many years. Can't ride anymore of course, but she can still run like the wind."

"She's beautiful," Trey said running his hand down her painted brown and white muscled shoulder. "Cierden also said to not be out after dark. Why?"

"At night, a variety of mostly mischievous creatures roam freely, such as imps, but some are very dangerous like the mountain troll I mentioned earlier. We've had many raids by a group of dangerous lizard-like creatures. Most of the cities are well defended against them now but you aren't safe out there. You know how to saddle a horse?"

"Yeah. I spent a lot of time on a horse named Earl at summer camp last year."

"What's summer camp," Karl asked inquisitively.

"It's a place where kids go to learn stuff schools don't teach us, but mainly for parents to send us while they work." Refocusing on the mission he said, "How's the swamp safe at night? Isn't it still outside?" Trey said placing the pad and saddle on Dolly.

"It isn't safe. The swamp has its own inhabitants that are there all the time. The bigger ones will generally avoid you. However, if you were to sneak up on a swamp bear or god forbid a wollybrougher, you'll have to use the knife and lots of prayer."

Trey shuttered at the thought of seeing another Wollybrougher.

"Anything else?"

"No. That's all I can tell you. You'll have to be smart and careful. Move slowly while in the swamp but don't stay in one place for very long. Know you'll be watched the whole time you're there. Don't give anything any reason to approach you."

"Got it."

"Take care, Trey. I hope you succeed where I failed. I truly hope to see you again."

"Me too Mr. Ropping. Thank you for helping."

"You're welcome. Now don't forget my knife!"

Trey chuckled, "Sure thing."

Trey mounted Dolly, then trotted down a back alley before entering the street Porter left him. He looked to his left noticing Porter's wagon was replaced with several well-dressed men with cigars amid a wispy haze. He reined Dolly to the right then lightly prodded her eastward.

The city gave way to tightly organized communities set up in grids on the outskirts. A large pasture held several horses milling around a bale of hay. He passed a large central building, possibly a school, made of wood and donned a bell tower, however, there were no children to be seen.

Trey passed through a large gate guarded by two men with long rifles as he left Hoppston. Young children played in the grass adjacent to the tall stone wall that served as protection in the night. The previously cloudy sky gave way to a mid-day sun that sweltered overhead. Trey wished he'd brought a hat. He rode out of the city perimeter facing a dry flat landscape spotted with low trees and bushes.

Trey rode for an hour.

Cl-clop, cl-clop, cl-clop sounded Dolly's hooves on the hard road.

Cl-clop, Cl-clop, Cl-clop.

Side to side Trey wobbled in the saddle. His eyes became heavy as weariness set in.

The hooves droned on.

Cl-clop, Cl-clop, Cl-clop.

He closed his eyes for just for a second, nearly falling off when Dolly lurched to avoid something in the road only to continue the monotonous pace.

Cl-clop, Cl-clop, Cl-clop.

With beads of sweat dancing down his face, Trey closed his eyes again, then slumped easily onto the horn.

He woke to find himself, surprisingly, still on the horse's back. Dolly lazily munched on grass several yards off the road. The sun sat well behind him. He looked around, finding the dark swamp several miles ahead.

"I have to get going. I'm running out of daylight. How long have I been out? I must be more exhausted than I thought."

He set his head down on the back of his hands which were resting on the saddle horn. Looking at the ground he became confused at what he saw. He trained his focus on a tiny creature standing no more than four inches tall next to the horse's front left hoof. It was staring up at him with wide yellow eyes. It was blue with two black stripes on its back. Its skin was smooth and snake-like scaly. Its orange lips opened into a wicked grin displaying a row of pointy teeth. It jumped onto the horse, then violently bit its leg.

Dolly reared back, neighing in alarm. She bolted away from the road, unaware of what was attacking her. Trey's feet weren't in the stirrups as he grasped the saddle horn tightly trying to not fall off. Flopping all over the saddle he saw the creature rapidly climbing the horse's pumping leg with its eyes still focused on Trey's – biting several times as it approached. Dolly bucked with each nip nearly flinging Trey off each time.

Trey flailed an arm, trying to knock it off. It

jumped, ducked and dodged each defensive attack. It leaped onto Trey's back, then began biting at the nape of his neck. Trey arched, rolled out of the saddle, sideswiped a bush, then landed hard on the ground. He slid to a stop, unable to catch his breath. As Trey tried to breath the miniscule creature jumped onto his paralyzed chest, then blew a raspberry inches from his face – tiny slobber pelted his cheeks.

It jumped off joining two others rummaging through his bag. Trey tried but couldn't muster the breath to make a sound. A few seconds later they jumped out with his food, the knife Karl's dad gave him and the pouch with the key.

"No! Come back here!" Trey screamed.

He painfully got to his feet, then ran after them. They disappeared down a narrow hole under a large rock seconds before he caught up. He could hear giggling for several more seconds. He dug at the dirt, but it was too hard, and the rock was too heavy to lift. He flopped down onto the ground in exasperation.

A rustling emerged from under the rock. Trey peered into the hole to find two soft green eyes glowing in the darkness. The remorseful face appeared only briefly before a package blocked the view. Trey's confused look didn't stop him from reaching in to pull out the remainder of the bread muffins Karl gave him. The imp was gone when the package was clear of the hole.

"Well, Trey," he said aloud as he held the package of muffins. "What else can you get yourself into?" He looked distantly and continued, "I have to get out of here." He looked around and said, "Where's Dolly?"

The horse was nowhere in sight.

"She's probably halfway back to Karl's by now. Dang-it!" he said stomping the ground.

He walked back to his pack, gathered the remainder of his things, then looked closely toward the scraggly trees ahead in the distance.

"It's only about five miles."

He began jogging.

"If I continue at this pace, I should be there before it gets too dark."

He regulated his breathing and timed his steps properly.

Tough runs don't last, tough runners do, Trey could hear his track teacher say.

The theme song to Rocky began to repeat in his head. Da. Da Du Da. Da Du Da. Da Du Duuuuu. He ran a mile with no problem. After mile two his breathing was heavy. The sun began to fade at mile three bringing on a sense of urgency. Filled with anxiety, Trey quickened his pace.

When the sun was completely below the horizon, Trey became aware of something quickly approaching from the right. Making sharp glances he was unable to make out the shape in the dim light.

At this pace it'll intercept me before the entrance. I'm only about a mile out. I can make it.

He began sprinting. His heart raced; his legs burned. He looked back – the dark shape still in hot pursuit.

It's so much closer now! I'll never make it!

He ran harder. Pumping his arms, stretching out his legs, he ran faster than ever before.

"Grip and pull, Trey! Grip and Pull!" he yelled to himself.

He could now hear the foot falls of the beast behind him. A growl bellowed. Searing pain engulfed his legs. He felt as if a knife was in his side. He continued to run as hard as he could. He could hear the breath of the animal.

"All most there! All most there! AAAAAAAHHHHHHHH!" he yelled the final yards.

A painful blow to his back sent him tumbling to the hard ground. He rolled into a ball and closed his eyes to protect himself from the impending attack.

A moment passed, nothing happened. He felt it near his head. Hot sticky breath permeated his nostrils. It sniffed him several times before Trey opened his eyes to find a massive wollybrougher with a shaggy dull burgundy coat pacing next to him. It easily had two-hundred pounds on Cedric and was leaner. It approached coming eye to eye with Trey. Thick drool slopped from slightly parted lips exposing jagged teeth. It sniffed, then blew balls of thick snot onto Treys face. Then again. Trey dared not wipe away the slimy goo. It let out a loud roar as if it would at any moment have a temper tantrum. It stomped furiously, sniffed again at Trey's neck then deliberately turned toward the swamp in frustration.

Trey watched it join six more near the edge of the tree line. The wollybrougher touched noses with each of the others. They individually regarded Trey before disappearing into the swamp.

"Oh my God!" Trey yelled laying on the ground. "Coming here was such a mistake! I don't even know what I'm looking for or if it's in there. This is the stupidest thing I have ever done."

He sat up rubbing his aching quads.

I don't know how much more of this I can take, he thought to himself. *How will I get home?*

"Will I ever see mom again? Uuugggg," he sounded, struggling to stand. He limped the remaining distance to the entrance of the swamp.

The Grey Swamp

Tall dark trees shadowed overhead. Biting cold etched uncomfortably into his skin. The musky smell of aged compost grew as he progressed along an overgrown path. Thick air layered him with dripping moisture. He put on the jacket, then donned the hood.

Maybe I should stop for the night? But the trail is clear for now and I should probably move a little further. Hopefully, I can find a place to rest soon. It sure is creepy here. I wonder if it's any better during the day.

He could only see a few feet in front of him while fearfully looking left and right expecting a wollybrougher or something worse to leap out at any moment.

He tripped on a protruding root sending him painfully to the ground. He laid still for a moment trying to control dreadful thoughts as something rustled in the bushes ahead.

Comfortable that whatever ahead was gone, he

picked himself up, rubbed his right arm then slowly continued forward.

He swiftly turned toward the sound of a creature leaping away through the tree branches above just as something grabbed him by the hood. He instinctively pulled away as he struggled with its grasp. He grabbed at a thin scaly arm with numerous rigid fingers. It snapped as he turned his shoulder into the lanky appendage. He then started laughing out loud – then fell to a knee and cried as the tree branch slipped from his grip.

"I'm never getting out of here," he sobbed.

He looked up and around through watery eyes. He then proceeded off the path toward an overturned tree.

A bird, Trey believed, shrieked in the distance. He removed the folded tarp and draped it over the tilted tree base. He found comfort in that it camouflaged the shelter well. He crawled inside, spread a portion of the tarp on the ground then curled up in total darkness.

He shivered as the adrenalin wore off. A bitter cold surrounded aching limbs – it seeped into his bones. Uncontrollable chattering teeth and re-stless arms and legs added to the misery. He laid on the cold ground curled on his side and closed his eyes, trying to force an unconscious state.

A branch snapped outside the makeshift tent bringing Trey back to full alert. His heart leaped. His eyes groped for light. He was unable to make out any shapes. Completely blinded by darkness, he imagined monstrous creatures lurking about, planning their attack on the helpless misled boy lost in a damp swamp chasing mythical items.

Rustling in nearby bushes put him on edge. A strange sound echoed through the night.

Chirrup, Chirrup. Chirrup, Chirrup.

He whispered, "Don't move, Trey. Don't make any

noise. Don't give anything a reason to approach." His teeth clacked like a firecracker in his brain.

The urge to shift was agonizing. His legs and feet wailed for repositioning. He dosed for what seemed like seconds before waking to a strong breeze shaking the tarp.

He risked using a match to light a tea candle. The diminutive warmth was soothing but comfort never again came calling in the night.

Trey woke cold and shivering in total darkness. His moral dropped. He thought it was morning. He dreaded the thought of spending another minute in the tarp – frightened of what might happen.

"I hate this!" he shrieked quietly. "I must get moving. I can't waste time, nor can I stay in one place for long. I'll have to make my way in the dark."

He emerged from the tarp amid darkness. Faint light penetrated the forest which refreshed his soul. He carefully folded and placed the tarp in the pack, found the path, then walked for nearly an hour watching vigilantly for signs of danger. He finally took a break on a boulder to enjoy the warmth of a rising sun.

Soothing rays of light caressed his face. The pungent swamp odor now seemed to be laced with the sweet scent of cinnamon. He breathed in big then slowly released.

"I have to figure out where I am before I continue."

He produced the map, then began studying.

"I came in this way, then walked probably two miles along this path. I shouldn't be too far from this fork. The fastest way to the pond would be to continue straight ahead. Karl was certain it was there. Maybe he just missed something."

While he sat deciding on a direction, a mantis crawled onto his leg. Trey focused his attention on the slow-moving insect as it crept onto the map resting on his lap. Pulling from the hypnotic state, he shooed the mantis away with his hand watching it fly a graceful arc.

That was pretty cool, he thought. The resulting smile floated optimism throughout his outlook on the dire situation.

He replaced the map in the pack, took another moment to enjoy the last nut bar then continued the perilous expedition.

He noticed a squirrel-like animal sitting on a limb paying him an inordinate amount of attention as he passed below. "Hey little squirrel," he said as if speaking to an infant. It darted away as if Trey threw something at it.

Past a grassy fork, the landscape became less forested. Pockets of shallow water dotted the trail. He walked a while longer on ground that squished like a damp sponge. Colorful red and yellow mushrooms and other fungi adorned the narrow path.

His mind wandered during the hike. The mid-morning swamp became incredibly humid. The previous night's coldness had long expired. He passed tall reedy plants with bulbous drab blooms. He brushed one of them with a hand releasing a vibrant orange dust. He waved the surrounding cloud away then continued on the trail.

His eyes burned lightly. He rubbed them as he began thinking of his mom. He wished he could see her. He hoped she was safe.

What if mom's not safe? The thought ate at him. "What if mom's not safe? What if Lyza was lying? What if Kathy isn't as tough as I was led to believe?"

He continued walking at an increasingly faster pace on the verge of hyperventilation. His progressively pessimistic mind spun around worries he had no ability to impact.

"What about Marcus?" he said aloud. "He's not safe without me to protect him!" He picked up his stride. "And the soccer team? What if coach kicks me off for not showing up for practice? How will I get out of here? I'm stuck in this stupid swamp! I have to get out!" he screamed.

Trey ran. He dashed past a tree. "I have to get back to Mom and Marcus!"

He mindlessly left the trail as he ripped through tall plants releasing clouds of orange dust.

"I'm going to die if I don't get out of here!" he screamed. "I'm going to die!" he yelled as he bolted through thick brush. Panic over came him. His mind was lost to the deathly poison of the cardis flower. He dropped his pack, he crossed a stream, he hurdled a boulder – then fell. In Trey's madness, he failed to notice the steep slope leading into a valley below.

He tumbled down. His body bashed end over end against rocks and scrubby brush. He skidded and rolled. He lost consciousness against a stump before finally resting violently against a large tree.

He laid there defenseless and nearly lifeless in an unknown valley in an inhospitable swamp consumed in an unnatural poison.

When he came to, his head throbbed. His left leg spiked with pain. Several places on his body stung with fading images of scrapes and minor lacerations rapidly healing from the fairy magic.

"Thank you Coméllula," he said out loud as if she were flying next to him. "What happened? How'd I get here?" The panic from the flower was gone but replaced with another. "Where am I?" he said as he viewed the underside of a scraggly tree canopy.

He pushed himself to an upright position against the crooked tree. Holding his head, he looked around to find himself in a valley surrounded by steep bluffs. A mucky stream set off to his right. He reached for his pack producing another round of intense dread.

"My pack! Oh god. I lost my pack! I don't know where I am. I'm lost," he said comprehending his plight. He tossed his head into his folded arms. "How will I ever get out of here without the map?" He gently wept.

A groan in the distance rocketed him to attention. Another groan followed by resounding footsteps spiked his body into alert mode. Something big was approaching. His eyes widened as he peeked around the tree. Just on the other side of the stream strolled a massive dark grey bear the size of a short-bus.

"That thing looks like it eats hippos for breakfast!" Trey whispered to himself.

It held a large black nose in the air as it walked a deliberate zigzag pattern.

It must have my scent, Trey thought. "I need to find a way out of here," he continued quietly.

Trey looked around for something to fend off the bear's possible attack. He analyzed the tree of which he was under, noting its impressive height and crooked trunk. He then quickly filled his pockets with large stones and prayed the bear would leave him alone.

The bear waded across the thin stream as if on an intercept course with Trey. Trey peeked around the corner again noting it was nearly twenty feet away which looked to Trey to be about as long as the bear itself.

"That's way too close to be coincidence. It's definitely coming for me."

Trey looked up, took a deep breath then scurried

up the tree. He rapidly grabbed branches and placed feet in crooked crevices. A penetrating roar came from the monstrosity. Fifteen feet up Trey saw the bear leap the distance between him and the tree. Twenty feet up the bear raised on its hind legs and nearly swatted him out of the tree as it easily snapped several branches Trey previously used as steps. Twenty-five feet up was just enough to remain out of reach. He continued to climb, nearly to the top only to stop as a branch broke beneath his feet, nearly sending him plummeting to his death.

Black razor teeth the size of his hand chomped at the air in anticipation of a new and interesting lunch. It smacked the tree nearly shaking out the scared boy.

"Now's not the time to panic," he said gathering his balance. "Hey buddy!" Somehow talking to it made him feel better about the situation. "Why all the fuss? I haven't bathed in days, I'm sure I taste horrible!"

The bear pounded the tree. Trey held on tight as the quake diminished.

Trey's face lit up as another stupid idea came to mind. "The force times the trajectory of the base along with the current angle of its lean will put me approximately there," he mumbled while looking at the nearest bluff.

He yelled, "Do you think you could move to your right just a bit?"

He threw a rock from his pocket. It bounced off the bear's head. The bear howled then swatted again at Trey, shaking the tree violently.

Trey continued to throw stones, aiming specifically at the left side of the great animal. The bear began to flinch at each toss and gradually shifted its position in response.

"That's it, little buddy. You're almost there."

He threw another stone, issuing another shift by

his increasingly angry opponent resulting in a long-lasting shaking by the great beast. Trey nearly lost his grip in the midst of the quake.

Trey looked just below at the ridge of the bluff of which he fell then threw another rock that pelted the bear in the left eye. It howled and fell onto all fours. It wiped at its painful eye with a shaggy paw, shifted slightly to the right then looked into the tree.

"That's it. You're there," he said confidently.

It bellowed an ear shattering roar that vibrated Trey's insides. It then raised onto hind legs.

"That's it!" Trey said breathlessly. Fear and excitement blended into a feeling of euphoria. Trey grasped nearby branches and yelled just as the bear slammed into the tree with a tremendous force, "I hope this works!"

The base of the tree snapped sending Trey down. Just at the right moment, he leaped from his position onto the ridge of the bluff. He rolled to reduce the force of the impact found his feet and started running. The tree smashed onto the bluff and rolled down the incline. A ferocious roar rumbled but seemed distant to Trey as he sprinted in the opposite direction.

"My pack!" he yelled as he grabbed it in mid-stride. He ran several minutes more until a trip forced him to take a breather.

"Holy crap that was close!" he said between heaving breaths. "I can't believe that worked!"

He rolled onto his back huffing frantically. He stared up into the clear blue sky peeking through the dreary trees, wearily yearning to be back home with his mom and her fried chicken.

"Dang, I'm hungry – and I don't even have any bars left. Stupid imps," he said scornfully.

He looked upward from his lying position on the

ground to find himself on the edge of a vast stretch of cardis flowers. "The flower!" he said sitting up. "The orange dust is the last thing I remember before the bear. What else is out to get me?" he said exasperated. "Don't stay in one place too long," he remembered Karl saying.

He rose studying the dreadful field. "I can't go around. I have to go through."

He took a calming breath, cinched the rain hood around his face then carefully tip-toed into the wild meadow. Large bulbs of dull green rested precariously upon lanky stalks. Each swayed independently as if dancing to a slow rhythm.

Trey arched backward, barely scraping by one that drifted too close.

"This would be easy If they'd just quit moving," he said upon stopping to reassess his course.

A bird flittered above as he watched a wafting butterfly pirouette among the deathly petals.

He moved into a small circular open space – the flowers seemed to all look his way as they quietly bobbled left and right.

He stepped over a short one then dodged two edging his path. He then continued the monotonous pace, zig-zagging his way toward safety. He felt confident near the end of the patch but maintained extreme vigilance. However, he failed to notice another short one when his head was turned. He caught a glimpse of his clumsy boot through the corner of his eye as it lightly grazed the bulb. As if in slow motion, the petals twisted slightly open to release a tiny orange stream that rose toward the tired boy.

He panicked as the rising orange snake circled his leg. He covered his face the best he could and ran.

Bursts of orange exploded as he pounded through the remainder of the field. Trey kept his head down and eyes closed – hoping he could stay in front of the psychoactive cloud.

He guessed he was near the end when he opened his eyes. Swiftly avoiding a tree, he continued to dart through the woods at full speed. Moments later he skidded onto the mushy trail, relieved to not see any signs of orange on or around him.

After a huge sigh of relief and the heavy breathing subsided, he thought, *this would be a good time to put on the waders.*

He unrolled the map, setting it aside, then removed the waders from the sack. He pulled them over his pants, then sat back against the tree. He closed his eyes a few seconds before looking down to find a mantis resting on the map.

"What in the world? These things must be everywhere."

He watched it watching him.

"Are you following me, little guy?"

It didn't move.

"You sure seem to be."

The mantis continued to look in Trey's direction.

It slowly spun in place reorienting toward Trey.

Trey gave it a suspicious look.

It jumped, then hovered a few inches.

Trey continued to observe the insect.

It jumped and hovered again.

Just before it settled back in its previous position, Trey caught an image on the map. He leaned in to take a closer look. The mantis shifted to the top edge of the map as if in response to Trey's movements.

"It can't be," Trey said in disbelief. "This isn't a map at all."

He glanced at the mantis then to the map, then

said out loud, "The depiction of the trail on the map, the one I thought I was walking, along with these shadings that I seemed to have mistook for representations of topography of the swamp...highly resemble the shape of a mantis."

He paused amid deep thought then said while looking blankly ahead, "I'm not following a map, I'm looking for a guide!" He looked back down at the tiny bug, "And my guide...is a mantis? You have to be kidding me."

At that moment, the mantis leapt away flying several yards to rest on a log far off the trail.

"Well, I guess it can't be crazier than all the other stuff I've seen recently," he said to himself. "So, I'm following a bug? Big deal. It's not the first time."

Trey tossed the map into the bag before setting out after the insect guide. When he reached the log, the mantis took flight again, this time soaring four times as far. Trey squished on the wet ground to catch up.

The mantis leaped onto the trunk of a tree, then began proceeding from tree to tree through a thin forest. It stopped just short of a murky bog stretching the distance of a basketball court and as wide as Trey could see.

He approached the mantis, looked out onto the stagnant pool and said, "No way. I'm not going into that." He thought about what Karl said regarding the boggers worm. He had a brief image of slimy ribbed worms burrowing into his skin.

He shook off the gross image when the mantis launched over the bog. Trey couldn't see where it landed but was sure it made it to the other side.

He desperately looked for another way to cross but the bog was too wide. "This point, actually, looks like the narrowest." He decided to test the water.

He eased a rubber booted foot into the bog. It sank

a little but remained mostly above the water as it found semi-solid ground. He stepped a little further out sinking just a little more. Then another, continuing the gradually declining pattern as he eased across the foul water.

He became accustomed to the slow presumptuous pace. He continued wading as water rose to the top of his boots when suddenly he sunk to his waist. He let out a startled yelp. He thrusted his hands into the air to prevent them from submerging in the water. He nearly lost his balance. He teetered on one leg for a moment. He looked down to find the chest high waders seemed to be keeping him dry. He regained his composure then began swishing again slowly through the water – ensuring each step was solid. His boot slipped off something hard. He lost his balance. Just before his hand submerged, he caught himself. He slipped only one more time afterward.

The water continued to rise above his waste and into a middle mesh pocket built into the stomach portion of the outfit. He was about halfway when he stopped, unsure if he should continue. He looked back from where he came. The shoreline seemed so remote, but he was sure he could get back safely. He looked toward the mantis, which he still couldn't see, only to feel dread and terror.

He took two steps back toward probable safety then stopped. He closed his eyes and said, "I can do hard things." He then turned back toward his guide and continued across the bog with only one additional slip after which he remained dry.

He slogged onto the shore after the perilous crossing, confident he wouldn't have to down the sickening medicine to prevent the boggers.

He caught a glimpse of the mantis flying through a thinly treed area. He took a deep breath of relief to be across the bog, then followed.

He came upon a trail, hidden within a span of tall bushes. The mantis launched to the right on the trail. When Trey caught up, it jumped onto his shoulder.

"I suppose you're just along for the ride now, huh?" he said looking at the tiny green passenger.

He walked the trail for only thirty minutes before approaching a body of musty water just larger than a pond but smaller than a lake. When he reached the edge of the water the mantis sailed off to the left to land on the first of a series of stones shadowed by a wide treetop. It hopped each stone before settling on the last and largest of the group.

"You want me to go onto the stones? In the water?"

The guide remained motionless on the last stone.

"Ok. Fine," he said remembering Karl's warning and shaking off the fresh feeling of crossing the bog.

When Trey reached the final stone, he looked down at the mantis and said, "Now what?"

The mantis seemed to slightly bow before flying away.

"But wait! What do I do now! Argg! Stupid bug!"

Trey sat on the rock and reviewed the map again.

"There's nothing here but sit, don't believe and rock. Ok. I'm on a rock. Check. I'm sitting. Check. What the heck does 'don't believe' mean?"

"Don't believe. Don't Believe. What's it mean? Don't believe. Unbelieve. Non-believer. Does it have something to do with religion? Think, Trey. Religion. Believe. Trust. Think. Believe. Imagine. I'm sitting on a rock believing I'm an idiot. Ok, focus. There has to be something to this. Don't imagine? Don't think. Don't think? Sit on the rock and don't think? That's not it."

But he couldn't get the notion out of his mind.

"Don't think."

Trey sat still on the rock. He tried to clear his mind. Thoughts of his mom wondering where he was, of whether he would lose his position on the soccer team again, if he would be able to get home all streamed through his head.

Slowly, each passing thought faded. The wind rustling the water and the bugs chirping in the trees diminished. A distant call from a falcon echoed into nothingness. Even the soft footfalls of the beastly creatures closing in evaded his senses until there was only himself but not his self.

His whole body vibrated as if he touched a live low voltage wire. His brain tingled while his skin pricked with a comfortable warm sensation. He gradually felt as if he were falling – no – sinking into the stone. He became minimally aware of light passing into darkness. He settled into the subconscious. He no longer felt physical senses. He thought it was much like the Etherios but not quite – the thought faded.

Dream-like images passed within his mind's eye: a shadowy congregation of people, Leslie's kiss, a dragon with golden tipped wings flying through clouds. Darkness prevailed as he continued to sink further and further into nothingness.

A dim ruby colored light shone in the distance growing in luminescence as he floated toward it. No thoughts raced through his mind. Only quiet – and the light.

He drew closer until he could make out its ring-like shape.

Yes. It is a ring.

He reached for the object, cautious but not afraid.

His slightly bent outstretched finger slowly drifted within a couple centimeters before he paused. The ring pulsed white and ruby light. The synchronous pattern increased in intensity as his finger neared until a final flash of light burst when the connection was made.

"Hello Trey. I am Master Olerand," the trim bearded man in an aged but clear voice said from across the silver ring. "Do not release the relic."

Only his head and chest appeared as if looking through a window.

"It's you!" Trey gasped.

"We are connected through time by Moridon's relic. We will remain in near physical contact as long as we are both touching the ring. However, I fear you do not have long and are in grave danger."

"Danger?"

"Yes. We must speak with haste."

"Time in the sense that you know is not linear. It may be easier to consider that time happens all at once. The ring allows us to open a window to various occurrences."

"Whoa, that's really deep."

"I summoned you here for selfish reasons – a wish, so to speak. However, if you succeed you may preserve your life as well as the lives of your ancestors."

"That's what you showed me in the dream, isn't it? That I have to face Khaitu or die?"

"You saw what you needed to see. I am merely the conduit for you to access the memory. I am not aware of what you are destined to do but I do, however, believe it does involve you facing his fury."

"So that city was real? He really burned it and everyone there?"

"Yes."

"Just like NamJai."

"Yes."

"How do I stop him?"

"That knowledge, hopefully, will come to you prior to your confrontation."

"That's all the advice you have for me?"

"Yes."

"Ok. Did you lead Mr. Hampton to find the key and build the portal?"

"Yes. I have been working diligently in secret to prepare you two for this moment."

"Why go through all the trouble? Why not just save them yourself?"

"I cannot interfere with the deeds of Khaitu. If I do, I will become an undead slave, unable to bind him in the upcoming ceremony."

"Oh yeah. The curse."

"So, you can't prevent Commerand from falling either?"

"No. Commerand will be an unfortunate casualty. We can only hope you will also free our brother. I'm afraid that my actions or inactions at this point will lead to the event happening. Do you understand?"

"I think so."

"You are my descendant's and your ancestors only hope."

"Descendants? Ancestors? What?"

"Before you go you must know the time ring facilitates viewing of the past and present but only what the heart desires which is how I saw my family's destruction as well as Commerand's fall. You must hold it in your palm, enter a quiet state and focus on your heart.

"It also allows communication through time which is what we are doing now.

"Finally, it allows travel through time for

imminently important means. You must sit in a relaxed position with the ring placed on your right index finger. Upon entering a deep meditative state focusing on exactly when you want to be, you will circle the ring over your head and pull yourself into the adjacent instance of time. It must not be used for personal gain."

"I don't understand. None of this makes any sense."

"You will understand when the time comes for you to understand. Also, as you have most likely become aware, the land in which we live provides our lineage with certain abilities. You must remember, the spirit is what controls magic. Magic is intentional. It cannot occur by accident. To utilize it effectively you have to learn to be one with our spirit. You must learn to release your mind as you did to enter this realm. Only then will you be able to use magic to fulfill your destiny. Quiet your mind. Become one with our spirit. These words must endure."

"What are you talking about? I don't understand. Lineage? Magic?"

"There will come a time when you will believe. When that time arrives, you will see."

"I must first believe before I see? What does that even mean?"

"Yes. It is that way with everything in life. You are very wise for your short years. I fear we have lingered too long." With urgency he said, "The protector of this relic has arrived! You must take the ring and go! Now! Run, Trey! Run!"

Olerand disappeared with the window. Trey felt himself slipping back into consciousness.

He grabbed the ring and woke with a jolt. He looked to find the ring in his open hand. It adjusted in size when he placed it on his right ring finger.

A colossal brown and grey falcon shrieked from above. It dove, grasping Trey with giant talons. It beat powerful wings just twice before broadsided by an airborne wollybrougher sending them all crashing into the pond. Trey rushed out of the water looking over his shoulder at the massive bird thrashing – slinging water and mud all about.

He darted across the shoreline down the hidden trail. He was startled by a familiar burgundy beast running along-side him. Recognizing its helping look, he grabbed a hand full of shaggy coat, then leaped onto its back. Two wollybroughers, one sliver the other black with a navy shimmer, joined in behind.

The falcon took to the air. It swooped down; talons outstretched toward Trey but was deflected by the black wollybrougher. It swooped back around grabbed the silver one on the left, tossed it into a thicket, then rose just out of reach of the black one leaping from the right. It dove again toward Trey, just missing him when Trey leaned precariously to the side of the racing animal. Dashing through the swamp at a break-neck speed, Trey rose from its side, pulling on a think tuft of hair just in time to avoid a passing tree.

The wollybrougher exited the trail into narrowly spaced trees. Trey raised his feet onto its back to avoid injury from the passing trunks. He looked like a small jockey riding an oversized Newfoundland. Branches and leaves battered him as they set a blistering pace through the dense forest.

The creature slowed to a walk as they approached the edge of the swamp. Trey noticed through the trees the falcon circling high above, waiting for them to emerge. The beast paced a few minutes periodically looking into the air, puffing furiously at the impossibility of Trey making it back to the city safely over land. It trotted back into the forest joining the other three in wait.

They set a brisk pace, darting through thickets, changing course periodically but always staying under cover. The falcon occasionally flew low just over the profuse canopy but never ventured into the forest in fear of confrontation with the pack.

They came upon a cave. The burgundy leader regarded the others who stayed behind. Trey dismounted as he was led into the dark dampness of the cave which was about a foot taller than his head. They descended slowly as the light from the opening of the cave behind them completely faded. After a few minutes of darkness, a dim light appeared in the distance ahead. Upon approach, Trey recognized the light coming from a hole in the ceiling. The tunnel widened near the opening.

The wollybrougher stopped just inside the opening not venturing into the light. Trey moved closer to take a look noticing they were most likely between Hoppston and the swamp but was stopped short of the light by a large paw. The wollybrougher drew Trey's attention to the ground. With an outstretched claw it carved into the cave floor a straight line with several additional lines branching off on either side. He looked at Trey, then back to the drawing. He scraped a claw down the center line then looked at Trey again.

"I understand. Stay on the straight path."

The wollybrougher turned and disappeared into obscurity.

Antonin

Turning his head from the darkness, Trey noticed his drenched clothing.

"Oh Crap! The Boggers!"

He tossed off the waders and fumbled in his pack for Karl's medication. He brought his hand into the light and looked intently at the small vile of brown liquid.

"...black and smelly. If not treated quickly it gets worse and requires amputation – and oftentimes, death," he remembered Karl say.

He downed the minty medicine which ironically reminded him of a chalky drink his mom makes him take when he has an upset stomach.

Pushing away the vicious side effects Karl warned him of, Trey continued through the tunnel for nearly two hours until he heard voices, small voices just ahead past an opening in the tunnel above. Trey became motionless against the edge of the tunnel. The miniscule voices became louder until three imps appeared in the light. One of them looked closely in Trey's direction before turning into a divergent tunnel.

He whispered silently to himself, "I'd recognize those yellow eyes and orange lips anywhere. Those are the guys that took the key!"

He held his stomach as it rumbled uneasily.

"Stay on the straight path," he said to himself as he stared down the dark tunnel. "But I have to get home."

He waited a few minutes in despair then followed them into the side tunnel. The chatty trio were easy to trail in the dark. Trey kept his distance, only stopping when they were quiet. The tunnel twisted into a steep incline with several flights of steps carved into solid rock.

His skin became clammy as cold sweat formed over his brows.

He climbed for what felt like miles on the rocky staircase.

His stomach twisted as his joints ached with each labored movement.

He slowed when he was assaulted by a pungent odor.

"Oh gosh that smell is putrid! It smells like old dirty socks threw up rotten egg salad! Yuck!" he whispered to himself.

He fell to a knee and vomited violently. His head panged afterward.

After regaining his composure, he continued higher until he reached an opening which led to a large cave. His stomach lurched again causing him to empty the remains of his stomach onto the dry steps. The odor was unbearable. His head pounded with each beating pulse.

He stopped to rest and gasped for breath amid hopeless fatigue. His weakened muscles ached. Out of the corner of an eye, he glimpsed an object rapidly approaching. Clumsily, he ducked as a large stone club smashed the rocks above his head showering him with debris. Trey looked up to find a dumb looking troll standing nearly ten feet tall with bulky muscles lifting a huge club made of solid grey stone. Wide set eyes refocused on their target. Quickly, Trey rolled to his feet to avoid another life-ending blow, then dashed into the dark smelly cave.

Hoping for a way out, he scurried toward a dim light while holding onto an aching head. He was distraught to find a small luminescent crystal sphere rather than an exit.

The sphere was among other items which seemed to be thoughtlessly piled – but no magic sack.

He picked up the sphere, which seemed to vary in intensity according to his thoughts on how bright it should be. Befuddled on the possibility, he barely evaded a large stone hurled by the troll.

He grabbed a large bone bladed knife, then used the sphere to find a temporary hiding place. He thought *off*, then the light disappeared. Shadows glanced off the walls as the troll approached, sniffing furiously.

He leaned against the cold wall holding the hand with the knife on his head, the other wrapped around the sphere on his stomach. All of his joints ached like he had an intense case of the flu. His stomach continued to sporadically lurch. He again, dry heaved uncontrollably.

When his spasms subsided, he noticed a large boulder just taller than the troll. He pocketed the light sphere then ascended the boulder to remain out of view. The troll entered the cavernous space – sniffing the boy out.

With a great moment of courage, Trey propelled himself off the boulder onto the Troll's wart riddled back. He grabbed hold of its clammy bald head and drove the knife deep into its right eye. It let out a great howl as Trey fell off its back and slammed to the ground.

Trey looked up aching and violently nauseous watching in terrified astonishment as the troll stumbled backward, regained its balance then pulled the knife out along with the eye. It then continued the assault with a massive club in one hand and bloody dangly-eyeballed knife in the other.

The troll towered over Trey with the raised club. Just as it intended to hammer him into a lifeless pulp, three consecutive arrows pierced the head and chest of the monster sending it sprawling down a deep gully.

Astonished to be alive, woozy and dizzy from the boggers medicine, he turned to find a foxlike creature holding a bow walking briskly toward him. Trey feebly pushed himself into a sitting position and sluggishly slid away from the fox's approach.

"Relax, Mate. No need to be afraid," he said in a thick Australian accent that Trey found vaguely familiar. The fox replaced the bow on his back and held out his hands in a gesture of trust. "Antonin's my name. You can call me Ant."

Through blurry eyes and weary muscles Trey began, "Ok. Uh. I..."

Trey burped, retched, dry heaved then passed out.

~ ~

"Hey there," Ant said as Trey slowly opened an eye.

"Wha..." he spit a wad of acrid leaves onto the ground. "Who are you? Where am I? What did you put in my mouth?"

"Take it easy there, Mate. You've had a rough time."

"What do you mean?"

"What do you mean, what do you mean? You talkin about the troll or where you are now or what you've been doin for the past hour? What do you remember?"

Trey sat up and leaned toward the warmth of a small fire.

"I'm freezing," he said as his teeth chattered. What's happening to me. Why am I so cold?"

"Let's work backwards, how about that and you stop me when you remember what's going on. Ok?"

Trey nodded weakly.

"You vomited, passed out and began convulsing, so I assumed you took something like Aravian extract to keep from getting the boggers. Am I right?"

"Yeah. How'd you know?"

"I didn't know, I just assumed. Good thing to because the rampus weed would have killed you otherwise."

"Killed me! What?"

"Don't worry. You'll be fine. But you'll probably have a strong headache till tomorrow...and possibly vivid hallucinogenic dreams."

"More crazy dreams? Just what I need. And the troll?"

"I think he's gone for good."

Trey looked at the fire and said, "Thanks for saving me."

"No problem, Mate. You really had that troll going! What the heck are you doing here anyway? Don't you know not to go in the mountain?"

"No. I guess not. I followed three imps through underground tunnels. They stole stuff from me yesterday."

"Imps you say. Hmm. Whatever it was is gone now

if those magical misfits have it.

"Magical? What do you mean?"

"Imps possess formidable magic."

"What kind of magic?"

"I don't know. It's just what I was told. I've never actually seen one."

"So, it's a rumor that may not be true?"

"I know people who have seen it firsthand. Believe me, it's real." Ant looked toward the mouth of the cave and said, "We'll set off to Roberton in the morning."

"I can't go back to Roberton. I have to recover my stuff and get to the lake."

"The lake! No way, Mate! We'd have to cross the river."

"What do you mean, we?"

"I can't rightfully leave you to your own, now can I. You would've been smashed by the cave troll had I not followed you. You have no business in this mountain."

"I'll be just fine. I appreciate your help."

"Fine? Really? You couldn't even keep tiny imps from taking your stuff. How will you be fine out there on your own? Grant it, you somehow got lucky with the wollybroughers. By the way, why didn't they eat you?"

"I don't know about those things. One licked me on the way to Hoppston. Maybe that had something to do with it."

"You're pulling my chain! You were snuffled by old man Porter's wollybrougher?"

"I guess."

"That's awesome, Mate! You know they think you're one of them now. They'll protect you like their own. That's why they didn't eat you and saved you from the felixis."

"You mean the bird?"

"Yeah."

"How do you know about Porter and the bird?"

"I started following you after you asked me where you were back in Roberton."

"Why were you following me?"

"You were dressed so strangely and didn't know where you were. I had to learn more. I followed you back to the library. After you left, Cierden asked me to keep you safe."

"I don't remember speaking to you in the city. Am I missing something?"

"Oh yeah, I forgot. Just one second." He stood and held up a finger which made him look like he was preparing to give a speech.

Ant then became blurry, like looking through a rainy windshield. Trey rubbed his eyes to be sure his vision wasn't being affected by the rampus weed. When Ant cleared up, a man with a rounded reddish-brown beard and no moustache wearing a brown hat and a casual buttoned coat stood before Trey.

"You're the guy I bumped into in the city! I knew I recognized your voice. How can that be?"

"I'm a Segralite, a race of shape-shifters. There are very few of us around today. Curiosity and our nomadic nature are our undoing."

"Really? Like how?"

"How we contribute to our own demise?"

"Yeah," Trey said wide eyed and ready to be entertained.

"Well, let's see. There's my cousin Oxnard. He died by getting too close to a wollybrougher. He kept saying he thought he could train one."

"Ah. That one's curiosity?"

"Yeah."

"I guess he was wrong."

"I heard of one guy who wandered into the

sandgrala desert and was never seen again."

"Nomad," Trey said quickly then smiled at Ant.

"My mother, who is still alive, told me about my uncle Lon who never had children because he never found the right shelia."

"Nomad! This is fun. Let's keep going," Trey said happily. "It helps me keep my mind off my headache."

"I think you get the point."

"Fine. I think your shapeshifting is amazing! Can you turn into anything?"

"Most everything I've seen before. I prefer animals. Humans are hard to mimic and take a lot of energy, but I needed some things in the city that day. What are you doing here?"

"Can you turn into a bird?"

"Yes. But I don't know how to fly."

"I would learn. Can you turn into a horse?"

"I can do a horse."

"How about a bear? No! Can you turn into a wollybraugher?" Trey asked with wide excited eyes and a cheesy smile.

"We're getting off track. Why are you here?"

"The librarian didn't tell you?"

"No. We didn't have much time for chatting. All he said was that you came through the special portal, whatever that is, and that you have to succeed in what you're doing. You also seem to have a little more than luck on your side."

"Luck? Why do you say that?"

"Cedric saw something in you worthy of the snuffle. You made it through the swamp, albeit with help from the pack. And you were doing well against the troll. What were you doing in the swamp anyway?"

"Wild goose chase, maybe," he said stealthily spinning the ring on his finger. "I don't know why I'm here. But for now, I just need to get my stuff from the imps and get to the lake." Ant took his flaky reason and didn't press the issue any further.

"What'd they get that was so important that you would risk your life to recover?"

Trey hesitated then said, "They got the key I need to activate the portal."

"Portal? You mean the one at the library?"

"No. I can't use that one again. I have to get to the waterfall at lake Oshugar."

"What are these portals?"

"I'm uncertain. I only became familiar with them recently. They seem to be doors to different worlds."

"Different worlds? You're not serious are ya, Mate?"

Trey with a straight face and lackadaisical sincerity said, "I'm not from your world. I'm from a place called Earth."

Ant's posture relaxed as he looked away then back to Trey. "Earth? You don't have to make stuff up. Just say you don't want to tell me."

Trey smiled and replied with more sincerity, "No, really. It's true. I came through a portal in the library."

"Ok. Whatever you say Trey from Earth. Grab some wood over there and let's keep this fire going."

After sitting at the fire for a while Trey asked, "Cierden really sent you after me?"

"Yeah."

"Do you work for him?"

"No. It's more like a favor. You see, C and I go way back. The guy never leaves the library, you know."

"Yeah. He told me he stays to protect the books and the portal."

"Yeah. That's it, Mate," he said leeringly. "So,

every once in a while, he'll call me to do some reconnaissance. You know, to find out what's going on in the real world."

"You mean he hires you to sneak around spying on people?"

"Yeah," he smiled. "Like that."

"But this is different. You could've been killed by the troll. He must mean more to you than just occasional work."

"Yeah. He is. He taught me read from the stories in those books. As you can imagine, my dad wasn't around much. I actually haven't seen him since I was eight."

"Nomad."

Ant looked at him angrily.

"Oh. Sorry. I couldn't help it."

"He caught me running by the library one day and asked if I was a Segralite. To this day I don't know how he knew. I, of course, said no and ran away. But curiosity got the best of me."

Trey's eyes lit up followed by a sideways squinty-eyed look from Ant who said, "Don't say it!"

Trey smiled and didn't say "curiosity".

Ant continued, "So the next day I went back and asked him why he wanted to know. He said he needed someone to be sneaky and unrecognizable which was right up my mischievous alley back then. I started coming by the library a few times a week. Cierden would give me a task and when I returned, he would read me a story. This went on for years and even some today."

"That's pretty cute that you still do story time."

"Hey! Don't make fun. Cierden's voice can be incredibly soothing."

"I don't doubt that. So, what you are saying is that when your dad bailed on you, the librarian filled in some of the holes?"

"You got it, Mate."

"Cierden is the one you believe about the imps isn't he."

"Yeah."

"I know now why you believe in the imp's magic. I feel he has a few magical tricks himself," Trey said.

"Cierden *is* pretty amazing."

"I have a guy like that. Not magical or anything. Mr. H has taught me a lot. He's been more of a father than my actual dad ever was."

"It's nice to have those people in our lives isn't it?"

"Yeah. It is," Trey replied with a warm reminiscent smile.

"What's the deal with the bow? You're pretty good with it."

"This old thing? It's my dad's. It was the last thing he taught me before he left. It was all I had to play with as a kid so you can expect to get pretty good at something if it's all you have."

After a few minutes of silence Ant asked in a way that indicated the question's only purpose was to continue the conversation, "Tell me about your Earth, Trey. Is it like here?"

"It actually is. It seems that the land features are nearly exactly the same in some instances. However, this mountain isn't back home. Also, the buildings, horses and what people wear are like Earth two hundred years ago. I go to school and my mom works at a museum. I suppose it isn't much different from here other than we don't have whatever nighttime dangers you have."

"There are dangerous creatures out after sunset along with the imps. The imps are very active at night."

"I've had enough of those guys."

Ant chuckled at the comment then said, "Is there a girl waiting on you back home?"

"A girl? I don't know." He looked down before continuing, "Maybe. It was sort of complicated before I left."

"Complicated is interesting. Tell me more."

Well, I've sort of had a crush on this one girl for a long time. Her name is Sarah. But she never paid me any attention until recently. But now she has this older boyfriend with a car and...I guess...I hoped we could have been something. I must have been mistaken with her."

"A car? What's that?"

"It's sort of like a wagon but has an engine and you don't need a horse to pull it. The engine makes it go."

"That's amazing! A wagon that moves without a horse. You must tell me more about these cars."

"That's about all I can say other than some go really fast."

"I'd love to ride in a car one day."

"If you ever make it to my world – maybe."

"Tell me how you were mistaken with the girl?"

"I'm not sure. I guess she's been talking to me recently and we walked home from school one day and that was really great. We made plans to walk again together but I didn't show up."

"You guess she's been talking to you? Was she or wasn't she, Mate? You're not making any sense."

"She was. She was definitely talking to me. But that's not all. There's this other girl, Leslie. I don't know what it is with her. I've never noticed her before this year. My heart speeds up when I'm with her and I can't help but smile. She's just so sweet. I've always had a thing for Sarah, but Leslie is totally different."

"Two girls! Whoa! You do have a problem, Mate!" he hooted.

"Why didn't you show up for the first girl?"

"Ha! Yeah... that's sort of the beginning of why I'm here. I was attacked by these weird gross things, then ended up halfway across the world fighting for my life?"

"Really?" Ant replied languidly.

"Yeah. That's why I'm here."

"What else have you done to get you here?"

Over the next hour Trey told Ant about the attack of the rogglets, Lyza, Simon, the Keeper and his dreams. He kept the events around the eye, the dragon and time relic to himself.

"You know. I thought you were full of it when you said you weren't from this world. You tell the stories like they actually happened."

"It's all true. I swear. Look at this." Trey removed the disk from his pocket. "The stone in this disk is what I pulled from the Keeper and right here is the scar the rogglet left when he grabbed my ankle." Trey looked confused. "Well, it was there. I guess it healed."

"You're something else. That's an amazing story."

"I guess. Thanks."

"You sure do guess a lot. I would expect someone that has prevailed as much as you have in such a short time would be more confident."

"I'm really just trying to stay alive, which I haven't always been successful at. Remember? I died defeating the Keeper."

"Yeah. I remember," Ant said with leery eyes. Ant walked away looking out the cave entrance, then said, "Like I said before. You have no business here. It's way too dangerous for a boy." He paused for a minute, evaluating the nighttime activity. "My father once told me – " he began as he turned to find two large lizard-like creatures hauling off an unconscious Trey deep into the mountain.

"Arggg! Trey!" He ran after the abductors but was unable to catch up to their brisk unrelenting pace.

King Koltek

Trey was tossed into a crude rusty cage with a pounding headache. He lifted himself up, then looked out into the vast cavern lit by a phosphorescent glow that casted ghostly shadows across dark brown walls. There were lots of strange noises about; a clanging here, a random screech there, grunts and grovels from numerous mysterious creatures. Trey became frightened and feared the worst.

His eyes adjusted to the eerie light to reveal various lizard creatures scurrying about a rocky terrain. Slimy vegetation decorated the walls. A sour smell, like expired milk left out in the sun mixed with stagnant pond water filled the air.

Trey hung his head in disbelief.

"I can't believe it! This is the end," Trey said in a sad wimpy voice. "After all I've been through, I get captured in this stinky mountain. There's no way I'll get out of this cage. I'll probably die here – alone."

Trey closed his eyes and rested his head on the crusty bars.

"Don't be distraught, little guy. I'll keep you company," a low cheery voice said from the shadows across the cage behind him.

Startled, Trey jumped around. A man-like creature with bulging muscles, sloped ridged forehead, furry waist and clawed feet sat across him in a cross-legged position. He sat because he was too large to stand upright in the small container. Trey on the other hand had room to spare when he stood and could move freely.

"Oh my God! I didn't see you!" Trey said alarmed at the hulking figure that somehow escaped his eye initially.

"Don't be scared. We can be buddies," he said with a welcoming smile. His low voice could have been any famous TV or radio host – pleasant and warm. It didn't match his appearance at all. "I'm Calhoun."

Trey calmed a bit. His voice wasn't quite as hysterical as he made the assessment that Calhoun, at the moment, wasn't dangerous. "Nice to meet you Calhoun," Trey said apprehensively.

"What brings a guy like you to a place like this?"

Trey assumed Calhoun was being silly with humorous banter, so he replied while examining the cage, "Well, the popular vacation spots are always so crowded. I thought I'd try something more, you know, exotic this time around."

Calhoun responded intensely serious, "Why would anyone vacation here? It's damp and smelly."

"It's a – nevermind," Trey replied, unsure if the beastly man was messing with him or not. "I was captured up the mountain by those things. I'm not supposed to be here."

Calhoun's expression remained the same as when Trey first arrived, "I'm not either. Take me, I was just minding my own business when they captured me."

"Minding your own business, huh? In this mountain? I know you have a better story than that?"

"Maybe I was trying to steal back the cradle and got caught," he said nonchalantly. "I'm not exactly sure how I got in this cage."

"Now that makes more sense. What's the cradle?"

He leaned forward. He became comically intense. "It's a large magical crystal that is the source of life for my people." His eyes bulged with sincerity. "It's what lights this cavern. It makes everything grow," he said spreading his arms in outward circles from lower to higher. "But Koltek's imps stole it years ago."

Trey nearly fell over. His mind spun as Calhoun continued, "He doesn't know what it is. He just uses it to somehow control the over-grown lizards that have been wreaking havoc on the surrounding cities. I just now found it. I have to get it back before it's too late and thousands starve." He began to speak again before Trey stopped him.

"Please stop for a second. Did you say this guy's name is Koltek?"

"Yeah. He's a real nasty guy."

"Is he a demon?"

"A what?" Calhoun replied with a curious face.

"You know, a demon."

"I don't know what he is. I just know I have to return the cradle to my people."

It has to be him, Trey thought to himself. *Logos said we were destined to meet.*

Realizing the futility in learning about Koltek from the bulky beast, Trey asked, "That one crystal is really all that stands between harvest and famine for your people?"

"Without the cradle, our land will soon be barren."

"I see. And the demon … I mean Koltek, is also responsible for the nighttime terrors around here?"

"Yes. These lizard things don't handle daylight well and do their plundering after sundown. The cities are usually well lit at night which thwarts the midnight raids."

"So, these are the creatures everyone warned me about."

Calhoun scrunched his nose and said, "Yeah. They're nasty boogers."

"Haha!" Trey laughed. "And they're green!"

Calhoun remained expressionless.

"You know?" Trey said laughing. "Boogers. They're nasty boogers...and boogers are green." Trey's laughter turned to a confused smile.

Nothing from Calhoun.

"So, uh, yeah." Trey cleared his throat. "They're the bad guys around here. What's that tattoo on your forearm?" Trey asked to change the subject.

"I was once a warrior for the Rasius tribe," he said shamefully, "before the great peace. All of us bear the scars of our turbulent past."

"Warrior? Tell me more!"

"It is not something I am proud of. I killed many of my brothers for a worthless cause." He held his head low and pulled his knees close to his chest.

"There never seems to be a good reason for war. Please go on," Trey said sincerely.

"The four tribes of my land lived in peace for thousands of years. As our numbers grew, we began arguing over resources and territory. Squabbles turned into a thirty-year war decimating large swaths of our people. We could have easily worked together to efficiently produce enough for everyone, but influential leaders took power and pitted each tribe against the others."

"How'd they come to power."

"That is the funny part. We chose them to lead us. We became convinced we needed someone else to tell us what to do in order to solve our resource problem. Each tribe chose a leader for representation in negotiations. It seemed to go well for a while until our leader, Oligan came to us saying we can no longer trust the other tribes and must defend our territory. We began building an army of warriors. Oligan soon-after pressed for preemptive attacks on the other tribes which led to the war. We were so busy with the war and lost so many good people our land withered. Crops failed; herds left. We were on the brink of starvation."

"It's amazing to me what power will do to a person. How'd the war end?"

"On a peaceful Sunday afternoon, the cradle crashed from the heavens to a neutral area between the four tribe lands. The land around the cradle soon flourished. Thinkers from all tribes studied it and learned how to harness its power to solve our resource problems. We soon realized our leaders were intentionally instigating war between the tribes to separate us. Once we were separated and began feeling superior over the other tribes, it was easy for them to manipulate us to do the things they wanted us to do. We all became subservient to the system they created. For thirty years we lived like slaves under the guise we were protected when in reality they were stealing the resources they were claiming to protect."

"And then?"

"We banished the corrupt leaders and once again became a flourishing society. The cradle enabled the land to sustain our growing civilization. That is until the imps came in the night nearly fifteen years ago and stole it.

We've managed since then but the decline in food is noticeable. I along with ten others were sent to find it. I must not fail my people for I fear war will resume."

"And you came so close but got thrown into this cage. I'm in a similar situation. I will help you recover the cradle," Trey said heroically.

"Thank you, small boy. But I have a hard time believing you can help, even if we get out of this cage."

"I'll do what I can, and after hearing your story, I feel we'll find a way out."

"How'd you get here?" Calhoun asked Trey.

Trey began to tell the story he told Ant when a large toady creature, bulbous and bloated, entered the room. He addressed a large crowd of fat toady followers. He angrily shook at Calhoun and said with a huge ribbed mouth, "How callous and stupid could someone be to believe they could steal from the great King Koltek!" He spit slobber about when he spoke.

The crowd roared while masses of large lizards scurried about seemingly aimlessly – some stood on hind legs while a majority on all fours close to the ground while others stationed near strategic points didn't seem to move at all. The still ones held gruesome looking curved bladed weapons with pointy tips.

"Looks like my party has started," Calhoun said dryly.

Amid the speech, Trey turned to the bulky man-ish creature, "Your party?"

Koltek wore a dull metal crown and waived a crooked wooden stick in the air when he yelled, "Bring me the thief!"

Trey quickly turned back to see an army of portly pig-bodied frog headed lackeys storming toward the cage. They brandished long sticks with white/green sparks popping from the tips. They rushed Calhoun's side of the cage and quickly subdued him with several jabs of the electric weapons. Each strike arced with a loud pop before sending him down in a violent spasm.

The mob brought Calhoun to Koltek who's globular human-like legs under well-tailored pants propelled him back and forth on the inset stone carved stage.

"This thief!" he spat but missed Calhoun wide to the left, "Tried to steal our sacred lifestone!"

The crowd yelled in unison, "Oy!"

"He tried to kill us all with starvation!"

"Oy!"

"His punishment will be – " he looked down at the minions and raised his hands high like a symphony conductor entering the crescendo then yelled in a deep throaty voice, "death!"

"Oy! Oy! Oy!" screamed the throng.

Trey watched helplessly through the bars as Koltek and his minions set out to execute the sentence.

As Koltek rambled on, one of the lizards snuck up behind the cage, then quietly said, "You want to come out to play? I mean, I like the king's boastful speeches and all but this one has gone on too long."

Trey shared a confused look.

"I promise I won't eat you right away, Mate. I'm just so very bored."

Trey continued to not understand the situation. Suddenly he showed a faint smile as he said cautiously "Ant? Is that you?"

"Yeah, Mate! And I know where your stuff is," he said excitedly then turned back into the fox. With a wink, he opened the cage door.

The rusty hinges creaked loudly. The room silenced as everyone looked their way.

Calhoun said politely to Koltek as he bowed respectfully, "I do appreciate your hospitality, but I really must be moving on."

Koltek gave a confused look then shouted, "Get them!" His jowls jiggled in fury. He then rushed through a company of armed guards into a room behind him and touched something anchored to the wall. Instantly the aimless lizards halted then all dashed toward Calhoun, Trey and Ant. The guards behind Koltek reformed their original order and remained out of the chase when he returned.

"Run!" cried Ant.

Several of the frogpigs bounced into one another. Calhoun ravaged numerous others with swift punches. He crushed one into a wall with a large foot. He then picked up three electric sticks and javelined them all at the same time toward Koltek. As Koltek clumsily avoided the barrage, Calhoun darted toward Trey and Ant. Koltek left the great room amid several frogpigs.

Calhoun caught up to Trey and Ant as they sprinted down a random corridor followed by an angry horde.

"We have to go back!" Trey yelled.

"What?" Ant exclaimed. He then continued, "Oh yeah! Your stuff is back there."

"What?" Trey asked.

"Your stuff. Remember?" Ant replied.

"My stuff?" Trey couldn't for the life of him understand what stuff Ant was talking about. All he could think about was how he could get Koltek to the Etherios. Koltek is huge and not to mention all the crazy creatures he has under his command.

"Yeah! It's back where we were!" said Ant.

"No!" Trey yelled but thought he didn't have time to explain that he needed to find a way to trap Koltek to save Grandpa. "My stuff? Oh yeah! I need the key to get back. It's where the cage is?"

"Yeah!"

"Dang! Think, Trey. How do we get back?"

His eyes brightened, then said, "I have an idea!"

"I hope it's a good one!" yelled Calhoun. "Cause we have about fifty sharp-toothed critters with long blades on our tail!"

Trey rummaged through his pack as they rounded a corner. "Up on that ledge! Hurry!"

He fished the bottle from his pack, then said, "I hope this works!" Ant gave a surprised expression, then said, "What do you mean you hope this works?"

Trey smashed the small bottle just as they leaped upon the ledge. A hazy fog surrounded them.

"Be still and quiet. They shouldn't be able to see us," Trey said quietly.

Shortly after, the mob rushed past without the hint of a look in their direction.

"That was brilliant, mate! What'd you do!"

"Cloaking potion. I nearly forgot I had it. I'm glad it worked."

"You mean you didn't know it would work?" Ant asked.

Trey huffed from the running. "No. I've never used it before."

"That was your first time?" replied Ant. His face was twisted in a confused and angry expression.

"Yeah."

"You chose that moment to try something new? When our lives were on the line?" Ant questioned.

"It worked didn't it?"

"Why couldn't you have tested it out before now? Didn't think that bit of information would have helped make your decision?"

"I'm sorry! I didn't know I'd be chased by creepy gargantuan lizards today!"

"Easy fellas," said Calhoun. "Let's just get moving. Good work, Trey. Do you think it'll move with us?"

"No sense in asking Mr. Scientist over there," Ant thumbed toward Trey. "He's all about real life testing and doesn't know squat about his materials."

"Let's all walk together and see what happens," Trey said ignoring Ant's cynical comment.

They began walking slowly close together. The fog didn't follow.

"That's it for our cover," said Calhoun.

"What's the plan, Ant?" Trey asked.

"I saw three imps leaving a chamber on the other side of the great room from where your cage was located."

"Maybe that's where my stuff is. Can you sneak over there and get it?"

"Yeah. Should be no problem."

"You're looking for a small green bag and a large black handled knife with a carved symbol in the handle."

"Got it."

He began to rush off when Calhoun stopped him, then said, "Where is the location of the cradle? Did you see it?"

"Cradle?"

Calhoun held up his hand with a forefinger and thumb in a circular shape, then said, "It's a crystal about this size. It's probably glowing."

"You mean the large glowing diamond that is set in a protective cage guarded by an army of lizard things?"

"Yeah! You've seen it?" he said excitedly.

"Yeah. It's in a room right in front of you when you were about to be impaled by Koltek. He rushed back and touched it just before the lizards took after us. I wouldn't have seen it if the guards didn't split to let him through. There's no way we can get it. It's too heavily secured."

"That's none of your concern."

"You can't do it alone," said Trey. "We'll help you retrieve it for your people."

"It's not your battle, young Trey. I can handle these pesky creatures myself," replied Calhoun gallantly.

"We'll help you get it but let's get Trey's stuff first. There may be other useful items in that room," said Ant. Calhoun nodded in agreement.

Trey looked distantly in thought as they crept down the corridor back to the great room. Three lizards rounded a corner rushing toward them. Calhoun stepped forward, smashed one's head into the ground with a clawed foot while catching another leaping. He tossed it into the wall, then grabbed the third by the tail just before it reached Trey. He slung it into the wall then threw it down the corridor behind them. Trey and Ant stood in astonishment at how quickly the big guy handled the attackers.

"Let's keep going," Calhoun said casually.

They arrived at the eve of a corridor just past the cage where they could remain somewhat out of sight.

"I'll go with you," Trey said to Ant.

Ant nodded affirmatively then said, "We'll go around on that back wall. I think we can use those pillars for hiding if necessary."

"You have anything else in that bag that can help us?" asked Calhoun.

"No. That's it. All I have left is this tarp, jacket, kindling and matches."

"That's good. I think we can use it for a distraction later," said Ant. "Maybe you should stay here, big guy. You're just too large to not be seen as we creep across. We'll enter the cradle room from the far side," he said to

Calhoun.

"Ok. Be careful. I'll wait for your signal."

Ant and Trey snuck to the far wall, low to the ground using the wavering shadows and pillars for cover – careful not to be seen. Several lizards scurried about like ants but took no notice of Trey and Ant's stealthy march. They eased along the wall to the far corner where they found a wide corridor with several doors on each side.

"That one," Ant said pointing to the second door on the right. "Let's go."

They closed the door behind them. The circular room was about the size of a small bedroom with no other doors. Shelves loosely organized various items along the walls.

"A small green bag, you said?"

"Yes."

Trey rummaged through the items finding various cloaks, a jeweled goblet with intricate carved images, knives, wooden balls and helmets. "There's no consistency here. It just looks like random stuff."

Ant opened a long wooden trunk with tarnished metal corners, then removed several quilted blankets. "Yes! Cal will love this," he said raising a three-foot long war hammer with a rounded blunt head on one side and a large spike on the other.

Trey smiled and said, "I hope we don't have to use that." He shuffled through drawers and shelves but couldn't locate the bag.

Something bumped the door. "Quick hide!" Ant whispered.

Ant jumped in the trunk, then closed the lid. Trey rolled under the blankets just before the door swung open. Three imps entered the room chattering away in an undecipherable language. One of them jumped onto the trunk setting something on a shelf. Afterward, it turned, looking suspiciously at the lump of blankets on the floor. It questioned something to the others pointing at the heap. Another responded in a frustrated tone. He answered disappointedly, leapt from the trunk, then left with the other two.

Ant jumped from the trunk as soon as the door slammed shut. "That was close. We have to go. Now!"

"What do you mean? Could you understand what they were saying?"

"Loosely translated, the trunk imp wanted to put the blankets away but the other said they had to hurry to prepare for the party."

"Party? That's what it said?"

"Some sort of gathering tonight in the main room. If we don't get out of here now, we'll never make it. Look, Trey! On the shelf!"

Trey turned to find the little green bag on the shelf above the trunk. "That's it and Karl's knife!" He took the bag, held it close to him with both hands, closed his eyes, then said, "Aroushidium." When he opened it, he found the key inside. "Yes! It's still there!" He closed the bag again, then said the word. He placed it in a zipped pant pocket. He kept the knife in his hand.

"Let's get back to Calhoun," he said but what he was thinking was that this may be the only chance he has to capture Koltek and save Grandpa. He thought, *I left the Etherios key at home. How will I ever rescue Grandpa?* He then had another thought that brought great shame in himself, *Logos didn't say I had to bring him back alive. I sent the Keeper there when I killed him with the sword.* He looked down then shook off the disconcerting shameful feeling.

Trey and Ant slunk to the entrance of the great

room.

"There's way more of them than when we crossed earlier," Ant said as he looked upon the mass of bodies milling about the main area. "I don't know if we can make it without being noticed."

"I'm afraid you're right. What do we do?"

"The cradle is straight across the room," Ant said pointing. "We'll have a hard time getting there in this crowd." That corridor," he said pointing to the left, "It opens to a space about half as big as this one. There are two corridors exiting that room besides the one through which we'll enter. Hopefully one of them leads out."

Trey replied sarcastically, "Hopefully? You didn't map this plan out ahead of time?"

"Ok, wise guy. Let's stay focused. I'm sure we can get to the room, but I'm not sure we can secure the cradle and escape. You sure you want to do this?"

"Yes. Calhoun's people are depending on us."

"How do you know he's not just some crazy thug only interested in stealing the diamond to get rich?"

"I just know."

"Yeah. He feels like a good guy to me too. Seems like he's trying to do the right thing."

Ant edged to where he could signal Calhoun. Once their eyes met, he pointed to himself then motioned with his hands like he was throwing something. He ducked back as a horde of lizards entered the room. Koltek boomed angrily as one looked to be reporting bad news – most likely the outcome of their escape. Koltek roared furiously then smashed a frogpig with the staff. It toppled over holding its head.

Ant peaked around the corner regaining Calhoun's attention. He brought his hands together facing down, then raised them higher to facing up. He pointed across to the corridor leading to the cradle room. Finally, he nodded. Calhoun nodded back. He slunk back behind the wall as Koltek began to address the creepy audience.

Ant ran back to the small storage room. Trey followed. Koltek boomed a speech to the crowd. Hundreds of livid roars followed. Trey shivered then closed the door behind them, muffling the revelry.

"What are you doing?" Trey asked.

"Hand me that tube over there."

"Trey looked to his right, then grabbed a thin metal tube."

Ant made a small hole of loose dirt in the floor of the room. He added water and mixed until a pasty mud formed. He set the tube upright on the ground, then scraped in the paste. He compacted it with a stiff rod. He removed the wick from a candle, thinned it with a knife then soaked it in the fluid from a lantern. He emptied the contents from a pouch he retrieved from his sack so that it filled in around the wick holding it firmly in place in the tube. He scraped and compacted more mud leaving a tiny amount of the wick exposed. "Let's go," Ant said.

Back at the entrance as Koltek continued a lively sermon Ant said, "Give me the jacket, kindling and matches." He removed a couple matches from the box, then placed the box and tube in the shirt with the kindling. He caught Calhoun's eyes, then once again nodded receiving a returning nod. He lit the edge of the match box as well as the wick and tied the sleeves to the back of the jacket forming a sack. Holding the makeshift sack in one hand while counting down from five on the other so that Calhoun could see he said, "Get ready to run."

Watching Ant's fingers: five- four- three- two- one. Ant slung the jacket high into the air. It sailed silently across the room, turning over and over until it landed with a thud on the dirt floor in the middle of a group of spectators. The startled group began murmuring. Koltek quieted. Others joined in on the confusion the increasingly smoking distraction had caused.

Calhoun began to stealthily cross the room.

"We don't have but a few more seconds," Ant whispered as he ushered Calhoun to hurry.

Calhoun nearly reached them when the matches ignited sending the jacket into flames. The growing group jumped back while others joined. "Now, Trey!" Ant urged under his voice.

Trey grabbed the war hammer as they quietly hurried toward the far wall adjacent to the crowd. Calhoun cut the corner of the room drawing the attention of one of the onlookers who raised an alarm.

"It's a diversion! They are after the lifestone!" yelled Koltek. "Stop them!"

"Run!" Calhoun screamed grabbing Trey like a running back holding a football as he caught up.

"No matter what happens, keep running!" Ant yelled.

They sprinted toward the far wall as an explosion filled the room. Many of the surprised pursuers dove to the ground in fear or scurried in the opposite direction.

"To the room!" Ant yelled to Calhoun who set Trey down and quickly bowled his way through a mass of frightened frogpigs.

Koltek bolted into the cradle room. Large numbers of giant lizards came to a unified attention throughout the mountain.

Trey and Ant easily reached the room as everyone seemed to be focused on the massive Calhoun. They stopped just inside facing a mob of creatures alertly guarding the huge diamond framed in the wall. Koltek loomed over the pulsing guard.

"I think you're gonna need this," Trey said holding

out the heavy hammer with two hands and all his strength to Calhoun which he took effortlessly without either of them removing their eyes from the guards.

"Grab the cradle, get out, then take the passage to the left. I think that leads to the first corridor we were on which I think will take us out of here," Ant said as he notched his bow.

Calhoun said to Trey and Ant before he stepped out in front of the armed guards which stood slightly taller than Trey, "Stay here. I got this."

As sweat dripped from bulging muscles he boomed, "Koltek! Return to me the Cradle and I'll let you continue your miserable existence."

Koltek slowly emerged from the throng. He shuffled close to Calhoun and began, "Your people are wretched – "

Like a homerun swing with lightning speed, Calhoun landed the hammer sharply against Koltek's slimy head. The king flailed and crumpled into the corner.

Trey watched the opportunity to rescue his Grandpa play out in front of him. The demon lie helplessly in the corner while they prepared for the imminent battle. He gripped the cold handled knife and thought about what he had to do.

Calhoun then let out a massive cry, "AAAEEEEEIIIIIIIIIII!" breaking Trey's attention. The crowd responded with a thunderous unified wide-mouthed hiss – Trey jumped back reflexively.

Calhoun leaped into the group, swiftly avoided razor-edged blades and crushed the first in his path with a powerful swing of the hammer as if he were chopping a large block of wood. The hammer drove the creature's skull through its gangly neck down to the floor causing it to rupture into an unrecognizable clump of bone, scales and blood. He then swung the deathly weapon upward catching another in the chest, launching it into the violent mass. He next swung it like a baseball bat taking out several attempting to encircle him.

He gripped the weapon in one hand then assumed an aggressive athletic stance. He growled before reengaging. He launched into the group yelling madly. He swung the hammer with one hand while grabbing and punching with the other. He laid out bodies everywhere he stepped.

He snatched a sharp staff from the grip of one and with a powerful slice, cut another in half at the waist – it slid apart into a pile on the bloody floor. He twisted the staff in his left hand like a half-time baton twirler then plunged it all the way through one and into another like a shish kabob. He then snatched the blade out through their side spilling their insides. He then swung to his left racking another with the hammer.

One disarmed guard chomped the back of Calhoun's massive leg before he smashed its head with the blunt weapon spreading gooey brain all over. He shook one latched to his arm into two others. He swung and toppled the three of them down. He continued pounding with the hammer and slicing with the blade. Green bodies flew into walls and the ceiling with each crushing blow.

Ant released arrow after arrow, taking down one, sometimes two, each time.

Trey glanced at the demon in the corner and said to himself, "This is my only chance." He focused his mind around ending Koltek as the brought the knife forward and left the battle.

He creeped close to Koltek as chaos raged in the background. Koltek was breathing shallowly. The massive creature lurched. Trey jumped back defensively but Koltek remained unconscious - barely.

The knife shook in his hand. "It's a demon," he said trying to convince himself what he was about to do was ok. He gripped the weapon in both hands and raised it above his head. His eyes widened, he tried to look away but didn't want to miss his target - the area where Trey thought his heart should be.

Do demons have hearts, he thought briefly before pushing the thought away.

He closed his eyes, tensed, opened them again then closed them as he plunged the knife down until it stopped firmly.

He opened his eyes to find the knife stopped before touching the demon's skin. Trey was confused. He panicked thinking Koltek was preventing the atrocious act. Trey tried to raise the knife up to try again but it wouldn't budge. He pulled and lurched and tried to wiggle it free but it just stayed there, motionless not even an inch from Koltek. He released the knife which hovered for just a moment before floating to his side.

Trey stepped back as the demon shifted.

"No! He's waking! Calhoun! He's waking! Help!"

A bloody lizard slammed against the wall to Trey's left. Trey saw his friends fully engaged. They were no help.

"Koltek will live and Grandpa will stay in the Etherios forever! No!"

Then something caught his eye. A pair of green eyes emerged from a dark corner. As the tiny imp approached him, it lowered a raised arm releasing the knife from its spell. The knife then fell to the floor with a thud.

Anger overcame Trey. "Why! Why did you stop me!" he screamed. The imp stopped and raised another hand sending a calm over Trey. He relaxed and watched the imp perform a series of movements. It looked as if the tiny creature were playing slow motion basketball without a ball.

Koltek's eyes opened. Clarity revealed itself – and he was angry. He stood, towering over Trey. He raised an arm as if to swat a fly then he began to scream – not a painful scream but one of terror as he took notice of the green-eyed imp. As the imp continued his magical basketball dance, Koltek began to shrink. The smaller he shrunk the higher pitch was his scream until only a sound like a hovering mosquito came from the miniscule demon. Then a capsule engulfed Koltek and floated effortlessly toward Trey.

Trey plucked the pill shaped capsule from the air and looked curiously at the imp. The imp bowed, rose, showed Trey reverent eyes then disappeared into the darkness.

A roar from Calhoun brought Trey back to the intense battle. Trey watched several lizards slash and bite at Calhoun, but Calhoun drove forward supported by Ant's lightening quiver. Ant notched and delivered an arrow into the skull of a scurrying lizard. He released another catching one in midair before it sliced Calhoun's bald head.

Trey dug the magical bag from a zipped pocket, said the word, and placed in it the capsule containing Koltek. He then said the word again placed the bag back in the pocket, grabbed the knife and rushed to help his friends.

Flush with the nerve to save his friends, Trey jumped in with a flying kick to one lizard, then with Karl's big knife, stabbed another through the top of the head on his way down. He slashed up in a twist, splitting the throat of another. He wished he had the sword that was resting peacefully in his mom's garden, rather than the knife. A bladed staff fell to his side. He regarded Calhoun who smiled following bashing the weapon's owner.

A steady stream of lizard's and frogpigs flowed through the entrance behind.

Trey swung the staff slicing the fat gut of a frogpig – it squealed and scurried out of the room followed by several other cowardly cohorts. Many others backed passively against the walls while others pretended to be effective in the fight. A couple seemed to be arguing about who would strike first.

Ant launched his last arrow just as Calhoun became overrun by a mass of green. Trey was knocked to his back by an attacking thick tail – the staff fell from his hand out of reach. One leaped onto Calhoun's head while three were scurrying toward Trey.

"Ant!" Trey yelled. "Help me!"

Trey's eyes were desperate. His hand reached out. Calhoun twisted in a throng of green bodies like he wore a bulgy green hooded overcoat. The lizards abandoned the use of weapons in a primal thirst for blood.

Ant was out of arrows; he couldn't help his new friends. He fell to the floor in anguish.

"Ant! Help!" Trey screeched as he flailed his legs to ward off the attacking creatures.

Ant closed his frightened eyes. He crouched on the ground.

"AAAAAAAH!" screamed Calhoun falling to the ground. He rolled his massive body trying unsuccessfully to free himself.

Trey kicked one of the lizards while another lept behind him.

Ant watched the failed attempt to recover the cradle which was ending with the lives of the three of them.

"Do it Antonin!" Ant said to himself with his eyes

closed and hands over his pointy ears. "You don't have a choice! But what if..." He waved off the frightful thought.

He bravely stood. His terrified eyes met Trey's one last time before he raised a waving finger in the air. Ant shivered with fear – of the unknown. Trey though he heard Ant say, "I hope I don't kill my friends," just before he watched the fox emerge from a blurred state as a slick reddish-brown wollybraugher.

Ant stood on all fours and growled ferociously drawing the attention of several guards. He leapt onto the lead of the three attacking Trey. He ripped its jaws apart, tossing the lower aside while dropping the remainder of the body as he turned to find his next target. He dug huge jaws into another, then flung it away while slashing the third with a clawed paw. He bounded lightning fast into the group, slashing and chomping Calhoun to freedom. He grasped one by the skull then ripped its spine from its back in a single gruesome motion.

All of the frogpigs scampered away squealing in panic.

Calhoun eyed the vicious beast, "Ant?"

Ant payed no notice as he pounced on an attacking giant lizard. With Ant's brutal assistance, Calhoun reached the cradle. More lizards poured through the door. Calhoun smashed lizards with the hammer as he removed the radiant diamond from the housing. He secured it in a pocket before clearing a way for their escape. Green bodies flew left and right as Calhoun mowed through with the hammer. Ant continued his personal massacre.

Calhoun threw Trey onto his shoulder, then fought his way through the exit to the corridor. Ant followed after decimating several more leaving the floor painted in fowl greenish grey blood.

"Trey! Your leg!" Calhoun said casually while looking at Trey's dripping red leg.

"I'll be ok," he replied. He could feel the leg healing as they spoke. "Just keep moving."

They set a brisk pace through the mountain. As a wollybrougher, Ant was substantially faster than the screeching followers and Calhoun's massive legs had no trouble keeping up.

"You really freaked me out, ole buddy," Calhoun said as he dashed down a wide corridor. "Don't you think it would've been a good idea to tell someone you might turn into a savage killer?"

Ant growled at Calhoun's remark.

"Easy now. I'm just kidding," Calhoun retorted.

Ant slowed and began shaking his head. He turned and lunged at Calhoun tackling him to the ground. Trey fell hard on the mountain floor. Ant stood wildly growling above the massive figure. Calhoun swiftly rolled and tossed Ant against the wall. Ant launched again as Calhoun reflexively stepped back and twisted to avoid the strike.

"Ant! What are you doing?" Trey screamed.

Ant swiftly turned toward Trey and snarled. He then stumbled and shook all over. He drunkenly lunged again at Calhoun who easily avoided sharp teeth. Ant fell backward then rolled on his side releasing a loud bellow. He regained his feet, stared uneasily at Calhoun, then Trey before he fell to the ground unconscious.

Lake Oshugar

"Ant's awake!" Trey said running from the edge of a swiftly flowing river.

"How are ya, buddy? You really had us worried back there," Calhoun said.

"Wha....What happened? Where am I?" Ant said as he groggily looked around at a distant mountain across a grassy plain.

"You passed out in the mountain. I thought you died. You were acting all crazy and attacked us. Calhoun carried you here."

"I attacked you? I'm sorry. I take on the instincts of whatever I change into. Wollybraughers are wild and callous. They're uncontrollable, even when it's me. In the room back there, I panicked and couldn't think of anything else. I put us all in jeopardy. I should have been more careful."

"No. You were great. Had you not changed, we would surely be gone," Calhoun reassured.

"As one of them, I could have killed you just as well as any of the others. I couldn't make the distinction on my own. We were left to the instincts of the animal to make the right decisions."

"Well, it worked and we're still alive. Please don't do it again," said Trey with a worrisome smile.

They all shared an uncomfortable laugh.

"Now how do we cross this river?" Trey continued.

Ant wearily walked to the edge of the water. He peered out over the wide swift river. He could barely make out the other bank. He looked left then right and shook his head from side to side as if saying no then hung his head for a moment.

He returned to the others and said, "I have an idea, but it's nearly as risky as the wollybraugher incident."

"Let's hear it," said Calhoun.

"Trey, remember the felixis?"

"No! That's a bad idea," stammered Trey. "That bird was nuts. Plus, you don't even know how to fly."

"Maybe I can practice? I just have to get us over the river and lake. It's not that far."

"I don't know. That thing was huge. What if you can't control it and you eat us both?" Trey replied.

"I don't know of anything else big enough to get us over, Mate. Do you have a better idea?"

"No. No, I don't have a better idea." Trey looked toward the river then back at Ant, "How about you start smaller, maybe a finch?"

"Ok. I'll try that. But before I transform, do either of you have any food. I'm famished."

"Take this. It's the last of the bread muffins Karl left me." Trey remembered the kindness of the green-eyed imp that brought back the muffins after their attack.

Ant took his time with the muffins, resting between bites. When he was finished, he said, "Ok. Let's learn how to fly."

~ ~

Ant blurred into a tiny bird standing on a patch of grass between Calhoun and Trey. He wobbled a little then began unsteadily walking one foot after the other. He fell over several times.

"He looks awkward. What's wrong with him? It doesn't seem natural," said Calhoun.

Trey replied, "You're right. What is it that looks so funny? It's like he doesn't know how to walk."

Ant waddled like a duck with stiff legs. His tiny bird tail wagged back and forth as his body tottered left and right.

"Wait! That's it! Finches don't walk they sort of hop. Try hopping rather than walking," Trey said to the tiny bird.

The bird regarded Trey for a moment, took a small hop, then several more.

"That's better," Trey encouraged.

The bird hopped, hopped and then hopped some more. Ant stood still and looked up to Trey and Calhoun as if seeking approval.

"You're doing very good tiny Ant," Calhoun praised.

Ant opened each wing one at a time, observing them independently as they stretched out. He began to slowly flap but not quite in unison – he tumbled over. He seemed to get it after several more attempts. He flapped harder, then slowly rose off the ground and toppled over backwards. Trey and Calhoun couldn't help but chuckle. He flapped them again and toppled over to the side. After several unsuccessful attempts, Trey and Calhoun sat as Ant struggled with flight.

"Do you think he'll ever get it?" asked Calhoun.

Ant stopped and looked up with his little cocked beak pointed at the massive guy.

"You know he can hear you," Trey responded to Calhoun with a frown.

Calhoun raised his eyebrows as if Trey said something personally offensive to him.

"It's ok, Ant. I believe you can do it," he said to the tiny bird.

Ant continued several more unsuccessful tries. He flapped in a frustrated frenzy then rested on the ground after toppling over.

"Just take a break, little buddy," Calhoun said.

Ant jumped up as if in defiance and once again began flapping. On the fourth attempt he sustained a ten-second-long hover. Trey and Calhoun cheered as if their favorite team just won the championship game.

He hovered a few more times, gliding forward a little further on each descent. Trey reached down, offering his hand to Ant. Ant hesitantly hopped on. When Trey raised his hand chest level, Ant leapt off gliding down to the ground several feet away. He hopped joyously back to Trey flapping his wings making each hop a little longer. Trey lifted the bird above his head. This time when he leapt, he flapped his wings sustaining a slow descent, making a few small turns to land back at Trey's feet a minute later.

Trey and Calhoun rejoiced.

The tiny bird hopped from the grass, then flew to land uneasily on Trey's hand. He flew off making several ascents, descents and turns before once again steadily landing on Trey's palm.

Trey held the little bird at eye level, then asked, "You are ready now?"

Ant launched from Trey's rising hand. He flew confidently in the air. He circled them before he hovered several yards above his mates. Then he blurred – and grew. When the blur cleared a magnificent falcon with black accenting a mostly white body emerged. Ant released a booming screech which shook fear into Trey. Ant soared high into the sky before landing softly with a powerful WOOSH of immense wings amid ecstatic applause from Trey and Calhoun.

Ant beheld them with penetrating black eyes then lowered his head. Trey hesitantly climbed onto his back. Ant clinched Calhoun with a mighty talon then lept into the air. They rose slowly as he furiously beat the great wings. Trey released a terrifying scream when they quickly lost altitude while Ant attempted to get a feel for the added weight. Regaining momentum, he made a wide circle before soaring over the river.

Calhoun yelled joyously like a small child riding a pony, "Wooooohoooo! This is great! Hehehehe!"

Trey thought while looking upon the rumbling waves of white water below, *there's no way we could have crossed that. It has to be a mile wide.*

Clearing the river, the group ascended over a lightly forested area of spruce, fir and aspen. Miles of trees dotted the landscape below. Various herds of prey animals rushed and dashed away from the large form above. The end of the forest gave way to an immense lake. Trey barely made out cliffs accenting the far side. Ant dove lower targeting the shoreline. He pulled up just in time to stall their momentum. He set Calhoun down before resting on the rocky ground. Trey climbed off, slipping a little on loose pebbles.

Ant blurred back into a fox, then said amid heavy breathing, "That's...harder...than it...looks." He sat roughly.

"You did great, Ant! That was wonderful flying!" Trey cried extatically.

"Yeah! It was pretty good wasn't it?" Ant said proudly.

"I was a bit uncomfortable. Maybe you should file your nails before you pick someone else up again," Calhoun said. Trey and Ant laughed at his stoic delivery of the comment.

"Now you can fly," Trey said happily. Ant responded with a proud smile.

They turned their attention to the lake.

Soft waves washed ashore as Trey walked to the water's edge. "Cierden said this lake is dangerous."

"Dangerous? In what way?" Ant asked.

"He said there was some sort of water beast."

"These waters are perfectly safe. We'll have no trouble crossing. Especially in the air," said Calhoun.

"You may be right. Cierden didn't say he knew for sure."

"I don't think I can do that again for a while. I wasn't sure if we'd make it over the forest. I looked for several places to land but decided to push it a little farther. I'm beat." He laid back on the rocky beach and closed his eyes.

"The last place we need to be is in the middle of the lake without a boat," Trey said looking onto the water.

The water rustled a few meters off the shore.

"Did you see that?" Trey said to the others pointing. "The water over there."

"Over near those small ripples?" asked Ant looking

sideways from a horizontal position.

"They were bigger before."

"Just fish. It's getting late in the afternoon. Probably dinner time," said Ant resting his eyes again.

"It was too big to be fish." Trey said.

"You guys have nothing to worry about," said Calhoun trying to allay their fears.

"There it is again!" Trey said as a large object churned the water.

"That was no fish!" exclaimed Ant briskly sitting up.

"You two are not listening," Calhoun said as he walked to the water. "There's nothing here that will harm you."

The words barely left his lips when a giant cerulean blue creature emerged from the water. It flopped onto shore easily overshadowing the hulking Calhoun. Trey jumped back while Ant scampered away on his backside.

It raised up like a cobra ready to strike, spreading a solid wavy fin that advanced along the entire length of its smooth body. Two thick antennae protruding from its head were tipped with bulbous black ends that reminded Trey of pinecones. It was accented by vertical black stripes that traversed both sides of its back. Long dark eyes seemed to favor Calhoun.

"Guys. Don't be afraid," Calhoun said walking toward the beast. "Hello Daisy," he said in a voice you would use with a small child. The creature lowered its head to meet Calhoun's. "It's so good to see you!" he said rubbing her side.

She made a harmonious sound as if a great celloist played a joyful tune. "What are you doing so far from home?"

She made more beautiful sounds.

"Isn't she lovely?" he said as he turned toward the

less frightened onlookers.

Trey edged a little closer becoming trusting of Calhoun's friend. "Yes. She is very beautiful. How do you know her?" he continued cautiously.

"Her and her family live near my village far down the river," he said pointing toward the eastern side of the lake.

"I don't think I understand. I grew up near a large river with lots of things living in it, but I never formed a personal relationship with any of them nor did I meet them on this sort of level," replied Trey.

"Daisy was injured years ago when I was just a boy. I found her washed up on shore. She was just a tiny thing back then. She had a large gash in her back. Look you can see the scar there. I think it was a spear from one of the other tribes. I never did find out. I took her to a pond and raised her back to good health. I visited her every day for over six months. She often came to see me after I released her back to the river. As she grew larger, she would take me on exciting rides. We would sometimes be out for days exploring these waters. It certainly is good to see you again," he said returning his affection to Daisy. "You think you can take me home?"

She released a jubilant melody.

"But first, I need you to do my friends a favor."

She regarded him lovingly.

Daisy moved effortlessly through the water. Her head and back raised above the surface, easily accommodated the three passengers with minimal wetness.

"This is amazing!" Trey said cheerfully.

"She's so fast," said Ant.

"Yeah! Nearly as fast as your flying, but way more enjoyable!" said Calhoun.

"I'll have to give her that," Trey said. "I was super

stressed out in the air. This is smooth, like riding in my grandma's car."

"Hey! That was my first time flying. I'll get better."

"I sure hope so, because you can't get any worse," Calhoun replied.

The occasional wet spray electrified Trey's face in the rushing wind. He couldn't contain an elated smile. Daisy made a few soft turns to mix it up before arriving at the shore next to a tall waterfall.

After debarking, Calhoun said, "I can't thank you guys enough for helping me recover the cradle. You didn't have to risk your lives for me and my people, but you did anyway. I'll remember you and tell your story to the end of my days." He hugged them both individually longer than expected and squeezed them harder than was comfortable.

"I think we all know that Ant was the hero today. I would be dead or stuck in this land without him," Trey said. "He saved my life at least twice."

"I agree," replied Calhoun. He lifted Ant into his great hands, "You are a great....whatever you are." He regarded Any lovingly then set him down and continued, "I must return the cradle to my land. It was great meeting you two and hope to see you again," he said as a tear streamed down his cheek.

"I'll miss you too, Cal," Trey said hugging him again.

"Till next time!" Calhoun said climbing aboard Daisy.

Trey and Ant watched Daisy slink off the shore then she darted away with amazing speed as Calhoun waved goodbye.

"So. Shall we be getting you on your way?" Ant asked to Trey.

"Yes! Let's go!" he said, eager to be home again.

They walked along the edge of the shore until they reached the colossal wall of water.

Ant hollered over the resounding falls, "You say it's behind the waterfall?"

Trey screamed, "He said at the base. Can we get behind it?"

"Yeah. Look. There's a thin ledge."

They followed along the ledge to the other side.

"Nothing but solid rock. Looks like Cierden was wrong." Ant yelled over the thunderous vertical river.

"It has to be here! He was right about everything else!" Trey exclaimed.

"There's nothing here. Let me fly us back to Roberton. Maybe the librarian can think of something else."

"No. There's nothing else he can do for me."

"You're sure he said it was at the base?" Ant questioned loudly. Ant didn't believe it was here but chose to continue the charade until Trey gave up looking.

"That's what he said. I'm sure of it."

Ant looked at the water plunging into the lake and said, "Maybe it's down there?"

"You mean, under the water?" He yelled, feeling a pain in his throat.

"I don't know. You said base and we walked through there. Maybe it's further down."

"Why would it be so hard?" he said wearily. "Ok. I'll try it. If I don't come back then you'll know I made it, or I drowned."

"That's really encouraging, Trey. You're not really going down there are you?" Ant yelled with a 'don't do it' look.

"Yeah. I don't have any other options. I'm a good swimmer. I placed second in the two-hundred-meter freestyle last summer," he said with a hopeful smile.

"I don't know what that means, Trey," Ant replied confused by the rationale for Trey risking his life in the falls.

Trey rummaged through his pack handing a knife to Ant. "Please get this to Karl Ropping in Hoppston. Can you do that for me?"

"Sure thing."

"Thanks."

Trey removed the bag from his pocket. He said, "Aroushidium", took out the key, said the word again then replaced the bag back in his pocket.

"When you see Cierden again, tell him thank you."

"You're really going to do this?" Ant asked worriedly.

Trey gazed into the eyes of the concerned fox, "Yes, Ant. I have to get back. Remember the bad guy? I have to stop him."

"But this looks hopeless. You're sure to drown," he replied emphatically.

"I'll be ok. I've battled worse things than water."

"If I can't stop you. I'll stay here to help if you need me."

"Thanks."

Trey looked at the metallic object in his hand, then said to himself, "Where do I need to go now? I remember the shape of the portal Lyza and I took in Egypt. I don't want to go back to Airhame. What was the one on the portal back home? Argg! I can't remember."

"I just want to go home!"

Trey formed the key into the shape of the Egypt portal, then thought to himself, *maybe I'll be able to get help when I get there.*

He looked at Ant, then shouted, "I just go down

there and look?" He had a frightened expression.

"Are you procrastinating? You're the portal expert. I wouldn't even know what to look for. You'll be ok. Just jump in and swim down. If you don't see anything, swim away from the current and come back. We'll figure out what to do then."

"Ok. Thanks for saving me today. I'm forever grateful."

"No worries, mate. You just get home."

"You'll be ok getting back from here?" he said stalling.

"I'll be fine! Just go!" Ant said urgently but also laughing.

"So just jump in and swim?"

"Trey! Go!"

"Ok! Here goes!" Trey jumped out into the center of the waterfall as Ant yelled, "No! To the side, Trey! Not into the falls!"

The water was cold. Not cold like you walk outside in the morning and get a chill or cold like a blistering headache after drinking an iced treat too quickly. It was numb toes cold. It was getting sucked out into space instantly freezing cold. But Trey didn't think of the bitter water. He couldn't, while thousands of large surging hands violently pushed him ever deeper. Tumbling, twisting and twirling – he became disoriented. He released his only breath in panic.

He pained for a single inhale. His lungs burned. His chest heaved. Wide eyes revealed nothing but cold wash. He was pushed further and further until finally, he spun out of the turbulence, bashing his head on solid stone, mixing blood into the chaos – nearly losing consciousness. He pressed against the brutal wall while rushing water grasped at his body. He frantically tried to scale the wall hoping to make it back to the surface. With the free hand he pulled and kicked his way up. His weak body failed to make significant progress.

I'm not gonna make it. I'm too far.

Terror overcame him. He hysterically scurried up the wall face. Unable to see as water rushed all around him, he wildly grasped for crevices and crags to help his ascent. Red filled his eyes from the gash. He nearly passed out. He jammed a finger on a protruding rock. He quickly grasped it to prevent descending into the abyss.

The world slowed.

Defeat was inevitable.

How easy it would be to let go – to peacefully drift away with the current. How simple quitting would be. How meaningless was all this pain.

Sleep crept in. Endless slumber hummed a tranquil melody.

He tenderly closed his eyes. He loosened his grip. His fingers slid from the smooth protruding stone face.

It's smooth! This is it!

He slammed the key onto the stone.

The Pheonix

He heaved and gasped for breath on the desert floor. Trey rolled to his side and coughed out water from burning lungs. He breathed in dry dusty air – the pain felt so good. He opened swollen eyes to the blistering sun. He stood on elbows and knees providing better leverage to empty his water distended stomach.

He gasped and panted. Long strings of drool clung to his chin. He said while facing sticky wet sand, "I never ever want to go swimming again!"

He folded over and laid there wet with sand tacked hands and clothes. He closed his eyes secretly wishing he would wake in his bed to the end of this foolish nightmare.

After several minutes of self-pity, he regained his feet feeling the south Egyptian sun already sizzling the water from his dark skin and odd clothes. He put the key in the bag, said the word, replaced the bag in a zipped pocket, then began walking unsteadily toward the small city ahead.

Rising heat from the desert road was unbearable – freezing water a distant memory. Parched lips and sweaty pits summarized Trey's two hour walk toward the city. Previously wet clothes were dry, and he had a chafe in a place he would never show. He flagged down a nice elderly man who didn't speak English. With the use of vivid hand movements, he conveyed a desire to go to the town ahead in the distance.

He arrived at the off-white stand-alone wood paneled building where he met Karim and Malory with Lyza just a week before. The door was unlocked but no one was home. He showered then helped himself to two ham and mayonnaise sandwiches along with a tall glass of milk. He laid on an uncomfortable scratchy couch taking a much-needed rest hoping someone would show. He woke several hours later still alone.

"I must get going. I can't waste any more time." He stood and continued talking to himself, "But what am I in a hurry for? I really have nowhere to be. I should just wait for someone to get here." He sat back down. "But what if no one shows?" He nodded to himself then stood from the couch. "Karim could be anywhere in the world."

He searched the house for useful items. He found a few Egyptian Pounds and an old cell flip phone of which to Trey's surprise still had service. He grabbed the charger, another sandwich and headed toward the door. As he opened the door to leave, he spotted a set of keys on a hanger. He walked outside to find a sport bike in a side shed. He smiled, then said convincingly to himself, "I'm sure he won't mind. Plus, it's sort of an emergency." He ran back into the house to locate the helmet which fit nicely. He also found a black leather jacket that was just a size too large, but he wore it anyway.

He wrote the following note.

Karim,

It's about ten A.M. Tuesday morning. I need your help. Please call the flip phone that was in the back room as soon as you get this message. The only person I know how to reach is the Phoenix so I'll head that way to see if he can help.

Trey

He left the note on the kitchen counter then exited the house. He secured loose items in the backpack before straddling the bike. The low sitting machine was comfortable to balance.

"One down, the rest up. Front brake. Back brake. This should be just like the dirt bike back at Grandpa Jake's farm," he said nervously.

He turned the key – pressed the ignition. The bike roared to life like a cougar launching at prey. After getting a feel for the throttle, he pressed down on the gear shifter. The machine bumped under his crotch as the transmission found first gear.

Easing onto the highway, he lightly twisted the throttle feeling consistent power from the finely tuned machine. He slalomed the center line a few miles as he moved through the first three gears, enjoying the ride while becoming accustomed to its handling characteristics.

With a rush of adrenalin and the next gear, he aggressively throttled the bike rocketing him along the deserted road. Rocks, palm trees and miles of sand whooshed past in a blur.

Fourth gear.

He twisted more and laid down behind the tiny windscreen. The thick jacket ruffled wildly in the turbulent wind.

Fifth gear.

He passed 100mph then 125mph continuing to push the bike.

Sixth gear.

The bike howled as the wheels hugged the hot pavement. He let out a scream of excitement, "whhoooooooaaaaahooooohooooohoooo!" as he passed 135mph. Every muscle in his body tensed as he walked the edge of chaos. He released the throttle at 150mph letting out a cry of ecstasy. He coasted while he caught up to himself. He maintained a speed of 100mph until he entered the city where he would learn a valuable life lesson.

Trey pulled into the parking lot lined with freight trailers. He parked the bike on the front sidewalk, hung the helmet on a handlebar, then let out a breath of relaxation. He itched to climb back on to feel the speed again. He longed for finishing this meeting quickly so he could return to the road. An uneasy feeling settled in his stomach. "Must be the excitement. I thought I'd be accustomed to that by now," he mumbled to himself.

Reluctantly, he turned to enter the building. He checked the flip phone to reveal no calls or messages before he walked through the stale waiting room toward the attendant. She said to him while standing, "Good morning, Mr. Roberts. He is expecting you."

"Thank you, Ma'am," Trey replied.

Expecting me? How can that be?

He thought about leaving. His instincts urged him to jump on the bike and fly away. But he continued because he knew not what to do and thought he needed guidance.

He walked vigilantly down the hallway. Two large men in black suits filed in behind, cutting off an escape. He paused when he reached the open door.

"Trey, my boy! It's so good to see you again," said the Phoenix wearing a pin striped navy suit and slicked back black hair.

The two guys behind pressured him into the room.

"Have a seat over there. We have much to discuss." He wore a deceptively pleasant smile.

Trey sat in an elegantly tufted dark leather chair stamped with leather buttons. It was uncomfortable.

"Trey. How've you been?" the Phoenix said behind the large desk.

"I suppose I've been ok," Trey said unsurely.

"And your mom? How is she?" his smile beamed with duplicity.

"Why would you ask about her?" Trey asked defensively.

"No reason. Just small talk. Let's get to it. I need your help," he said walking around the desk. "We are in a very tight situation. Your friend, Lyza, has betrayed us. She is working with Commerand to free Kahitu."

"That can't be true. She's risked her life several times to keep the relics from his possession."

"Has she now? Or is that what she told you she was doing?"

"What do you mean?"

"Think about it. When you were last here, her only concern was to recover the sword only Khaitu can wield."

"Ok. I suppose that might be true."

"And when you recovered the eye, did she actually risk anything to help or did she arrive just in time to secure the eye into her possession?"

"She, uh, helped us...well. I guess she did get there

just in time. And she wasn't anywhere near the fight. But if she were working with Commerand, why didn't she just let him get us?" Trey thought for a second then continued, "How did you know I recovered the eye?"

"Trey, my boy. It's my business to know things. Didn't Lyza tell you?"

"Yeah. I guess she did. Why do you think she betrayed us?"

"She needed leverage. Without the eye, she had no bargaining power with Commerand. My sources tell me she hasn't yet turned it over to him. We have to hurry. I need to know everything you know about the location of the eye. We must recover it before Commerand can use it to find the relics!" His urgency seemed unauthentic but passionate none the less.

He doesn't know that we lost the eye to Clievan. So much for your great info skills there buddy. A smug smile creeped onto Trey's face.

"But she saved me from the rogglets. None of what you say makes any sense."

"Tell me. Trey. What do you know about the story of the great King Khaitu?"

"First I know he wasn't great. He was an evil king that killed lots of innocent people. When he was banished, the benevolent queen hid the relics and ruled the land until she died."

"Is that the story you know? She ruled until she died?"

"Well, I just assumed that's what happened."

"Take a look at this." He handed Trey a tablet with pictures and hieroglyphs.

"This is a depiction of King Khaitu and Queen Raferti. The description below reads, "...and he took the former king's daughter as his wife. An exquisite beauty standing over three cubits, which is about six feet by the way, with flowing dark hair and dark blue eyes. Tell me, Trey. Does that description and image remind you of anyone?"

Trey's expression didn't change. He dismissed the evidence by saying, "It can't be. That was over three thousand years ago."

"What is time to you, Trey? Have you not met anyone else that is still alive from ancient times?"

Trey thought about Seth and Simon. *But they aren't human.*

The Phoenix continued, "It's true. Lyza is Queen Raferti. She was granted immortality in the very ceremony intended to bestow it upon Khaitu. She's been trying to free her beloved husband ever since."

"Lies! She said I couldn't trust you. Now I know why. Making up a crazy story like this."

But what if it's true. It does sound like her and she does have the book of relic locations and possibly the eye. Maybe she's out at this moment recovering the lost relics!

"You know I'm right, Trey. Don't be a fool! Do the right thing and help us. She must not succeed in freeing him," he said more forcefully.

"Even if I believed you, I don't know where she hid the eye or where she is now."

Brrrriiiiinnnnnggggg! The phone in Trey's pocket rang. Trey looked at the Phoenix with astonished eyes.

"Well? Won't you answer it?" the Phoenix said slyly.

Trey slowly reached into his pocket.

Brrrriiiiinnnnnggggg!

He pulled out the dated phone

Brrrriiiiinnnnnggggg!

He looked once more at the Phoenix then flipped it open. "Hello?"

"Trey! We're coming for you. You must maintain

your composure for my next words, then only say ok if you understand what I'm asking. You are in grave danger and must escape as soon as possible," Lyza said then paused.

"Ok."

"I believe in you, Trey. You can do this. Now hand him the phone."

"Ok."

Trey handed the phone to the Phoenix who was now standing next to him with a strong hand on his shoulder.

"My Queen! How may I be of service?" the Phoenix said in a joyful tone that hinted of derisiveness.

Trey's mind raced. *I can't trust anyone. Nick was right about Lyza. And Lyza was right about this creepy guy. I have to get out of here on my own.*

He wiggled a little in the seat. The Phoenix increased the pressure on his shoulder in response.

"Let the boy go. He doesn't have a part to play in this. He's just a boy," Lyza pleaded.

"You know I can't do that, your Majesty. I will, however, make a trade. Bring me the eye and I'll let him walk."

"I don't have it."

"Then get it! You have till the end of tomorrow." He flipped the phone closed, then tossed it onto the desk. "Trey. It has truly been a pleasure." He motioned to the two guys that followed Trey into the room, then said, "Show him to his room." The two suits grasped each arm and toted him out.

"I can walk, you jerks!"

One walked in front one behind.

They brought him to an interior room with no windows. He heard the locking bolt slide after closing the thick solid wood door. Trey sat in a leather office chair saying to himself, "Now, what do I do?"

He looked around but found no inspiration in the room decor.

He removed the ring from his finger, pondering it for a moment. He placed it in the palm of his hand, closed his eyes, focusing on the sound of each slow, steady breath.

Thoughts rolled across his mind like flitting leaves in the wind – briefly occupying his attention before disappearing into nothingness. Distant images of people and scenes shadowed his subconscious.

Drifting deeper, color spilled into awareness. A serene setting of this room emerged. Outside the room, typical activities remained undisturbed as he floated through the office building. He became filled with dread while witnessing the Phoenix sitting at his desk discussing movements of trailers with the two suits who brought him to this room.

A violent eruption of mayhem ensued as rogglets flooded the building, rushing from all sides, breaking windows and busting down doors. They scurried down hallways in a frenzy, searching for something.

"Searching for me!" he said in alarm awaking from the trance. "Commerand is coming! But why is he looking for me? The ring! He must know I have the ring! I have to get out of here. Now!"

Trey slipped the ring back on his finger, then beat on the door yelling, "Hey! You have to let me out! They're coming! We're all in danger! You have to let me out!"

He received no response. He kept beating and yelling until his hand hurt.

"They aren't coming. I'll have to do it myself."

He placed the crystal sphere, rope from his pack

and the disk onto the desk. "How can I use these to escape? The rogglets will move fast when they get here. Maybe I can use this rope?"

He tied a section of the rope several inches off the floor just a few feet inside the doorway, securing it with the desk and a couch. He removed wall hangers from several framed pictures of which he uses to suspend another section of rope across the top of the doorway. He secured the desk chair precariously with the loose rope so that one of the legs hung just in the path of the door. After about an hour he finished his rudimentary traps.

While inspecting his work he heard dampened gun blasts then a thump on the back wall and several muffled screams.

"They're here!"

He rushed back to the desk replacing the sphere into a zipped pocket. As he reached for the disk, the door burst open. The chair above the door toppled onto the first two unwary assailants smashing them to the floor. Two more entering in behind tripped over the taunt rope stretched across the doorway. Trey grabbed the disk then easily hurdled over the collapsed bodies into the hallway. Gunshots rang in distant parts of the office space and outside the main building.

He sprinted toward the way the suits brought him but skidded to a stop seconds later as one of the Phoenix's suited cronies slammed lifelessly into the corner wall ahead. The body crumpled onto the stained carpet. Rogglets followed it around the corner toward Trey. He quickly spun around and ran in the other direction. He tic tac'd on the wall to avoid one emerging from his previous room. The rogglets that succumbed to Trey's traps joined the chase.

He turned the corner just as Commerand emerged from a far room, setting a brisk pace toward Trey.

In great surprise and fear he tried to stop but tripped on the rugged carpet hurling him uncontrollably into the air. He fell on his stomach several yards from Commerand. The disk propelled from his hand, bounced on the carpet, rolled past the undead sorcerer and finally settled against the far wall. Commerand seemed to be unconcerned with the artifact.

"Bring me the Eye of Kartho," rang the raspy voice as he continued to approach.

Trey was too frightened to understand that Commerand still believed he had it. He instinctively hid the hand bearing Moridon's ring.

"What eye? I don't have it!" Trey exclaimed.

"You insolent boy! Tell me where it is!"

"Why? Why should I?" Trey stalled hoping something miraculous would happen.

Commerand raised the staff, magically lifting Trey from the floor. He pulled the staff toward him. Trey floated with the movements. He forced Trey to look into cloudy dead eyes. The stench of rotting flesh molested Trey's gag reflex – he fought back a surge of vomit.

Commerand said, "IIIII muust have the eye to end thissss misery. IIII mussst free him so IIII can diiie along with this forsaken world! IIIII wiiill haaave it!"

Trey tore his eyes from Commerand's and yelled, "I don't have it!"

"Then you will die!" Commerand said definitively as he clutched the boys throat.

Trey caught a glimpse of the disk on the far side of the room. He closed his eyes, then said a silent prayer to be out of the grasp of this horrifying creature. The disk became focused in his mind. He imagined himself standing against the wall holding it. He held onto this image as he felt Commerand's skeletal fingers clinch like a vice. Trey fought with all his might to live. He never lost the hope he will escape. Trey opened his eyes to intensify his resistance only to find himself standing at the far wall with the disk grasped firmly in his hand.

Flabbergasted at his immediate freedom but not more so than Commerand who swiftly turned to continue the assault. Wide eyed and ready, Trey sprinted out of sight before Commerand could catch him with the powerful staff. Rogglets filed in the hallway toward Trey from the lobby. He dashed through a side door which led to a large warehouse full of freight containers. He ran down isles of stacked containers.

"What do I do?"

An explosion behind startled him out of the thought. Lyza and Karim along with several others dressed in white garb, armed with machine guns, emerged through the blasted hole.

"Lyza!"

"Trey! You escaped!" she said surprisingly.

"No! Not yet!" he replied.

"We have to get you to a safe place!"

"I'm with you there! Let's go!"

They turned to exit the warehouse but were met by a swarm of rogglets. Commerand along with several others approached from behind.

"What do we do, Lyza?" Trey said concerningly.

She looked at him gravely, "You need a weapon to protect yourself. Call the sword, Trey."

"What?"

"Call the sword. You need to use the sword."

"No! I'll die! We'll all die!"

"Put away the disk and call the sword!" she said more urgently as the assailants approached from all sides. "It will only harm you if connected with the disk!"

"Tell me, Lyza, if that really is your name, how do you know all this stuff?" he said accusatively.

"Not now, Trey! Call the sword!" she screamed as rogglets commanded by Commerand attacked.

"I don't know how!" screamed Trey.

Loud cracks from automatic weapons echoed off warehouse walls. The group surrounded Trey protecting him from the onslaught.

Trey closed his eyes.

"There are too many!" he heard a man scream in the distance.

Trey focused his mind on an image of himself holding the sword, then thought, *sword come to me*, over and over again. *Sword come to me. Sword come to me*, until he felt it's warm handle in his grasp. He thought it could burst into flames at any moment.

Rogglets broke through their defensive formation. Trey raised the sword slashing it down on one of the attackers. He spun upward from a crouched position slicing three more. He finally thrusted the flawless blade through another.

He tossed the lifeless body aside which cleared a hole for them to move further into the warehouse. The team spread out as they pelleted assailants with bullets. Rogglets infiltrated their tight formation scattering the group throughout the warehouse. Trey became lost in the maze of containers while desperately trying to reunite with the group.

He darted through several isles until coming to the end of a row.

"Maybe I can hide in one of these," he said as he studied the door of a large shipping container. He lifted the latch with a bang, raised the counter-weighted door which pulled from his hand rolling all the way up. He fell off the back consumed with intense horror as he met hundreds of dead eyes filling the enclosed space.

"Zombies! Oh my god!" he screamed scurrying

away from the horrendous sight while maintaining eye contact as if to avoid a surprise attack.

Undead glassy eyes were unfocused and unmotivated to move the standing listless decaying bodies that softly bumped and swayed in place.

"These are Khaitu's zombies! This is part of his army! The Phoenix has them ready to deploy!"

Shots rang throughout the cavernous building as Trey regained his footing. He backed up to get a better look at the warehouse full of containers stacked three high. Shocked by the sheer number of containers, realizing each may be packed full of deathly servants brought a tremendous sickness to his stomach. He sat amid a strong spell of dizziness.

"This will not end with us escaping from this warehouse," he said to himself with an unfocused stare while coming to terms with the decision he has made. "I have to end it. It has to be now."

He placed the sword on a crisscrossed lap. He closed his eyes. He transferred the time relic from ring finger to index finger.

He drew his mind to an image of the small village from his dreams. He imagined the thicket, the woman selling pottery, the children playing an ancient version of street soccer. He imagined standing next to the woman and child. He felt the sand in his toes, he smelled the sweet aroma of freshly baked dough.

Trey slowly circled his right hand above his head. He sensed centuries passing before him. His fingers stroked an illusory edge of a bewildering universe as if he were in a shallow well only needing to pull himself out of the abyss of life's unbroken challenges. Carefully, he pulled down the veil of time to envelop himself in a contorting theory of entangled madness. Closed eyes revealed within his inner vision, vivid images of twisting stars in a kaleidoscope of brilliant colors. As his hand rested on the floor of the warehouse, the images and colors faded. A stale warmness engrossed his body. Darkness prevailed; urgency ensued.

257

Birth of a Prophecy

"He's in Dahshur," Moridon, a tall dark-skinned man in dark blue robes with an aged face said to Olerand. "This risk is great, Master. We must focus on the ceremony. These people's lives are miniscule to what Khaitu will do if he gains immortality."

"This is something I must do. I must try to save them. I was afraid he wouldn't make it, dear friend. I thought all was lost. I have very little time to put things in order. I will return later to meet with Khaitu this evening."

"Very well, Master."

"Palonis! Prepare a boat for travel," he said in the local language.

~ ~

Trey opened his eyes to find himself sitting on a

woven wooden rug resting on a sandy floor in a tiny dark building. Light peaked through cracks in the structure.

No. Not any building. This is someone's home, he thought.

The sword remained resting on his lap. "Thank goodness these passed with me," he said to himself referring to the artifacts travelling with him. "The theory of quantum physics holds through time! An object from separate instances of time can be in two places at once. Nick's gonna get a kick out of that one."

He replaced the Roberton attire with a wrapped linen garment secured by a cloth belt over his pants, formed a make-shift sheath to conceal the sword on his back, grabbed an interesting looking piece of bread, then emerged into the bright midday sunlight.

"This is all wrong," Trey said anxiously as he looked around. "Where's the thicket? Where's the cliff? This village is way too big. What did Olerand say? Focus on where you want to be. Did he say where or when?"

An elderly dark-skinned woman carrying a slender clay pitcher gave him a strange look as she overheard his conversation to himself. He offered an embarrassed smile before turning right down the narrow pathway.

"He must have said *when* because I am clearly not *where* I need to be." His stomach teemed with anxiousness at the thought that he was in the wrong place and that he made another big mistake.

After walking nearly half a mile down a sandy street lined with small clay buildings, a river came into view.

"Ok. That must be the Nile. I followed that North from the portal to the Phoenix's warehouse. Cairo is just north of the warehouse and the place I need to be, according to the eagle dream, is west of Cairo or northwest of here, assuming I'm right to assume I only traveled through time and not geography.

"I hope I have enough time to get there," he said to himself with great concern in his voice.

He walked northwest for fifteen minutes through a casual ancient city – a city that would accurately represent any he had previously seen in textbooks. Dark-skinned people of all ages and sizes were hocking wares, providing services and loitering about. A small, thin boy standing under a tall palm tree seemed to be offering him a bracelet made of stones and tiny shells.

He strolled through a bazaar admiring the intricate detail on clay pottery when his eyes were drawn to a familiar face. He ran to the man, nearly knocking down another on the way.

"Karim! Is that you?" Trey looked closer at the startled man's face. "It's you!" he exclaimed again pulling away the surprised man's turban. "It's you Karim! Oh my god it's you! How can this be!"

The man replied in an indecipherable language.

"What? What did you say? I don't understand!"

Karim continued to speak, then motioned to his friend. They exchanged a few words while looking precariously at the unfamiliar boy in hysterics.

"Of course! You don't speak English yet! Come with me!" he said elated while grabbing Karim's shirt. Karim was reluctant and pulled away.

"You have to come with me," he said with urgency and a hopeful glare. He pulled at Karim's sleeve again who looked once more at his friend then followed Trey.

Trey led a more curious Karim to a secluded area behind a tarped structure.

He faced Karim and with a serious face and voice he said, "You don't understand a word I'm saying and I'm not real sure why I am still talking."

Karim watched attentively at the young boy try to convey to him a very important message.

Realizing the futility in more words, Trey stepped away from Karim. He looked to make sure no one else was around. With wide eyes he presented with two hands the sword from behind his back, then said, "I need to see Olerand."

Karim jumped backward covering his mouth releasing a flurry of incomprehensible words. Panicked eyes spelled the acknowledgement Trey was after. Karim urged him to replace the sword then briskly led him through the village to a one roomed square structure standing nearly fifteen feet tall. It looked like a meeting place – like a conference room – lined with stacks of sand colored bricks Trey assumed were used as chairs. He ushered everyone out before facing Trey with a serious expression.

Trey looked into the eyes of the frightened man, then pointed at himself while saying, "Trey Roberts." Next, he opened his hands palms up. He pulled them to his chest while forming a claw shape with his fingers saying, "want." He then said, "Olerand."

Karim stood in immense disbelief for several minutes. He repetitively shifted his hand from his mouth to his hip to his forehead – deep in frenzied thought. He looked as if he were doing an Egyptian version of the macarena.

Trey became uncomfortable – unsure of what would happen next. He started fidgeting with his makeshift tunic – flopping and flapping the fabric to and fro.

Suddenly, Karim nodded then quickly left the room. He instantly returned ushering Trey to sit. He held outstretched palms, indicating for Trey to stay. Trey did as commanded – for a little while.

~ ~

Karim ran back to his friend, then said urgently, "I need a boat. Fast."

His friend replied in a jovial voice, "They are very expensive. You could never afford one in three lifetimes."

"No. I just need to borrow one. I have to get to Memphis as fast as possible."

"Why would you go there?"

"I must find someone that can help the boy."

"What's the deal with the boy? He was speaking a strange language. You should not help him. The gods would not approve."

"I don't have time for lectures, Femi. Please help me."

Femi regarded his passionate friend then said, "I know someone that may take you to Memphis. Come with me."

"Thanks," he replied as they hurried toward the port.

They approached a shaggy bearded man in his early twenties loading items into a boat with a small square white sail hoisted upon a single mast. It was longer than a full-sized pick-up truck. When he saw Femi, he quickly approached with wide arms and a jubilant smile.

"Brother! How good is it to see you today?" said the man.

"It is very good to see you too!" Femi said grasping the man in a warm embrace.

"Adom, my good friend, this is Karim. He needs to get to Memphis in a hurry. Can you help him?"

"It is very nice to meet you, Karim!" he said embracing Karim in a side hug. "I am heading that way now. I just have that last container to load."

"This one?" Karim asked as he picked up the last container.

"Yes. Thank you for your help. Please set it next to the others."

Karim loaded the container and remained in the boat made of tightly tied papyrus reeds. Adom bid farewell to Femi then joined Karim in the boat. They pushed off into the swollen river.

~ ~

Trey sat in the room for what seemed like hours. He became shifty and bored. He drew the sword and role played a pirate in a great battle.

"Arrrg! Ya slimy cuss. How dare ye try ta steal my booty!"

He sliced and jabbed a few times then laughed at himself before he sat back on the sandy brick.

He set the sword aside and tapped a beat on the brick. With both hands working as drumsticks, he sang under his breath, "Whoa- Oh! Livin on a pray-er! Take my hand uh uh-uh uh-uh uhhh-uh!"

After the song he laid on the floor and tossed the gold coin many times into the air – challenging himself to catch it every time.

He heard a commotion outside and sat up. "What was that?" He looked at the carpet draped door. Shadows peeked underneath.

He laid back down but didn't throw the coin. He sat up again and looked toward the door as someone shuffled by. He stood and moved closer. He edged his ear near the door. He heard voices of several people passing by as he zipped the coin in a pocket.

"Maybe I'll just take a peek." He moved closer then said, "No. I better stay in. Karim said to stay."

He sat back down on the brick and stared at the door. He heard a group of kids run by. "They sounded like they were having fun. I wonder what they're doing."

He stood and moved back toward the door. He lifted the edge of the carpet door open, but no one was in sight. He closed it again and sat back down.

He stood again and paced around the room, minding the door each time he passed. The third time around he peeked again.

Nothing was there.

He opened it more to reveal nothing.

He peeped his head around the door to look down the other side of the road which was clear.

He stepped out.

The narrow road was clear. He relaxed as the sun warmed his face. He closed his eyes to passing thoughts of the outrageous circumstances that brought him to this moment.

A startling commotion broke out far to his right. He looked to see an elderly woman with a slender clay pitcher standing with a well-dressed man. She looked right at Trey and pointed as she fervently told the man something. The man seemed surprised at what she said then raised his hand in the air and yelled something in Trey's direction. Trey looked behind to find no one behind him. He looked back to see the man briskly walking in his direction. The woman stayed behind with a troublesome smile.

"Oh crap! That must be a policeman. What could she have possibly said that would get me in trouble?"

Trey started for the door but remembered he left the sword out in the open. He then casually crossed onto the path across from the door. The policeman yelled again as Trey ducked out of sight.

Trey ran.

He turned down a tiny pathway that opened to a larger road. He turned left and sprinted toward a group of structures. The policeman hollered loudly as he gained on the frightened boy.

Trey hurdled a heavy barrel then turned again down an alleyway. He dodged hanging cloths as three small children watched him pass. The children smiled and chased after.

Trey looked behind at the cackling kids and said, "What's the deal? Now I have kids chasing me?" "Who else wants to join in on the fun?" he said out loud as he passed a group of people sitting under a wooden shelter.

The policeman yelled again and a man from the sitting group jumped up and joined the chase.

Trey looked back as the new man shouted incomprehensible words at him. "I was kidding! Please stop chasing me!" Trey frantically shouted.

The new man ducked down an alleyway to the left while the policeman overtook the children as he continued to lessen Trey's lead.

Trey turned left at a T intersection and just as he approached another crossing the new man emerged from the alley on the left and blindsided Trey in a magnificent tackle. They both tumbled diagonally up under the eave of someone's home.

As the policeman approached Trey said while still on his back, "What'd I do? What'd I do wrong?"

The policeman grabbed him by the sleeve, said some angrily toned words, snatched him to his feet and drug him down the sandy street.

"What have I done? I've messed everything up. There's no way I'll make it to the village in time."

~ ~

After several minutes on the river, Adom said, "Tell me, Karim, what brings you to Memphis?"

"How well do you know the city? Do you know many people there?" Karim replied, avoiding the question.

"I've been running supplies to the royal complex for twenty years. I began with my father who knew King Ronodan well."

"He really knew the Great King?"

"Yes! My grandfather was there when Ronodan emerged from the Earth. I still remember his words today after seeing the king in all his splendor. He said when approached, Ronodan asked only for water and shelter. My grandfather took him into his home as one of his own. The king told him, 'on this day forth, your family will be the supplier to my kingdom. Recognizing he was in the presence of a truly benevolent king, he gave his allegiance at that moment. Our family never wavered to the kingdom until Khaitu came to power. Since then, my business has nearly diminished entirely."

"You are still close with the king and his people?"

"What do you mean?" Adom asked with a concerned look.

"I need to find someone within the royal elite."

"Those outside the royal elite aren't welcome within the complex. I'm not sure I can help you get inside. Who are you looking for?"

Karim hesitated then said, "Olerand. I need to speak with Master Olerand."

"That's impossible," Adom said briskly. "No one

sees Master Olerand and he never leaves the complex." His voice became ominous and deep. "Many say he is a demon that is under the control of Khaitu. They say he is heartless and will kill for no reason at all. Also, if he kills you, you are lucky. He is said to have evil powers granted directly from Set, the god of violence and chaos, with which he will curse your soul for eternity."

"I have heard those same rumors. Nevertheless, I need to reach him."

"I cannot help you. Even if I knew how to get to him, we would never be able to get through the gates. What in the name of Ra could you possibly need with that evil creature?"

"I can't say, but I believe I have a very important message that will somehow change the world as we know it. I believe it with all my heart."

Adom's stare seemed to last several minutes. He looked down shaking his head.

"I can get you to the gates, you'll be on your own after that....unless....It can't be," Adom said in astonishment. "The gods may be looking favorably upon you, friend."

Adom ruddered the small boat to the left on route to intercept an inconspicuous boat sailing upriver.

"What are you doing? I am in a great hurry!" Karim said anxiously.

"Easy, my friend. Ahead of us is a royal vessel only used for discrete travel. I have not seen it out since the fall of King Ronodan. The coincidence of your urgent mission and this vessel out today is highly suspect. If you say your message is intended for Olerand himself and is of great importance to our people, then maybe the gods have also placed Olerand in play as they have you, for the specific purpose of meeting on these rural waters."

As they drew near, two royal guards emerged from

the cabin brandishing spears. The guard on the right said in a strong forceful tone while raising the long spear in an aggressive position, "Turn away!"

Startled by the forthcoming attack from the previously unnoticed guards, Adom quickly steered the boat away.

"No! I have to speak with him!" he said to Adom. Realizing Adom's reluctance, Karim yelled across the slowly moving river, "Master Olerand! I have to speak with you!" "Master Olerand! Trey Roberts needs to speak with you!" Karim cried hopelessly.

One of the guards briefly returned to the cabin before reemerging saying, "Peasant boat! Come to us!"

"What have you done! You imbecile! You have surely killed us!" said Adom in a terrified and angry voice.

Adom pulled the small craft alongside the royal vessel, then pleaded, "Please forgive my passenger. He does not know what he says. He – "

"Hush!" the guard said stopping Adom's appeals. "You! Master Olerand will see you," he said to Karim.

Karim hurriedly boarded the royal boat.

The guard said to Adom, "Be gone to finish your duties to the kingdom!"

Adom set off with the command, meeting Karim's frightened eyes one last time before he disappeared into the cabin.

The elderly man didn't fill Karim with dread or concern. He noticed a feeling of comfort and welcoming.

"Please sit, young man," Olerand said.

Karim did as directed.

"Why do you seek my counsel on this fateful day?"

"Master, I met a boy today. A very strange boy that speaks a strange language." He hesitated then said, "The boy has asked to meet with you."

"And this boy's name is Trey Roberts?"
"Yes, Master."
"You will take me to him."
"Yes, Master."

Upon reentering the port, Olerand magically disguised himself to look like a laborer. Pale wrinkly skin turned dry, dark and weathered. Long grey hair shrunk into ridged barely noticeable stubble. His trim beard smoothed away into a square jaw.

They emerged from the boat, then hurried to the building where Karim previously left Trey.

At the door before entering Karim said to Olerand, "Shall I leave you two alone?"

"No, dear Karim. We have much to discuss."

They entered the room to find it empty aside from the sword lying on the floor. "Trey! Where are you!" Karim said in the local language.

"Master. He isn't here. I left him just a short time ago. I don't know where he could have gone. I fear something bad has happened."

"It is most urgent that you find him, Karim. Go now. Waste no time!"

"Yes, Master."

Karim burst through the door. He looked both ways before heading toward the busy part of the village.

Along the way he passed a group of people, "Have any of you seen a small boy? Maybe one you wouldn't recognize?"

They all shook their heads no.

He hurried toward city center hoping Trey wandered into a populated area out of curiosity. He approached a young mother and asked, "Have you seen a new boy in town? He would be wearing strange garments over his legs,"

She replied no and turned away.

"Argg! Where could he be!"

He turned to find a child tugging on his shirt. It was Aleki, one of his former students."

"Hey Aleki. I'd love to play but I don't have time."

"You're looking for the boy with strange hair, aren't you?"

"Yes! Yes, I am. Do you know where he is?"

"He's in jail," the young boy said with a frown.

"Jail? Why would you think that?"

"Officer Bacchus chased him through the village. Me and my brother ran with him for a while, but they were too fast."

"Jail! Oh no!"

The child said as Karim was leaving, "Do you think they'll cut off his hands?"

Karim quickly turned and said, "No! No. Why would you think that?" He dashed off without receiving Aleki's answer.

He rushed across the village to the guard house. He entered to find Trey sitting in the corner while two guards and an elderly woman discussed Trey's predicament.

Trey stood and said, "Karim! Please get me out of here!"

Everyone looked curiously at the boy with the strange language.

Trey watched as Karim entered an intense discussion with the guards. Karim turned toward the woman as one of the guards pointed. The woman lividly responded with words as well as pulled on her shirt and put her hand into her mouth like she were eating something.

The other guard entered by saying something to Karim, pointing at Trey and then back at the woman. The woman nodded as if in agreement.

Karim disagreed with a loud voice and his hands raised forward as if saying stop. He then looked as if he were pleading as he looked back to Trey with soft eyes and then back to the guards.

One of the guards looked as if he asked Karim something then they all turned toward the woman. She replied with eager words and a smile. He then turned back to Karim who pulled a cloth sack from the inside of his pocketless shirt, looked inside then shook his head no to the guards.

As it looked like the conversation had been settled with Karim's head bowed, Trey finally caught on. He fished for something in his pockets then rushed to Karim. Karim turned toward Trey with sad eyes. Trey then grabbed his hand and placed in it the gold coin that just days ago Karim had given him in Egypt thousands of years later.

Karim's flabbergasted look ensured Trey read the situation correctly. Karim presented the gold coin to the woman who seemed ecstatic to receive it. She quickly left the building. Karim addressed the guards apologetically. He returned to Trey, leaned over, said a few encouraging words Trey couldn't understand then led him back to meet Olerand.

"Olearand! It's really you! I can't believe you are actually standing here!" Trey said as he entered the building.

Karim quickly looked to Olerand noticing he returned to his former self.

"Yes, Trey Roberts. You have achieved a great deal

making it this far. But the true test of bravery awaits, and we are desperate for time."

Trey picked up the sword, regarded it a moment and placed it the sheath on his back.

Karim looked at them both and said in the local dialect, "I can't understand a word you two are saying."

"Yes. Indeed," Olerand replied. He clasped his hands over Trey's ears. He chanted a short phrase that was indecipherable to both Karim and Trey. He then said, "That should do it."

"Do what?" Trey replied.

"You can speak our language. What was that other you were using earlier?" Karim asked to Trey.

"No. I don't speak your language but now you can speak mine. How is that so? I'm talking like I normally do. Aren't I?"

"You can now understand the local dialect as well as many others," Olerand said to Trey.

"Really? That's what you did with the ear thingy?"

"Yes," Olerand said proudly.

"That's pretty cool. It sounds just like you're speaking English!" Trey said excitedly.

"It will be a valuable skill in your future journeys," Olerand said.

"Future journeys? I don't think so! I'm done with travelling. I'm never leaving the house again!" he said. He continued in a depressed voice, "That is, if I ever make it back home. What do I do now? This is not the place in our dream. I'm far away. Am I too late?"

"No. You would not be here if you were too late. We still have time."

"I don't understand. Is the boy in the dream, me?"

"No. The boy in the dream is my son and the woman's name is Sharina. She is my wife."

Karim looked at Olerand in astonishment.

"Khaitu forced me to look upon the ring to the future of his kingdom, but as I said before, it only shows your heart's greatest desire. My greatest desire is my wife and child. The ring showed me their demise by the fire of Khaitu's sword – the very one you stow upon your back. I am risking the lives of many, including your life and my eternal damnation to save them."

Trey unconsciously felt the blade on his back then said, "I've seen lots of movies about time travel and they all say interfering with the past leads to massive time distortions or other destructive unforeseen events."

"But don't you see, young boy? The future already reflects your actions today."

"The future already – what? Are you saying...? That's what you were talking about when you mentioned your family and my ancestors! You're my ancestor?"

"Yes, Trey. We were able to connect primarily through our lineage. Had my family not survived, you would not exist to save them."

"That's some crazy chicken and egg paradox," Trey said sitting back on a woven rug on the floor.

"Time is not paradoxical. It is as we weave our instances together to form the continuum we experience. Time only exists when we perceive it with our minds and consciousness."

"It's dead and alive at the same time," Trey mumbled.

"What was that?" Karim asked Trey. "Did you say something about being dead?"

"It is a theory by a famous physicist. Schrodinger theorized that if you placed a cat in a box with something that could kill it, it would be both dead and alive at the same time. It would only be either when the box is opened to perceive the animal's state."

"So, in a sense, it is both dead and alive?" Karim

responded in a confused manner.

"Exactly," replied Trey.

"Karim. Please gather two camels for Trey's journey," Olerand said handing Karim a bag of gold pieces. He took the bag then quickly left the room.

Returning his attention to Olerand he said, "Ok. Let's get this straight, I have to go do something that I've already done?"

"Yes. You have perceived it in your mind. You know what to do," said Olerand.

"No!" Trey panicked. "No, I don't! The dream was incomplete. I tried to tell you that last time we spoke. I only found the woman and child. I don't know what I did to save them. That's why I sent Karim for you! You have to tell me what to do!"

"I know not what you did. I only witnessed the destruction. Trey, I must implore, if you don't remember what you did and fail, you will not exist. You have to remember. You must succeed in this instance or the entire time continuum as you know it will change, and..." he looked away with a miniscule tear in his eye, "my sole purpose for existing will die a fiery death."

"So, I'm once again on my own."

"I'm afraid so," replied Olerand. "You must be off. You have a long journey ahead. But first, I will give you this." Olerand handed Trey a small black orb that was soft and cold to the touch. It was small enough to fit into his closed hand. "Smash this and all telepathically controlled entities will be temporarily incapacitated."

"Great! This will definitely be handy," replied Trey with a smile as he secured it in a pocket.

"You must protect them, Trey," Olerand commanded.

"I will. I will do everything I can."

Karim returned and said, "I have the camels."

"Tie them together," Olerand directed.

"Trey. Have you ever ridden a camel?" asked Karim.

"I've been on a horse."

"What's a horse?" Karim asked.

"Seriously? You've never seen a horse?"

"No."

"It's sort of like a small camel without a hump."

"And you ride them?"

"I have, but not often."

"I am interested to learn more about the strangeness of the future."

"Don't worry, buddy. You'll learn plenty about the future," Trey said with a knowing smile.

Karim and Olerand in disguise walked Trey to the northern edge of the village. The fastest way will be to take a north by northwest route through the desert. All you need to do is keep Memphis and the plateau to your east and you should easily arrive at the village.

Trey looked up at Olerand, then said, "I don't think I can do this. I just don't know what to do. I feel like I'm going to my death."

"That may very well be so, but you have no choice. No one can do this for you," Olerand replied. "You must save our family. Please be careful. Act swiftly and confidently."

"Thanks, Master Olerand. Will I see you again?"

"No. I'm afraid this is our last encounter in this timeline."

Trey rushed to hug him tightly.

"Now be gone, boy! Time is not on your side!" Olerand commanded.

"Good luck, Trey!" Karim said. "I hope to see you

again!"

"If I make it through this, I'm certain you will!"

Karim lifted Trey onto the lead camel, then tapped it on the rear to get it going. The camel let out a loud gurgling groan before it eased off with the other trailing behind.

Karim and Olerand watched for nearly ten minutes as Trey rode off into the horizon. Afterward, Olerand turned to Karim, then said, "Now for your part."

Karim returned a curious expression before they walked back to the house.

Believe Before You See

Trey travelled in a dusty desert pathless direction for several hours deep in thought. He replayed vivid dreams in his mind, desperately looking for the answer that would save him from impending demise. His thoughts travelled from the dreams to his friends to his mom. Sadness filled his heart as he ached to be with her again. Sadness like watching the last fading petal fall from a lonesome rose which once held tremendous beauty.

If I could have but hugged Mom one last time. Had she known that would be the last time, would she have loved me any greater? If I could have spoken to dad – I miss him so much.

Soft tears streamed down his face. Unashamed in solitude, he let them fall onto the scorched desert as he stared thoughtlessly in deep sorrow. The muffled thud, thud, thud of the camel's steps in the sand played a backbeat to his heart's desire.

He woke from the daze with a camel's groan. He

noticed the sun remained to his upper left as the plateau formed far to the east. It brought an ominous feeling as he recalled the dream upon the cliff's edge.

"The sun is just higher than what I remember in the dream! I have to get moving! I may have less than an hour before the village is ravaged!"

He prodded the camels to pick up speed. Setting an easy trot, he settled back into the saddle scanning anxiously ahead for signs of the village.

~ ~

Ruminating in his chamber room, Olerand awaited the call when a knock at the door broke his meditation.

"SahRa requests your presence!" commanded a harsh voice.

Olerand stood, replaced his hood, then walked with the messenger to a garden just outside the royal quarters.

"Master Olerand," addressed King Khaitu standing nearly seven feet tall with a full thick wavy black beard which tapered gracefully to a rounded point several inches below his chin. His open tunic embroidered with light weight black armor on the shoulders and sleeves, revealed a light brown chest covered to the neck in ancient hieroglyphs that seemed to shift with each muscular movement. He was striking as a man – an evil and powerful handsome man.

"Yes, SahRa?"

"Come with me. We have much to discuss."

"As you wish, SahRa."

Khaitu spoke with elegance in a low toned voice as

they walked through the lively plots. Long flowing black hair trailed down sculpted cheeks as he spoke downward to Olerand. "These vegetables, Olerand, they grow in the dirt I provide. They consume the nutrients I feed them. They survive on the light I allow to penetrate them. These vegetables grow because I permit them to grow. They live because I deem it possible for them to do so. For that, they are grateful to be eaten by my people. That is their purpose, to be eaten. Otherwise, they would not exist. I would not allow them to live if they served no benefit to the kingdom."

Olerand walked in stride without acknowledging Khaitu's words with emotion or reaction.

"Furthermore, this garden is like my kingdom. It is orderly. Each plot has a specific purpose that serves the greater good of the kingdom. However, it requires regular pruning. The dead and dying must be removed for the whole to survive and prosper. More importantly, if an invasive species, such as the lotus weed were to proliferate, the threat of it rapidly spreading throughout the remaining plots is great. Therefore, it must be plucked and destroyed."

The imposing figure turned to Olerand with blazing yellow eyes, then continued, "There is a lotus weed emerging in Saqqara. It wishes to grow and spread revolution throughout the kingdom." He paused, then said with a wide sinister grin, "You and I will go there and pluck it from the garden." He placed a gauntleted hand onto Olerand's depressed shoulder. They vanished in a wispy black fog.

~ ~

Trey's eyes widened when the village came into view. As he drew near, the thicket became prominent on the west side.

"Hopefully, I'll remember what to do when I get there."

He spurred the camels to a run. Amid multiple bellows and groans from the galloping ungulates, Trey contemplated his rapidly approaching fate.

He entered the thicket from the south. After dismounting and tying the lead camel to a tree, he slowly approached the edge closest to the village.

A peaceful day permeated the bustling village sitting a football field away.

He looked back at a slowly sinking sun and said, "I don't have much time. Think, Trey! What do I do! What did I do?"

He spread the few items he possessed onto the ground, then said in frustration, "None of this stuff will help me save those people or defeat Khaitu!"

He sat before the items, closed his eyes in failure, then said in exasperation, "I've come this far just to fail now? I should've let Commerand kill me. Then this whole thing would be done!"

He closed his eyes and held his head in capitulation. He opened them and said, "Wait a minute. I have to first believe it before I can see it," he said in a hopeful tone. "That's it! I have to believe before I see!" He stood up and said, "I hope this works!"

He recalled the dream where he followed the wolf through the village and tried to remember each intricate detail.

"Ok, Trey! You can do this! Let's go save your ancestors from a scorching death!" he said attempting to motivate himself to action.

~ ~

From a cloud of black smoke, Khaitu and Olerand emerged before the lively desert village. Olerand's heart sank. He didn't expect to arrive so quickly.

He thought to himself, *I am afraid Trey had not enough time to prepare. My family is doomed if I can't stop this madness.*

"SahRa," Olerand said wisely, "I will go into the town and make an example of the dissenters? That will be lesson enough to dissuade anyone else to plan a rebellion. We will spread the word to the surrounding villages. No one will question your wisdom and power."

"No, Olerand," Khaitu said calmly as he stared upon the village. "That is not enough. I will make this village a graveyard. When I am finished, it will only be suitable for the dead for millennia to come."

"But, SahRa," Olerand said maintaining his composure, "I must implore you reconsider." These people are necessary for your projects. This village's laborers are currently assigned to your monument. We cannot afford the time lost with their absence."

"I have instructed Palomis to activate laborers from northern territories. They are arriving at the camps tomorrow."

"SahRa! These people are valuable to your kingdom!"

"These people will die, and their ashes will scatter in the wind. This place, located so close to Memphis, will be an enduring reminder of the fate of those who plot against me."

Khaitu turned cold evil eyes upon the meek looking Olerand, "Your incessant advice is becoming aggravating. Tell me, dear friend, what connection do you have with those insolent humans?"

Surprised at the accusation but thankful for the delay he replied, "I have no connection with them. I find humans interesting and useful. They are resourceful and moderately capable of solving problems on their own. I think it best to have as many around as possible to ensure the viability of your great kingdom."

"Intelligent you say? Look at them down there, muddling around in their own self-worth. Each of them wishes to be better than the next. If given the opportunity, any would strike down the next to gain an advantage. It happens every day in these miserable villages. Their quest to be better than their brother, sister and friend naturally divides them. When they are divided, they are simple to rule.

"However, Olerand, if they were to organize. If they were to plan and work together, they could easily overthrow us no matter what magic we used upon them. Their numbers are too great. But they won't do that as long as they believe they are separated from each other by family lines, village boundaries, social or economic status. That is the purpose of designing their social system in this manner. That is why we benefit some over others. We create envy, they create the separation. We create the illusion of protection, regardless of the hardships we actually put them through, and they accept the inordinate rules. Intelligent they are not. Otherwise, they would work together for the benefit of themselves and their race as a whole regardless of where they live, work, worship or play."

"I see," Olerand searched for words, "and you believe there is a group within this village that intends to organize?"

Khaitu turned his massive body to face his

conscripted sorcerer. He looked upon him with such force that any mortal would have been crushed. "They have already organized, and the weed has spread to the upper ranks of my cabinet. The humans in this village are but a distraction from the greater purpose you serve. I summoned you into my service for a single task. That time is now threatened due to your weakness for a human. Tell me, Olerand. What were you doing in Dahshur today?"

Startled by the unexpected knowledge of his surreptitious activities but maintained a calm composure Olerand plead, "Surely you would not annihilate all those people for rumor and conjecture?"

"These people are of no concern to me nor the wretched souls in Dahshur. It is too late for mere humans to rise against me. My time as a mortal has come. My only focus is the red moon ceremony. You must complete the assignment. After which, you will return to her in the spirit world," he said coldly as he removed, from a waist scabbard, the sword with completed disk firmly mounted in the pommel.

Khaitu's face and skin dimmed to charcoal as the sword erupted into a dark red and orange blaze. Yellow eyes turned jet black. His hair and beard became alit in flames angled in the same direction of each strand. His body was consumed in a fiery hell.

Olerand rapidly retreated several steps to avoid the immense heat.

"SahRa! You mustn't!"

Khaitu never heard the words as he was consumed with destruction and mayhem. He raised the flaming sword.

~ ~

Trey took a deep breath facing the items. He turned toward the village said "twenty" then sprang into a run.

"Nineteen," Trey said as he dashed across the desert. "Eighteen – seventeen – sixteen." He entered the village. "Fifteen," he said out loud as he passed children kicking a ball. "Fourteen – thirteen," as he rushed through the bazaar. He hurdled a group of chickens that were too slow to move out of his way. "Twelve," as he passed the laughing man and an argument over a bag of grain. "Eleven," he said uneasily as he was losing his breath when he turned left past a woman selling pottery.

"I'm too late!" he shrieked as he saw the great flaming object in the distance. The woman and child were just ahead. He ran with all his might. Each step propelled him farther and faster as he used every ounce of might to push his muscles to their maximum. "Ten!" he yelled as he slid in front of the startled and immensely frightened woman and infant like a baseball player stealing home plate. The baby cried furiously.

"Olerand sent me! You have to trust me!" he cried.

The woman looked at him with terrified eyes but nodded in agreement.

"Nine – eight," he said turning toward the assault. The flaming object erupted into a brilliant light. Instinctively, Trey unsheathed the sword. He held it out as if defending a downward strike just before the melting ball of plasma engulfed the village.

~ ~

"HAHAHAHA!" the flaming demon roared at his moment of devastation.

Olerand fell to his knees in disbelief. Never had he seen such an atrocious example of power from Khaitu since the annihilation of King Ronodan and his army. But this time Olerand had a personal attachment to the destruction. Sheer horror pervaded his soul at how effectively the sea of molting plasma consumed the village. Shrieks and screams faded into pops and snaps like a campfire on a cold night. The old sorcerer closed his eyes and wept for his lost loves.

Continuing to laugh in exhilaration, Khaitu sustained the raging torrent.

~ ~

Trey held firm a clear image in his mind of the storm of lava deflecting from his sword away from the village,

"Seven!"

The woman and infant screamed behind him. His arm wobbled, slowly receding to the volcanic flood. He supported it with the other at the wrist.

"Six!"

"Five!"

The melting heat became unbearable. His arms bent visibly at the elbows.

"Four!"

The image of the city in his mind faded to a small protective ball around him and his dependents. He weakly held unsteady ground.

"Three!"

The roaring blaze rushed over and around them drowning out all other sounds.

"Two!"

His feeble arms wavered. Heat ravaged his body. Flames licked his hands and arms in excruciating strokes. The horrible stench of burned skin and hair saturated his nostrils.

"Ooone!"

He was unable to focus. He lost the image in his mind. Consciousness faded. He collapsed.

Courage

The roar subsided. Trey laid on the ground surrounded by trees and bushes. A baby screaming and a woman sobbing became more and more present as he regained consciousness.

He rolled his head to see the woman and infant unharmed by the blaze. He rolled his head toward the village to find it engulfed in a lake of fire.

He cried profusely – unconcerned with the throbbing pain from burns throughout his body.

With tears still draining down his face, he turned to the woman and placed a blistered red hand over her mouth, "You must be quiet. He can't know we're here."

She looked at him with wide light brown understanding eyes. She controlled her sobbing to a low muffle but couldn't stop the tears. She immediately fed the infant to calm it down while she shakily rocked back and forth.

Trey held them both with his eyes closed as the

destruction continued for several more seconds. A cloud of black smoke originating at the source of the fusillade signaled the end of the assault.

Trey released the woman and gazed at the disk in his hand. He peered out upon the slowly blackening village. Realizing nothing could have survived he wailed in a river of tears.

"I couldn't save them! I'm so sorry! I tried but I couldn't save them!" he moaned to the woman uncontrollably. "Please forgive me!" he continued. She pulled him close and held him as if he were her own child. "Please forgive me," he whimpered into her arms.

~ ~

Trey helped Sharina and her child onto a camel. He climbed aboard his and they set out on a slow southeast journey toward Dashur.

They were warmly greeted by Karim upon reaching Dahshur. Trey's former major burns, now minor injuries, were treated by an old shaggy black-haired woman. He changed into a less charred wrapped cloth shirt and belt similar to the fabric he wore before – it hung well below his waist. His pants remained mostly intact with only a few small burn holes.

Trey described in a flurry of tears, the fire and destruction of Saqqara and how everyone but the woman and infant perished.

"You were quite brave to face the challenge. I know no one with that kind of courage, including myself. I will personally see to the protection and comfort of Sharina and her child. Will you stay with us for the night?

It's nearly dark out."

"I must return to my time. I have a lot to finish," Trey replied.

"Very well. Olerand wanted me to tell you one last thing before you leave us."

"Yeah? What was that?"

"He said to trust the queen. She will be a valuable guide in your future quest."

"The queen? You mean Lyza? The tall dark headed beautiful woman?"

"Yes. That is a good description," Karim said chuckling.

"I will and I do," he replied. "Will you walk with me to where I arrived?"

"Sure."

Sharina approached Trey. She grabbed him by the waist and lifted him in a great hug.

"Thank you for my baby's life, young boy. I am eternally grateful for your heroic acts." He hugged her back with no verbal reply.

Trey and Karim found the hut in which Trey arrived to be vacant. The old woman was nowhere in sight.

Trey sat on the floor. He looked up at Karim and said, "Thank you, Karim. Thank you for helping me today. You didn't question any part of it."

"You're welcome, Trey. But I had prepared for this day. You see I've been having these weird dreams."

Trey laughed, then said, "You too, huh? One more thing."

"What is it, Trey?"

"The next time you see me, please don't squeeze so hard."

"I don't see how we'll see each other again but Ok. I'll be careful," he said with a questioning look.

"Also, thanks in advance for letting me use your bike."

"Bike? What's a bike?"

"You'll see in a few thousand years," Trey said smiling.

Trey placed the ring on his right index finger, closed his eyes, raised the hand above his head, imagined re-emerging in the warehouse at the time he left. He pulled himself back into his proper timeline leaving Karim in astonishment at Trey's gradual top to bottom disappearance.

~ ~

"Trey! Get up, dude!" he heard Karim yell.

It didn't work, Trey thought. *I'll be trapped in the ancient past forever.* He opened his eyes to reveal a shipping container full of zombies and Karim urging him to move.

"Karim! It's you!"

"Yeah! Now move it!"

Trey stood then began running through the warehouse with Lyza, Karim and the remaining rescue force.

"What are you wearing, Trey? Where did you get that crazy shirt?"

Lyza's questioning ignited Trey into action.

"No! Wait!" Trey said sliding to a halt, his ancient tunic ruffled with the momentum.

He turned facing the oncoming horde.

"Trey! No! We must escape!" Lyza shrieked.

"I know! Come to me!"

"Puzzled at the change of confidence in the young boy, the team stopped. They flanked Trey on either side and behind.

"What are you doing, Trey! You're going to get us all killed!" yelled Karim.

Trey glanced at the concerned ageless man as he removed something from his pocket. Just as a surge of rogglets began a forceful attack they all fell to the ground motionless upon the busting of the cold black object in Trey's hand.

"Run for that exit! Now!" Trey pointed.

"What did you do!" Lyza exclaimed.

"I'll explain later, just run!"

"Now is the time you left?" Karim looked at Trey as if Trey were a dog dressed as a clown walking a tightrope or something else just as absurd. "You left for ancient Egypt during this fight?" he questioned Trey who responded with a shrug.

Karim shook his head in disbelief as they exited through a door to an outside parking lot. As they rushed past the blasted hole in the wall, Trey eyed Commerand emerging alone from the large warehouse. Trey stopped to face Commerand at a distance.

"I will free you, brother!" Trey said passionately.

Commerand taking advantage of the moment, lifted Trey off the ground with the staff then crashed him hard on the concrete pavement.

Lyza yelled, "Trey! Noooo!" as she and Karim turned to assist the young boy.

Commerand whisked them away with a wave of the magical staff.

Trey wearily stood. He straightened tall and unsheathed the sword.

Commerand continued the assault by hurling Trey into a parked semi-truck leaving a dent in a side panel. The sword dislodged from his grip and clanged loudly against the pavement several feet away.

Before Trey gained solid footing Commerand, still a distance away, reached with lanky fingers and raised him off the ground by his neck.

Trey fought for leverage but couldn't grab a foothold on the truck's smooth surface. He flailed his arms wildly. Commerand swiftly moved him left breaking the trucks' mirror with Trey's shoulder then slammed him hard against the door cracking the window with the back of his head.

Trey fought for air. Blood struggled to find a vital pathway through choked arteries. He grasped at his throat attempting to thwart the telekinetic clutch.

Freedom seemed hopeless as Commerand held Trey's near lifeless body in a death grip. Strength seeped from his muscles as consciousness became cloudy.

Commerand stood emotionlessly holding the staff erect with the base resting on the hot pavement and the other hand outstretched toward the feeble child.

Lyza and Karim watched helplessly from afar as the young boy began to give up. One of Trey's hands fell from his throat. Moments later the other. Trey dangled limply against the truck.

Trey's eyes searched feverishly for a solution but found none. He cut them desperately at Lyza. He reached out to her. His eyes bled with fear. She ran to try to help but Commerand held her away with the rise of the staff. He closed them briefly before opening quickly again to search once more. Finding no help, he closed them gently as his hopeful arm dropped to his side.

A whirlpool of colors grew bright behind closed eyes. Reds, blues and yellows spun into a brilliant white. Trey eased near the sharp but painless light. He reached for it. He wanted it badly – more than anything else he'd ever known. But it was too far. He tried to move closer, but it stayed at an unreachable distance. It pulsed with each beat of his heart – each time brighter and more spectacular. He reached again, screaming in his mind to grasp it. *Just a touch,* he thought, would make the world right. *Just a touch would end this pain.*

Commerand strengthened his grip, ensuring a quick end to the child that defied him – the child destined to set him free.

Trey admired the light. He became complacent and happy to be in its presence. He smiled inside as his body was nearly finished. He reached easily again to caress the light – to bathe in its glow. It pulsed brighter than any other time – like a supernova – to only happen once.

Trey found himself holding the light. Joy overcame his mind. He smiled physically. Then, a blade of recognition coursed through his soul.

Lyza watched as the sword rose, flashed a brilliant white then rocketed into Trey's hand. He then circled the sword around breaking Commerand's grip. Trey fell to the ground gasping for breath. He nearly caught his breath when he rose to a knee and defended another assault from the deathly sorcerer. Trey maintained his footing. He briefly conjured an image of the sword fending off Commerand's attacks.

Upon Commerand's next move, Trey successfully thwarted it with a matching wave of the sword. His eyes blazed as he sturdily rose to both feet and assumed an aggressive stance with the sword firmly in front. He looked through cold hazel eyes as Commerand was visibly surprised with the boy's successful resistance.

The dark sorcerer continued unrelentingly as he overpowered Trey into a slow retreat. Several rogglets regained consciousness and took to the battle.

The two danced an imaginary sword fight from a distance as Commerand attacked while Trey matched in defense.

"Look, Lyza!" Karim exclaimed.

"I know. He's starting to believe!"

"Over to that car! Quickly!" Karim said to Lyza.

In a brief moment, as Commerand sliced the great staff down, Trey countered with a side-step and a lateral lash that threw Commerand off balance enough for Trey to disengage the powerful sorcerer in time to tumble into the open back door of a slowly passing car.

Karim powered the car away from the warehouse, skidded onto the highway, then out of sight.

Home Again

"That was too close!" Trey exhaled. "You got there just in time!" He breathed heavily while holding his throat.

"I thought you were gone," Karim said to Trey who was sprawled out in the back seat.

"I think I was. I don't really know what happened."

"You did good, Trey," Karim said proudly.

Lyza added, "No, Trey. You did great! I've never seen that before. It was amazing."

"Why is it that…" Trey took a labored breath, "…everything amazing has to come from me nearly dying?"

Lyza laughed uneasily, "It seems that way doesn't it. We'll have to change that, now won't we?"

"Please do," Trey promptly replied.

They all shared a brief laugh.

Lyza continued, "We had no idea Commerand would be there. We thought we were just dealing with the

Phoenix's men," said Karim.

"What happened to him, The Phoenix?" Trey asked.

Lyza looked back over her seat and said, "We don't know. His men were mostly eliminated by the rogglets, so it seems that he was also surprised by the attack."

"I'm sure he ran away. That coward," Karim added.

"What about the loads of zombies?" Trey shivered at the memory.

"There's nothing we can do about them right now," Karim replied. "Commerand controls the warehouse. It'll be nearly impossible to penetrate while it's occupied by so many rogglets. By the way, good thing Olerand gave you that orb."

"So, you do remember after all those years? It was just this afternoon to me." Trey said laughing. "Oh my god, Karim, how are you still alive?" he continued in astonishment.

"All the protectors are ageless while in possession of the relics," he replied.

"You're a protector of a relic? Which one?"

Karim looked at Lyza who nodded in agreement. "He turned to where Trey could see him holding out the tiny staff charm attached to a titanium neck chain. "I have Olerand's." There are only two people who know about it besides me, You and Lyza."

"Don't you mean, Queen Raferti?" Trey said accusingly.

Lyza looked at Trey sternly.

"Don't you look at me like that!" Trey said in an angry tone. "You lied to me! You were...still are Khaitu's wife. How do we know you aren't just looking for the relics so you can free him yourself?"

"How did you find out who I am?"

"The Phoenix. He told me. He told me you wanted to free Khaitu."

"Do you trust him?"

"No. I don't guess so. But I do trust Olerand. He said I should trust you. So, I guess I will. Sorry, I yelled at you. It's been a hard day."

"Olerand?" Raferti said clearly surprised. "When did you speak with Master Olerand?"

"Who O? He and I go way back," Trey said laughing. He closed his eyes and said, "I just want my bed. I'm so tired."

She smiled and said, "Ok, Trey. Let's get you home."

~ ~

"Trey! It's time to go!"

"Just a few more minutes," he mumbled.

"Trey! Get up, it's time to go home," she said budging him on the shoulder.

"Home? Huh?" he asked groggily. "Home! Yes! Let's go home!" he said sitting up.

"I called Nick. He'll be waiting for you. Do you have your key?"

"Yeah, it's in my pack," he said as he pulled out the green bag.

"Aroushidium," he said then pulled out the key as he regarded the pill shaped capsule containing the demon Koltek. He thought, *there's no reason to let them know what I'm about to do. Grandpa will fill her in in time. Probably best no one knows about the key – just yet.*

"That's a neat bag. What've you been doing since you've been gone?" asked Raferti.

Trey closed the bag quickly then said with a big smile, "Wouldn't *you* like to know."

"We'll have to have a sit down soon to discuss all of this," she said with a sly smile.

Trey's brow furrowed and he looked down into the floorboard. "My family and friends still aren't safe, are they?" He then looked up. She saw at that moment the young boy that was thrust into a perilous world against his will.

"You are as safe as you've ever been, but not to freak you out you're definitely on Commerand's watch list. Fortunately for you, he's still focused on the relics and I don't believe he knows you have one. Otherwise, he wouldn't have let you leave the warehouse with it. He also doesn't know where the rest are, so he'll be looking for the eye and the book, if he even knows the book exists."

"And you still have people watching us?" Trey asked

"Yes. Well, most of them are people."

"I'm not sure I like how you worded that."

"They are...."

"No. Don't tell me. I've had enough for today. What's the shape of the D.C. portal we used before?"

"It's like this," she said as she drew the shape in the air with an outstretched finger. "Form a star then leave an 'L' down here at the bottom."

"I wish I could have remembered that back in Roberton."

"Where?" She asked.

"Our sit-down. Remember? We'll discuss all that at our sit down," Trey said with a crafty smile.

"Oh yeah?" she said laughing.

"Take care, Trey. We'll be in touch."

He hugged them both tightly, then said, "I'll miss you guys, but I certainly don't want to see either of you for a long time."

They all had a brief laugh then Trey said, "Till next time."

He bent the key and was again amazed when it animated to form a perfect star and L. He touched the key to the portal. He appeared in front of Nick standing next to the old well.

Nick rushed to hug Trey, then said, "I'm so glad to see you! I thought I'd never see you again."

"It's good to see you too," Trey said lovingly to the man who filled in many empty spaces that his father left behind.

"I thought I'd have to tell your mom what happened. They'd lock me up you know?"

"Yeah. They would," Trey smiled.

He stood back, then continued, "What on earth are you wearing? Here, Lyza said you would need a change of clothes." He handed Trey a pair of jeans and a hoodie.

"You'll never be able to tell this story. Don't even try," Trey said as he shook away the surreal memories.

They got into Nick's car then drove to Trey's house.

~ ~

Trey rushed in through the kitchen door and grabbed his mom around the waist.

"I'm so glad to be home, Mom!" he said hugging her tightly.

"I'm glad to have you back too," she said happily with a confused look.

"Teenagers. You know. All the hormones and such," Nick said reassuringly at the door.

"Thanks for bringing him home, Nick."

"No problem, Janet. I hope you all have a nice evening together."

"You too!" she said.

"Thanks for the ride. Mr. H! See you at school Monday!"

"Later, Trey," he said walking to his car.

Trey turned back to his mom. "Did I already tell you it's great to be home?" Trey said as he hugged her tightly again.

"Yes, you did. And you stink like you haven't bathed in two days. You go on and get a shower."

"Yes, Mom," he said smiling.

"And put away that sword! It's not right to be carrying around a weapon!" she said worriedly.

"Yes, Mom!" he yelled from down the hall.

Trey showered, placed the bag full of magical items on the bed post for quick access then removed the bag holding the portal key and Koltek.

Grandpa Patrick

Trey set the small bags on his dresser. He said Aroushidium then removed the capsule. He held it to his eye and thought he herd a faint buzzing sound. He then grasped the other bag in the same hand as the capsule, paused to reflect on what he might say, then turned the contents out onto his other hand.

"Logos, I have returned with Koltek. Release Patrick Roberts."

"Indeed, you have," Logos replied almost before Trey could finish his statement. "There is but one more thing – leave with me the Ragnastant's key and I will release your grandfather.

"That wasn't part of our deal. Our deal was –"

"I know what our deal was, human. The key does not belong in the human realm. I cannot risk any further meddling."

"No," Trey said firmly. "You honor our deal. Release my Grandpa."

"Ah yes. Of course. There is but one more task you may need the key for. I am in agreement."

Logos's presence faded. An image appeared. It was a hand. Trey felt love and grabbed the hand as he released the capsule. He watched the capsule float then expand into Koltek then blur away in a cascade of every color of light. He then regarded his grandfather holding his hand.

"Grandpa! Is that really you?"

"Yes, Trey. It's me," he replied in a familiar Cajun accent.

"I know. I can feel you."

"Indeed, you can," Grandpa replied stoically.

Trey moved quickly away from the entity but continued to feel Grandpa's love.

"Trey, Trey! 'm jus kiddin. T'was a bad joke," Patrick pleaded.

Trey rushed toward Patrick and said, "Please don't joke around like that again." He turned the key in his hand as they hugged tightly.

Patrick released him as they stood in the middle of Trey's bedroom. He quickly held a finger to his mouth indicating Trey to be quiet. He whispered, "I don t'ink i's a good idea do let anyone know 'm back, specially your mother. 'Ere's a lot I mus' uncover before we dell anyone, including Don. Ok?"

Trey looked down disappointingly. "So, you're leaving?"

"Yes."

"Right away?"

"I 'ave to. Lot's has happened and while you've performed spectacularly, 'dis burden on you mus' be lessened. I will catch up with Lyza then you meet me at Ricardo's Pizza next Wednesday at six PM. 'Den you can dell me all 'bout your adventures."

"Ok, Grandpa. Wednesday it is."

"I understand you have a key?"

"Yes." Trey said the word and handed the key to Patrick.

"'Das a neat bag you 'ave 'dere." He looked at Trey curiously and asked, "Cierden?"

"Yeah! You know him?"

"I've met 'im," he smiled. "I tink I should hold on to Ragnastant's key also. I don' foresee you needing it anytime soon. I will return it when the time is near."

"Ok, Grandpa." He handed over the bag with the Etherios key and said with relief, "I'm so glad you're here. I'm so happy we finally get to meet in person." His brow furrowed and fear etched his face, "But how will we ever –
"

"You don' worry about Khaitu just yet. We'll deal with him in due time."

Trey seemed disappointed but felt even more relieved knowing Grandpa seemed to have a feel for what to do. "Ok," Trey replied.

'I'll go now. It'll be morning in Egypt. Remember, don' dell anyone I'm back."

"I won't say anything. Tell Lyza and Karim I said Hi. Boy won't they be surprised when they see you! I feel like I should warn them."

"It will be great seeing them again. I sure did miss them. I assume Karim still has the place just north of the South Egypt portal?"

"If you mean the little white house then yeah."

"Ok. Trey. I'll see you next week. I love you."

"I love you too, Grandpa. Oh yeah. Lyza has people watching us."

"Thanks for that. I'll avoid them."

Patrick quietly left Trey's room and snuck out of the house through the back door. Trey watched him stealthily avoid Trey's house guards which left Trey feeling significantly less secure. *If an old man can get by these guys, then Commerand should have no problem.* "Geesh!" he said quietly.

Relieving Trey of the keys and Grandpa sounding so sure in his words set Trey at ease. His sense of mission became less urgent as he began placing faith in Grandpa Patrick to lead them to victory. For the first time he felt he no longer had to make life changing decisions. That night he got the best sleep in weeks.

~ ~

Monday in the hall at school Davis approached Trey. He wore a usual scowl and walked briskly. Trey stepped back wondering what he was angry about this time.

His face remained ridged as he said, "Marcus told me what you did last week."

Trey searched his memories for everything he told Marcus last week but couldn't think past the battle with Commerand which clearly happened later.

Davis continued with the glare, "I'm still really mad at you. What you did was unforgivable." His face softened. "But I just wanted to thank you for getting Lenny to take the video down."

"Oh Dude!" Trey said thankful Marcus didn't reveal any of his secrets. "No problem. I hated myself for doing it. I'm sorry. I meant to say that earlier."

"It's ok now. I deserved it. My dad told me later that I wasn't taking responsibility for my actions. I was blaming you for everything."

"We all do that. Heck, I just did it a few minutes

ago." They both laughed. "Does this mean you'll get back on the team?"

"If coach will have me back."

"Dude! There's no chance he'll say no. You're too good."

"Thanks Trey. I needed that." He started to go then stopped and asked, "When do you find out if you made the high school team?"

"I don't think there's any chance I made it. I mean, I didn't even go to practice the last two days. I think I'll find out next week, but I'm sure I'll be with you guys for the rest of the season at least."

He nodded to Trey and said, "I'll be glad to share the pitch with you again. Hopefully I'll see you at practice this afternoon."

"Yeah. I look forward to it," Trey said with a warm smile. He stood watching his new friend walk away and was filled with a happiness that could only be realized by helping someone else.

At lunch, Trey was telling Marcus about the wollybroughers and how he nearly died in the mountain.

"Look, this is the ring," he said holding up his hand. "I'll show you some of the other stuff when we get back to your house."

"That's an amazing story. You really did all those things didn't you?"

"Yeah, Marcus. It's all real...and there's something else," Trey said with a sneaky smile.

"What? What else could you have possibly done?" Marcus said with an excitable look.

"I learned a new way to communicate." He then smiled a big toothy smile.

"Yeah? What's that?" Marcus said even more confused about what Trey was insinuating. His eyebrows scrunched together, and he held his mouth slightly open as he searched for the answer to Trey's elusive statement. Then Marcus' eyes bulged as it dawned upon him. "You didn't move your mouth!" He then thought a second, "Did you? Did you move your mouth when you spoke to me?"

"Nope," Trey projected.

Marcus couldn't suppress the inappropriate word that followed the shocking realization that Trey was telepathic.

Silence followed. Marcus' eyes darted left then right. They brightened then squinched as he stared into Trey's.

"I can't read your mind. It doesn't work that way. I can only project into yours."

"Oh. That sucks for you. But still cool you can speak without speaking."

"It's come in handy a few times."

"It's all so unbelievable." He looked out over the crowded lunchroom. Then as if the magical conversation never existed, Marcus returned to middle school life and said, "You know Sarah and Kenny broke up over the weekend."

"Really?" he replied with an extra beat of his heart. He then spied Leslie across the lunchroom talking to a friend. He smiled and said while still looking in Leslie's direction, "Sarah's a nice girl. She'll find someone else quickly."

"She asked about you Friday. Was wondering where you were."

Trey brought his attention back to his friend. "Did you tell her I was off in another world fighting crazy creatures?" he said laughing distantly.

"What are you guys talking about?" Leslie said sitting down next to Trey.

"Hey, Leslie," Trey said happily. He affectionately bumped his shoulder into hers. "We're just talking about, you know, guy stuff."

"Guy stuff, huh?" she said tickling his lower ribs with her finger.

"Haha! Stop that!" he said laughing. "Maybe I'll tell you about it later. Can I walk you home from school today?"

"I'd really like that, but my dad is picking me up. I'm free tomorrow," she replied with a cute smile.

"Tomorrow it is," Trey said happily.

"Did you ever figure out the purpose of your dream?" she asked.

Trey looked at Marcus. They both laughed. "Yeah. Yeah I did."

In Utah

Trey walked home alone – happy with how the day went. It was a nothing tried to kill him, Grandpa was alive, Davis was on the team again, the crazy dreams were gone kind of happy day. As he rounded the corner past Sarah's neighborhood a man appeared in front of him – Trey thought from behind the big tree next to the road but couldn't be sure. It was Lamar.

"Cool Dude. Your dad's in Utah," he said as silver flashed unnaturally in his eyes.

Till Next Week

Trey's adventure continues...

Trey stood in astonished disbelief on a Monday afternoon – the Monday after he used Moridon's relic to travel back in time to save his ancestors from being decimated by fire. He watched the skylien formerly known as Lamar, a thin dark-skinned man he originally met at Donald's apartment complex the night Don Smith returned home from The Highlands, awkwardly propel itself into the sky and fly away with the information he so desired – the information that would lead him to his lost father.

"My dad's in Utah!" He looked left then right as if he missed something in the interaction. "I have to tell mom." He launched into a sprint then stopped. "I can't tell mom. She doesn't know he might be in trouble ... and she'll try to talk me out of finding him."

He looked around again, hoping to find the answer.

"Mr. H! "He'll know what to do. I hope he's still at school."

Trey entered the park he once avoided in order to steer clear of his former bully now good friend Donald. Donald was sitting on a bench talking to Carl, one of Donald's cronies who turned out to be quite an intelligent and nice kid but hid it from Donald amid low self-esteem.

"Hey Trey!" Donald hollered as Trey came running toward the couple.

"No time to talk, buddy! I know where my dad is!" Trey said enthusiastically.

"What?" Donald exclaimed then took chase. "I'll see you tomorrow at school, Carl!"

Trey slowed to let Donald catch up.

"You found your dad?"

"Sort of," Trey said amid heaving breaths. "I know, well, I think he's in Utah. I'll tell you more when we find Mr. Hampton."

The two boys launched through the double doors, ran past Principal Papperton who only gave a questioning expression at their rush then they skidded into the science lab. Nick was not there. The lab was empty. The boys took a minute to catch their breaths.

"How'd you find him?" Donald asked.

"It's sort of hard to explain," Trey said as he took a seat in a front row desk. Donald leaned against another and crossed his arms.

"You remember that guy I was talking about when I was at your apartment last week? Lamar? The guy that no one seemed to know?"

"I remember you asking about him. Why?"

"I told him about my dad when I left your apartment that day. I'm not sure why I did but it didn't seem to go anywhere, so I left and didn't think about it again."

"You told him all the stuff dad told you? The stuff about the portal and that he's protecting you?" Donald said in a way that made Trey fell like he did something wrong.

"No. I just told him he was missing. I sort of hoped, you know, with all the weird magical stuff that's happened, that maybe he was someone that could find him."

"And he found him, didn't he?"

"Yes! He did! Well," Trey looked at the floor before continuing, "he said he did."

"But you don't trust him, do you?"

"No. That's the part I wanted to talk to Mr. H about."

"What's Mr. Hampton got to do with Lamar?"

"He met him when we brought your dad home. He's familiar with the guy and, um – "

"What is it, Trey?"

"I uh – "

"Dude. You can tell me."

"I'm not sure I should. You have enough on your plate with your dad and all that happened at the park last week."

"I'm ok with all that. I've seen the guys following us. Look, there's one right there," Donald said as he pointed at the man in the red ball cap that saved them from the rogglet attack in the park last Saturday.

"Yeah. That's Charlie." Charlie waved nonchalantly at the boy's acknowledgement of his presence.

"Ok. I'll tell you but you can't get freaked out about it."

"Ok. I promise," Donald replied but looked a little freaked out and edged slightly away from Trey, as if a large spider just crawled toward him.

Trey tried to prepare Donald with trusting eyes then said, "Lamar isn't human."

Trey was pleased that the comment didn't seem to faze Donald. He continued, "He's a skylien."

Donald's expression slightly tilted toward the fearful side, but he maintained composure and asked,

”What's a skylien?”

"That's the tricky part. I don't know. But what I do know is that they take the shape of other things and that their real form is a super scary version of a skeleton with black shriveled skin awkwardly stuck to random places and a sharp claw at the tip of each bat-like wing. It was really creepy...especially at night."

Donald's expression became blank, like he was trying to think of an excuse to leave.

"But the worst part about it when I first saw it was that it looked and sounded just like Mr. H."

"Um Hum. A flying black skeleton you say?" Donald asked distantly.

"Yeah."

"That takes the shape of our science teacher," he said as he looked out the window – possibly expecting Lamar to show up and rip his heart out with a ruthless claw.

"I think it can take any shape," Trey said calmly while continuing to assess Donald's state.

"Right. Because this one looked like Lamar."

"Yeah, but I don't know the real Lamar. I've only met the skylien...I think. I suppose it could have been the real Lamar at some point. I don't know."

"You know, Trey. All this really freaks me out," Donald said with a tremor in his hands.

"I know, Buddy. But I need you to stay focused. We're in this together."

"I get that, but why are there so many monsters? Why me? What did I do to deserve this?"

"Nothing, Donald. None of us asked for this. It's all gonna be ok. I'll find my dad and he'll know what to do. He and Grandpa will help me make it all right."

"But your Grandpa is dead, isn't he?"

"No, Buddy. Well, he's not dead yet."

"I'm not sure I'm ready for all this."

"You need to stop with all the negative self-talk. You're Donald Smith, the toughest kid in school."

Donald looked at him with a painful grimace and replied, "I was mean. That's not tough."

Trey smiled and said, "Yes. You were mean but you had a good reason and you changed when that reason no longer existed. That was smart and the best thing for you...and change, especially when it involves admitting you're wrong, is very hard to do. You're a great friend now. So just let the past go and face these challenges with us, regardless of how scared we are and believe me, I'm plenty scared most of the time."

"You? No. You're always so confident."

"No, Donald. Most of that confidence you see is just me trying to survive."

"I guess we all hide our weakest parts."

"I don't see it as weakness anymore. When I'm scared, I know I'm alive and that I have something to live for. I find that I'm more capable to take decisive action because my own and oftentimes the lives of people I love are depending on me. It's not hard to be confident or courageous when lives are on the line."

"That does change your perspective, I bet."

"It sure does...and I hope you never have to make those decisions because while it's happening, I feel I'm wrong every time. It's agonizing."

"I don't envy you at all, Trey. I'm glad it's you and not me. I'd be sure to fail."

"You'd be just fine," Trey replied as he became frustrated with Donald's consistent self-doubt. "We'll have to work on your confidence. In the meantime, it doesn't look like Mr. H is coming."

"What do we do now?"

"I know of someone else that's familiar with skyliens," Trey smiled at his friend who returned a questioning frown. "Let's go find Marcus. He needs to see this," he said happily.

The boys left the main building and entered an adjacent building through the front then walked swiftly toward the sounds of various horns, strings and percussion instruments undulating the tune of the 1967 Disney hit, The Bare Necessities.

Trey peeked through the narrow window to see Marcus waiting patiently for his part. Marcus glanced up as if he felt Trey's glare and waved at this friend in the window. He then held up five fingers indicating he'll be out in five minutes. He then looked startled but gracefully tucked the old German violin under his chin and drew a strong bow across the strings. A melody so thin and playful lept from the instrument. Trey realized this was the first time he ever heard his best friend's passion – and was deeply ashamed.

Trey shushed Donald's comment so that he could take in Marcus' talent. The joyful tune set Trey's mind at ease and reminded him of a simpler time when he and both parents took in a movie about a young boy fighting for a cause larger than himself.

Marcus emerged shortly after the music ended. "Kid! What are you doing at band practice? Shouldn't you be at soccer?"

"It's not until later. Something big happened. By the way, you play wonderfully. I'm sorry I haven't seemed interested in your music until now. I never knew you were so good."

"What? You mean in there?" Marcus replied by pointing into the music room. "That's nothing," he said looking down shyly. It's the first time Trey ever noticed bashfulness in his friend.

Who is this guy, Trey thought? It's like I don't even know my own best friend.

Trey appreciated Marcus' humble attitude. "Dude, you're really good. I want to hear more. But not right now. I have something else you'll be interested in. Let's go before we miss her."

"Where're we going?" Donald asked.

"Fifth street."

"Why fifth street?" Marcus questioned.

"Would you guys just come on," Trey commanded. "You'll see when we get there."

The trio shot out of the school, crossed the yard and hit the sidewalk. From there, they walked nearly three miles to an abandoned construction site with a large half built concrete structure that stood nearly thirty feet high and open at the top. The boys entered through a doorless opening.

Donald asked nervously, "What are we doing here, Trey?"

"Just wait for it," Trey replied. He was almost giddy.

"What's up with you, Kid? Why are you smiling?" added Marcus.

Trey's grin shined as he regarded his friends but didn't attempt to answer their questions. He looked to the sky fervently.

"Trey. Seriously," Marcus continued. "What – " he began then continued in a shrill scream, "is that!"

Suddenly a large fiery object descended upon them rapidly. Bursts of plasma torched the interior walls and glassed the sandy ground. A booming screech rocked their very souls. Tornados of twirling sand and dirt pummeled their bodies, sending them staggering about. Marcus squatted with his hands over his head and Donald fell down in the torrent. The partially constructed building became a furnace in the flaming attack.

Another thunderous screech echoed across the empty structure – then silence as the dust settled – then hyena laughing prevailed. Marcus looked toward Trey who was on the ground holding his belly amid uncontrollable laughing. He then looked past Trey at the monstrous green dragon towering above the boys. Marcus screamed and stumbled backwards over a pile of broken concrete pieces. Donald remained cowered with his hands over his head screaming "Please don't kill us! Please don't kill us!"

"Oh My God, Tanny!" Trey said within a burst of ecstatic laughter. "I was scared out of my mind. I actually questioned whether you forgot we were friends – or were mad that I called you here. Oh my god! I need a moment," he continued. "That was amazing but please don't ever do it again."

"You said to make a dramatic entrance," Tanny replied with a reptilic smile. Her voice carried a metallic but elegant British accent as a dragon.

"I know, but I imagined you gracefully flying in and maybe hitting us with a burst of wind from your wings. I didn't expect Tanarkin the Killer Green Dragon from hell!"

"He he! Maybe next time you will be clearer in your request, Fire Tamer."

"No doubt. Lesson learned!" Trey replied.

"Trey!" Marcus exclaimed excitedly. "This is your dragon friend?"

"Yes. Come meet Tanny."

Donald peeked from his cower to assess the situation. He then rose angrily. "That was not funny. You should have told us," he said staring at Trey.

"Dude! I didn't know she was gonna do that. I'm sorry. I just thought it would be more interesting if she made a dramatic entrance than just appearing and me saying (in a low goofy voice), hey guys, this is my wonderfully nice friend Tanny the Green."

"It was freaking awesome, Kid! Can you do it again?" he said excitedly to Tanny as he crept toward a massive wing to steal a touch.

She regarded Marcus for a moment then said. "I think that's enough dragon for now." She then spun into a graceful older woman wearing a flowing green dress with long autumn colored hair and bare feet.

"Whoa," Marcus said as he stared at the woman who was once a dragon. "That was amazing. How did you do that?"

"She's a wizard, Marcus," said Trey.

"So, you can cast spells and make people turn into toads?" Marcus replied.

"I'm not that sort of wizard, but I suppose if I were to become inclined, I could do the toad. Why? Are you looking to transform your life into something more amphibious?"

"No Ma'am. Not today!" Marcus said with raised hands as if he were trying to push away an evil spell.

She smiled and returned her attention to Trey. "You said something about the skylien from the ballpark?"

"Yeah. I'm not sure if it was the same as the one in the ballpark. This one was disguised as a man I met in Donald's neighborhood. It said my dad is in Utah."

Tanny got real serious with Trey and said, "Did you agree to its terms?"

"Terms? What – "

"Tell me, Trey. Did you enter into a contract with the skylien?" she said angrily.

"No! No, I didn't. It didn't offer any. It just told me my dad's in Utah then flew away."

"Is that all it said?"

"Yeah. Well, no. It said it would return to me in two days."

"That must be when it will present its terms and the contract."

"Contract? You mean the agreement to get it to do something for me? To get it to get my dad?"

"Yes. It will present you with the contract in two days and you will only have the one opportunity to accept or decline. Afterwards, it will do what you ask or go away for good."

"Oh. Ok. I thought I'd have some time to think about what it wanted from me."

"Under no circumstances should you agree to its terms. There's never a positive outcome with those wretched creatures, even when you get what you agreed to. Understand?"

"Yeah. Don't deal with the skylien," Trey said sadly. "But what about my dad? How else do I find him?"

"What's the big deal?" Marcus asked. "If this guy Lamar knows where your dad is, why can't we just let him tell us?"

Tanny replied, "First, you can't look at Lamar as a man because he's not. Second, skyliens will only accept something of great personal value for the conscription – and the sacrifice is never worth the prize."

Marcus nodded as if he understood the warning.

"As of now, we must believe he's safe and is choosing to stay away, like dad said," Donald butted in. If my dad was right, he's ok and doesn't need our help."

"But – " Trey began.

"No buts," Tanny remarked. "Your friend is right. Do not agree to the contract."

"Ok," Trey said in a low voice.

Donald approached his friend and said with a hand on his shoulder, "We'll find your dad. Now we know where to start."

"Thanks, Donald." Trey replied with a worrisome smile then turned to Tanny. "Did you take care of that thing we discussed last week? Is it safe?" he asked in regard to the Clutched Rose they won from a lion-headed demon with a turtle's body in a ball field amid a flurry of fire.

"You need not worry about it any longer, Fire Tamer. It is in good hands."

"Good. Thank you. I may need to get it back soon, but for now let's leave it where it is."

"Why is that?" She said with a concerned glance away. "The Azuliposians will not be pleased with this news."

"I didn't know what it was then, but I think it's one of the relics. They'll just have to get over it."

"I see. It is safe until then."

"Great! Thank you for coming today," Trey said appreciatively.

"Yeah! Thanks for making this the most awesome day of my life!" Marcus said to Tanny.

"You're very welcome, young handsome friend of Fire Tamer."

Trey couldn't believe it, Marcus actually blushed at her complement.

"I'll be in touch," she said to Trey just before she leapt from the weed covered dirt and spun into a magnificent green dragon with leaf-like scales and roots for claws. A torrent of wind whooshed over the boys sending dirt and dust everywhere. She disappeared just outside the roofless building as if she hadn't even been there.

"I know you will," Trey said softly as he continued to look toward wispy clouds in the blue afternoon sky.

"Trey!" Marcus yelled so enthusiastically his oval wire-framed glasses nearly fell off. That was so awesome! Holy crap! I can't believe dragons actually exist!"

Trey looked at his friend.

Marcus continued, "I mean, I know you already told me, but until just now they were stories."

"You thought I was making it up, didn't you?"

"No! Dude! You showed me the disk and – "

"It's ok. I wouldn't have believed me either. I would have thought I was insane...and did for a little while."

"No. It's not that. It's just different – "

Donald finished, "When you see it in person." He then looked distantly, most likely reminiscing on the beautiful day those stories became a reality for him in the park.

"Yeah! That's it," Marcus said. He looked off into the sky and said tenderly, "She's the most beautiful dragon I could have ever imagined."

"Hey guys," Trey said, "you can't tell anyone about what you saw or what we've been talking about."

Marcus rejoined the conversation and replied, "No duh, Sherlock. We'd look like crazy people."

"You also have to know that all of this is no joke. It's not just a fun game of dragons and magic that you read about. This stuff is real and the possibility someone gets seriously hurt or worse is always possible. Donald will back me on this. I brought you here today, Marcus, because you need to know what's going on...just in case."

"In case of what? In case they get to me?"

Trey looked up at his friend from sorrowful eyes.

"And I trust you over just about anyone. I know when I need you, you'll be there."

"Back at ya, Kid," he said then donned a big closed lip smile.

"What do we do now?" Donald questioned.

"You guys can do whatever you do. I have to get to soccer practice before I get booted off the team. I bet Coach Rafiq is furious that I missed the last two practices with the high schoolers."

"I'm heading that way. I'll walk with you," Donald said.

"I'm this way. I'll see you guys later," said Marcus.

"Hey, buddy. Thanks for being here with me," Trey said sincerely to Donald.

"You know, Trey. I've been really scared since

that day at the park and today didn't really change that much." He smiled a big smile and continued, "However, it does make me feel much better that the dragon is on our side."

"No doubt!" Marcus added and gave him a high five.

"See ya later, Marcus," Trey said after they finished a round of rhythmic hand slaps.

"Later, D!" Marcus yelled as Trey and Donald walked away.

As the two boys walked the sidewalk toward the soccer complex Donald began, "That dragon – "

"Tanny," Trey added.

"Yeah. Tanny. She was sick. That fire she blasted all over the walls was pretty frightening. I couldn't imagine what you went through to save my dad. I have no idea how anyone could have survived that."

"Your dad didn't tell you how I did it?"

"No. He's not much for details."

Trey watched his steps as he said, "I took a potion that kept me from burning up." He then looked up to judge Donald's reaction.

"A potion? Really? Like in witch's brew and stuff?

"Yeah. Evidently there're people that make potions that do all sorts of stuff.

"People make those?"

"Well, I suppose they might not be actual humans."

"Donald gave Trey a 'Don't tell me anymore look.'"

"When I battled Tanny, I used two fireproof

potions and a levitation. I was still nearly burned alive. It didn't work half as well as I'd hoped. I could feel the fire melting my skin – I could even smell it."

"Eww. That must have been horrible."

"It was. Believe me. You don't ever want to get near that stuff."

"Today is as close to it as I hope to ever get." He thought distantly for a second then said, "If you were burned so badly, how come you don't have any scars?"

"That's a little more difficult to explain." He looked at Donald, trying to decide what to say. "I have rapid healing capabilities that I received from a bunch of fairies in a forest."

"Fairies? Dude," Donald replied in a disbelieving frown.

"It was fairies, I swear. Why would I make it up after what you've seen?"

"Exactly. I'd be easy to fool based on the fire breathing dragon experience."

"It was fairies, I promise I'm not messing with you."

"Ok. I'll believe you for now." They walked a few more steps and he added, "I think I could handle seeing fairies. They seem safe."

"They're pretty awesome. They brought Tessie back to life."

Donald got excited and said, "I love Tessie! She's so cool. It was funny. The other day I was shuffling though the apartment in a thick pair of wool socks when her tiny little blue self-sparked onto the shelf next to me. I could feel the static electricity building up so I pointed my finger at her to see what would happen. I popped her really good with the shock.

She made a high-pitched peep that made me feel super bad that I might have hurt her. But then she popped me back and it hurt so bad that I laughed. The cool thing is that I think she kept charging me, so we popped each other until I fell on the ground laughing.

"Dad says you understand her."

"That's right. Another gift from the fairies. Turns out that I understand many languages now."

"How's that?" Donald questioned with a curious face.

"It's a long story that involved an ancient wizard and lots of fire. I'll tell you about it another day after soccer practice."

"That'll be cool."

"I'll see you later, Donald," Trey said as he turned to enter the through the gate at field 1 – the middle school field."

Donald followed him in.

"Hey buddy, what you doing? I have to get to practice," Trey said to Donald.

"Yeah!" he said with a huge smile. "Me too. I'm your new keeper."

"No joke?" Trey said excitedly. "That's awesome! When did this happen?"

"Last week when you were with the high schoolers. When I went to your game the weekend before, I thought about how good I would be at keeper. I mean, I'm pretty fast for a big guy and that's what counts. Coach said Craig is off the team due to poor grades so it just sort of worked out."

"That sucks for Craig but good job to you! We're gonna crush it!"

"Trey!" Coach Rafiq hollered from the sideline.

Trey felt his stomach cringe. "I'll see you on the pitch, Donald."

"Good luck, Trey," Donald said hoping Trey understood his concern about what Rafiq would say about his missed practices last week.

"Good to have you back, Trey."

"Good to be back, Coach."

"How's your grandmother?"

"Who? Oh yeah. She's fine. You know, she just does normal grandmother stuff. Nothing too exciting."

"Coach Wood was disappointed that you missed the last two days." He gave Trey a pained look.

"I didn't make the varsity team, did I?"

"No. He said you did great Wednesday but got pushed around the other two days. He said you have a lot of potential but since he only had the one day, he didn't feel comfortable with what he saw."

"I understand." He found he was tremendously disappointed. He hated playing with the high schoolers but after his successful showing last Wednesday and the battle with Commerand at the Phoenix's warehouse, he felt he had the confidence to perform at a high level, regardless of how big or skilled the high school teams were – but mostly, he felt he missed a great opportunity.

"If it's any consolation, I'm happy to have you back on my team," Rafiq smiled.

Trey looked over the soccer field at Donald successfully defending the goal from Davis' strikes and became grateful for his current opportunity.

"I'm really happy to be on your team, Coach."

Rafiq ruffled Trey's hair then said, "Let's get out there and prepare our new keeper for the match this weekend!”

Trey’s face lit up and he said, “You got it, Coach!” They both trotted out to join Davis and the rest of the team at Donald’s goal.

After practice Trey became excited to see a familiar auburn-haired girl wearing a ponytail sitting on the first row of the stands. He ran to her with a big smile.

“Hey, Leslie!” he said as he attempted a sweaty hug.

She pushed him away playfully and said, “Gosh you stink!”

“Oh, come on. You know you like it!” he said as he briefly chased her around the sideline.

They naturally stopped then Trey said, “What’s up?”

“I just stopped to say hey.”

Donald walked up and greeted them both.

“I didn’t know you played soccer,” Leslie said to Donald.

“Today’s my first day!” he said enthusiastically.

“Oh my gosh! Fun! What do you play?”

“Keeper.”

“Oooo, that position’s tough.”

“No. I’m really good at it. Once I figured out the trick, I only let one ball through the whole practice.”

“Really? That’s amazing,” she replied. “What’s the trick?”

“I started watching their eyes and, in my peripherals, I paid attention to the ball. If the ball moved in relation to their eyes then I would lean toward their eye movements, if they weren’t moving together then I knew they were trying to fool me, and I went in the opposite direction. Nearly every time, I got a jump on them...many times I got lucky."

"I'd rather be lucky than good any day," Trey commented. "Can I walk you home?" Trey asked Leslie.

"I'd love that," she replied.

About the Author

Lee Magnus is an American author who began creating the stories he wrote with his children in a storytelling game he called "Let's Build a Story" where each participant would, in turn, orally create a few lines at a time until there was an eventual conclusion. The Trey Robert's series and several of the characters came directly from this wonderful activity.

Born in a small South Georgia town, Lee Magnus was raised by an English teacher who encouraged reading at a young age. He is a proud UGA alumnus, plays various musical instruments but is particular to the piano, and has two boys with wide imaginations. He currently lives with his family in Florida. Visit him at www.leemagnus.com